W9-BSD-941

THE GIRL IN THE WOODS

Patricia MacDonald

This first world edition published 2018
in Great Britain and the USA by
SEVERN HOUSE PUBLISHERS LTD of
Eardley House, 4 Uxbridge Street, London W8 7SY
Trade paperback edition first published
in Great Britain and the USA 2018 by
SEVERN HOUSE PUBLISHERS LTD

British Library Cataloguing in Publication Data
A CIP catalogue record for this title is available from the British Library.

ISBN-13: 978-0-7278-8778-8 (cased)
ISBN-13: 978-1-84751-894-1 (trade paper)
ISBN-13: 978-1-78010-957-2 (e-book)

All Severn House titles are printed on acid-free paper.

Severn House Publishers support the Forest Stewardship Council™ [FSC™],
the leading international forest certification organisation.
All our titles that are printed on FSC certified paper carry the FSC logo.

MIX
Paper from
responsible sources
FSC
www.fsc.org   FSC® C013056

Typeset by Palimpsest Book Production Ltd.,
Falkirk, Stirlingshire, Scotland.
Printed and bound in Great Britain by
TJ International, Padstow, Cornwall.

PROLOGUE

The din on the bus was deafening. The students were like a pack of wild animals, freed briefly from the confines of the dun-colored junior high, only to be restrained again on the dilapidated, yellow school bus. They resisted vehemently, bouncing on their broken-down seats and screaming. They poked and provoked those in nearby seats and communicated solely by shouting at the top of their lungs. Every so often the driver would turn around and yell at them to '*Zip it*'. This only served to provoke cascades of laughter and insults.

Blair Butler sat silently by the window, trying to stay still, and not draw attention to herself. She only turned her head a few times to exchange a smile with Molly Sinclair, who was seated next to her. Molly, petite and self-possessed, with long brown hair, was Blair's best, her only friend, and today, Molly was making a rare after-school visit to Blair's house. Molly had obtained a permission slip to ride on Blair's bus for the occasion.

Usually they hung out at Molly's house, which was on another bus route that ran along the opposite side of the woods in the Pocono mountain town where they lived. Today, Apres Ski (the coffee house on Main Street which Molly's family owned) was closed, so that Molly's parents could both go to a trade show in Philadelphia. Molly's parents didn't want to leave her home alone. The police had been called several times to the house next door in recent months. Their neighbor was a mean drunk, who took his frustrations out on his family with his fists. The Sinclairs wanted to take Molly with them to Philly, but Molly had a presentation to give that day and wanted to go to school. So, much as Blair dreaded having anyone over to her uncle's, inviting Molly to her house seemed like the obvious thing to do.

The bus snaked its way slowly up and down the hilly streets of Yorkville, letting off students at intervals. It turned a corner and trundled down Main Street. There were not too many people on the downtown streets on this bleak, weekday afternoon in early November.

The trees were bare, but the snow, which brought winter sports and prosperity to the town throughout the winter, had not yet begun to fall. As the bus made several stops along the Main Street, Blair pressed her nose to the window and looked out. They passed by the coffee house, the five-and-ten, the newspaper office and several sweatshirt shops. A woman, bundled up in a parka and a knitted hat, was being pulled along the empty street by her dog on a leash.

Blair turned to Molly. 'How's your dog?' she asked.

Molly had recently been allowed to adopt a puppy from the animal shelter. The furry golden-haired pup had big eyes and her bark was still a yip. The thought of such a companion was bliss beyond imagining for Blair, although she knew that it would never happen to her.

'We took her to the vet for her shots. Pippa wasn't even afraid. Dr Kramer says she's healthy, though she had some fleas. We had to get some medicine to put on her once a month.'

'Who's taking care of her today?' Blair asked.

'She's in the basement and we've got paper spread everywhere cause she's not trained yet. They left her food and water. Mom says Pippa will be all right till they get back. They're supposed to be back by seven thirty to pick me up. She'll be ok till then.'

Blair nodded as if she understood, but in fact, she knew nothing about training an animal. There had never been a pet in Uncle Ellis's house. The only animals he was interested in were the ones he killed during hunting season. A lot of the other men he knew had hunting dogs, but not Ellis. Dogs were too much trouble according to him. Dogs and nieces, he would say, referring to Blair and her older sister, Celeste. But Ellis had no choice about the nieces. Blair stifled a sigh.

'Not too much farther now,' she said anxiously.

The bus left the downtown area and almost immediately was surrounded again by the woods which covered these mountains. The bus wove down through the narrow streets and stopped at the corner of a dirt road.

'This is us,' said Blair.

Molly followed Blair down the aisle of the bus. The population of homeward bound students had thinned and had lost some steam, but Blair and Molly still had to dodge projectiles and desultory hoots and curses. Blair looked straight ahead and pretended not to notice, but Molly, who was not easily intimidated, turned and glared at their tormentors.

'Assholes,' she pronounced.

Blair stifled a smile and wished she had that kind of courage. Together they descended the bus steps and jumped off. The sudden silence around them, except for the rushing of a mountain stream, was a relief. Blair took a deep breath of the cold, clear mountain air once the bus had pulled away. Then she pointed down the road about five feet to where the dirt road met the macadam. The girls began to walk.

On the other side of town where Molly lived, the few houses built there were well-kept, nestled among the tall pine trees. The road to Uncle Ellis's house was dreary and overgrown. Celeste and Blair's mother, Tina, had grown up in this very house at the end of Burnham Lane. It must, at one time, have been a nice house, but now the road was dotted with rundown trailer homes and the Dietz's old house looked as if it was going to implode on itself. The paint had peeled off the shingles and there was automotive junk everywhere in the yard. The front porch had a giant hole in the floorboards. Rather than repair it, Ellis had put sawhorses around it. Most embarrassing was the oversized, ripped, faded confederate flag, which was spread out and fastened to the front porch wall, completely covering one window. Blair cringed at the sight of it. Worse was his collection of Nazi memorabilia in the living room. The thought of anyone seeing those swastikas made Blair feel sick to her stomach. She avoided going in there at all costs. Those are my uncle's beliefs, she wanted to say to anyone who came to the house, I'm not like that. But a glance at Molly's face reassured her. Molly didn't need convincing. She already knew that.

Blair led the way up the steps and unlocked the door to the house. Ellis was still at work. His truck was not parked outside. She called out, on the chance that Celeste might be home. She was not surprised when Celeste did not answer. Beautiful Celeste, with her long, black hair and perfect figure, was never home. She stayed away as much as she could. She cared nothing about school work, so she didn't come home to study. And she had friends with cars now, so escape was possible for her in a way that was not yet possible for Blair.

Blair turned on the lights on the first floor and led the way into the kitchen. Knowing that Molly was coming, Blair had cleaned it up as much as possible last night. The linoleum was old and worn and the table and chairs felt greasy. She thought of the shining, stainless steel kitchen island in Molly's house, but then she put it out of her mind. At least there weren't dirty dishes on every surface. She had made sure of that. She went into the ancient refrigerator and took out two orange sodas which she had bought for the occasion. She also had a pack of peanut butter cookies for them.

'Let's take them to my room,' she said. Just in case Uncle Ellis comes home, she thought, but she didn't have to say it. Molly took her share and they went upstairs to Blair's room and closed the door after them. Blair locked it behind her.

Blair had picked up and made the bed in the narrow room. They sat down on the bed and had their snacks. In no time, thanks to the irrepressible Molly, Blair began to relax. They began talking and joking, sharing their bits of gossip from the day. They progressed to polishing their nails and searching through Facebook on Molly's laptop. Lost in their own world, they could have been anywhere. This is pretty good, Blair thought.

At virtually the moment she entertained that thought, she heard the front door bang open, and the sound of her uncle's heavy tread entering the house. She could hear him muttering although he did not call out, either to her or to Celeste. He never did. She remembered her early childhood, when her mother was alive and would always be glad to see them when she picked them up at daycare, or when she woke them in the morning. It was getting harder to visualize her mother's face these days. Tina had died eight years ago, when Blair was five and Celeste was nine. Their father had left them years earlier. Blair did not remember him at all. And when Tina was diagnosed with stage IV lung cancer, that was the first time Blair remembered meeting Uncle Ellis.

Ellis was married at the time to a plump, blond woman named Sheree, who wore rhinestone studded jeans and who insisted, after Tina died, that Ellis had to take his nieces in. There was room in the big, old house, Sheree argued, and she longed to be a mother to the girls. So Blair and Celeste were packed up, removed from their foster family in the city and hauled off to the Poconos. Within a year, Sheree had met another man and left town, leaving her angry, disgruntled husband with his two unwanted nieces to raise.

'I think I'll use this gold-flecked one on my toenails,' said Molly, holding up one of the bottles of nail polish.

'Yeah, that's good,' said Blair.

'Whatsa matter?' Molly asked.

Blair could hear Ellis trudging up the stairs. She glanced at the door of her room.

'Nothing,' she said.

'Just ignore him,' Molly advised.

Blair nodded, but she couldn't help thinking that it was easy for Molly to say. She had a father and mother who adored her. They never yelled at her, or tried to scare her, or lock her out of the house when they got mad about something.

'I will,' she said.

But it was never that simple.

'Blair,' he bellowed, stomping down the hall toward her room. He grabbed the doorknob. 'Open this door.'

Molly looked up, wide-eyed, her sanguine advice forgotten as the doorknob jiggled crazily.

'Just a minute,' Blair said angrily, getting up from her seat on the bed and going to the door.

'How many times do I have to tell you? Don't you lock this door on me.'

'Sorry,' Blair mumbled. She opened the door and Ellis filled up the doorway, glowering. He was a tall, lean man, with unkempt, graying hair, a stubbly beard and purplish pouches under his wild, malamute eyes. He wasn't always loud and cranky. He could be almost normal when he wasn't drinking. But once he had the first beer of the day . . .

'What's this?' he demanded, waving a piece of paper in his hand. Blair could not see what he was holding.

'I don't know,' she said. 'It looks like a letter.'

Ellis peered at the paper he was holding and then he shook it at her.

'It's a letter all right. From the school.'

Blair tried to think if she had done anything wrong, but nothing came to mind.

'What does it say?'

'It says that your application for the computer science camp at the university during the winter break has been accepted. And that it will cost two hundred and fifty dollars.'

Blair's face flamed.

'Oh right,' she said.

'And where are you going to get two hundred and fifty dollars, may I ask?'

'I was going to . . .'

'You want to go to computer camp? That's the one time of year when a kid can make a buck around here. You can work at the Lodge or one of the ski shops—'

'She should go,' Molly spoke up defiantly. 'She's smart in science.'

Blair's heart sank. She loved the way that Molly always spoke up for herself, even with grown-ups, but it didn't pay to be brave around Uncle Ellis.

Ellis stopped in mid-tirade and leaned over, peering at Molly.

'Who's this?' he demanded, though he had seen Molly coming and going many times. Blair could smell liquor on his breath, but she had already recognized the signs. He was ready for a fight, as he often was when he stopped off at the VFW bar on his way home.

'Molly,' said Blair.

'Well, Molly, why don't you just mind your own business? I'll decide what Blair can and cannot do—'

'That's not fair,' Molly insisted. 'Computers are the future. My Dad always says so.'

'Oh, your Daddy says that, does he? Well if he knows everything, then maybe he'd like to pay for it.'

Molly glared back at him, but did not answer.

Ellis ignored Molly and turned to Blair.

'Ok, that's enough,' he growled. 'Stop playing around and get started on dinner. Where's that sister of yours, by the way?'

'I don't know. Probably at Amanda's,' Blair mumbled. Amanda Drake was Celeste's best friend, and they were practically inseparable.

'They're probably out chasing boys. The two of them,' said Ellis. 'Up to no good, as usual. You,' he barked at Molly. 'You run along. Blair has work to do.'

'I invited her,' Blair protested. 'She's supposed to stay here until her mother picks her up.'

Molly's cheeks were flushed. She began to gather up her stuff. 'That's ok, Blair,' she said in a shaky voice. 'I'll walk home.' 'No,' Blair protested. 'It's getting dark. You can't walk all that way.'

'It's not that far. I know the way,' said Molly.

'But your Mom didn't want you to be home alone. She was worried about that guy in your neighborhood.'

'I won't be alone. I've got Pippa. She's like a guard dog.'

'But we promised your Mom. I'm coming with you,' said Blair.

'The hell you are,' Ellis bellowed. 'You'll stay right here. You've got chores.'

Blair wanted to yell out how much she hated her uncle when he was like this, but she hesitated, afraid of how he would react.

Molly met her anguished gaze gravely. 'I'm going,' she said.

'No, stay,' said Blair. 'We can do our homework together. I'll make us supper.'

'Let her go,' said Ellis. 'I don't want her here anyway.'

Molly walked up to the bedroom doorway which was blocked by Ellis.

'Excuse me,' she said coldly.

Ellis stepped out of the way. Molly walked past him and started down the stairs. Blair jumped up to follow her.

'Don't go, Molly,' she said.

'Come with me,' said Molly in a low voice.

'I will,' said Blair. She grabbed up her jacket and tried to follow Molly out the door and down the hallway. Ellis's fingers closed like a vise around her upper arm.

'You're not going anywhere,' he said.

Tears sprang to Blair's eyes, but she would not give him the satisfaction of pleading.

'I hate you,' she said.

'Don't open your mouth to me or you'll be sorry.'

Blair blinked away the tears and tried to shake herself free from Ellis's iron grip, as she watched Molly marching down the stairs toward the front door. As Molly pushed the door open, she looked back up at the landing and met Blair's gaze. Her image was distorted by the tears in Blair's eyes. Then Molly walked out, letting the door slam behind her.

Blair wanted to cry out at the unfairness of it all, as she slumped hopelessly in her uncle's grip, watching her friend depart. Years later, when she looked back on that afternoon, she could recall a welter of emotions. She remembered anger and shame and an inchoate misery, longing for her late mother who was never coming back to rescue her. But even in the depths of her misery, it was fair to say that Blair had no premonition, no inkling at all, of the disaster this day would finally bring. Of the fact that she would never, ever set eyes on her best friend, Molly, again.

ONE

Blair sailed through the streets of Philadelphia, weaving in and out of traffic on her sleek, silver racing bike. On this windy November day, she was far from alone. The streets of this once stuffy, historic city – now a mecca for the young – were thick with bicycle riders, eschewing the lumbering SEPTA buses, for a green, efficient way to navigate the streets. Blair's apartment was the first two floors of a federal style brick building, but she worked thirty blocks away in the thriving Drexel University neighborhood north of 30th street station. Blair, whose graduate degree was in computer science, and two friends from the medical school, had taken a leap of faith and opened a firm that had developed a 3D computer printer capable of printing body tissue. Their process had produced immediate interest, a flurry of grants and an avalanche of work which came with it. The way it took off had taken them all by surprise. One of her partners, Anna, had recently had a baby, who had a crib in Anna's office. Her other partner, Todd, lived almost next door to their offices in a loft with his husband, Louis.

Blair took her bike into the building and up in the elevator. She always rode her bike, except on days when she went to yoga after work, her yoga class being far across town. Those days she drove her shiny, new Nissan just because she knew that she was more likely to go if she could get there quickly. And she needed the workout and relaxation. But, in truth, she felt more herself on the days she rode her bike. Blair rolled it off the elevator and parked it, beside the bikes of six other employees, in the spare, open reception area. Blair felt almost more at home here at work, than she did in her apartment. The apartment was beautiful, with shining floors and exposed brick walls, but it was more of a reflection of her success than it was a home. After all these years, she was still trying to figure out how a home was supposed to feel.

Blair passed through the main work area which was spacious and flooded with light from the floor-to-ceiling windows. Across the floor, in between desks and printers there were pieces of robots and life-size human models in varying degrees of detail. They gave the office the appearance of a workshop dedicated to creating human pods. Blair always felt exhilarated stepping into the workspace. We made this, she thought. We dreamed it and we made it come true. There were young people, casually dressed, yawning, texting and sipping from coffee cups. Blair spoke to everyone she passed. Her crew. This place was where she belonged.

She had a cubicle on the floor by the windows, which had no door or walls to separate her from the action. It was just a desk where she could organize her day. She sat down in her leather chair and looked at her phone. Just then it rang and she looked to see who was calling. Her heart sank and her hands began to shake. She took a deep breath and answered.

'Hi Uncle Ellis,' she said.

'She's on hospice now. You better get here pronto,' Ellis replied bluntly.

Blair knew exactly what he meant. She had been dreading this call for a while.

'Ok,' said Blair. 'Let me tie up a few things, and I'm on my way.'

Blair looked longingly around the office which was just coming to life for the day. She wished she could stay here and keep the world out, but that wasn't going to happen. This day had been coming for a while. Celeste had fought a battle with the same vicious cancer which had taken their mother, twenty years ago. Now, it was about to claim Celeste, who was only thirty. Blair had taken Celeste to the best medical centers in Philly and sought out cutting edge treatment for her sister, but even the most advanced treatments had only bought a little time. The last time Blair went out to the old house in Yorkville, Celeste had been weak and emaciated; her skin a sickly mottle of gray and yellow.

With a sigh, Blair pushed her chair back and put her phone into her purse. Her bespectacled young assistant, Eric, came up to her desk and set some papers on it.

'You going out?' he asked.

Blair nodded. 'It's Celeste. I have to go. I may be gone for a while.'

Eric looked genuinely stricken. 'Oh Blair, I'm so sorry,' said

Eric sincerely. He had been Blair's right hand through her frequent absences from the office. He knew all about Celeste's illness and the prognosis. 'You know we've got you covered here. Not that that's what matters . . .'

'It does matter,' said Blair. 'This place is . . .' She looked around the workroom fondly. 'It's my baby.'

'We'll take good care of your baby,' Eric promised with a wry smile. 'I'll keep you updated. Don't worry.'

'Thanks. Really,' said Blair. She could see that Eric wanted to hug her, but she drew back before he had the chance. Eric knew better than to take it personally. That was Blair. 'Let the others know?' she said. 'I don't want to have to . . .'

'I know. Will do,' he said.

Blair waved without looking back and went to pick up her bike and head back to her apartment. There wasn't a lot she needed to accomplish. She had no pets and her refrigerator was empty. Her clothes were virtually a uniform. Jeans, a heavy leather jacket, long-sleeved T-shirt and running shoes. These days she wound a long, fine alpaca scarf around her neck in deference to the weather. Her beauty routine was non-existent. All she needed was lip gloss and some coated bands for her pony tail. She would throw a few Ts and some underwear in a bag. Then, she would just lock up, get her car, and be on her way. She had no idea how long she would be gone. As long as Celeste needed her there. It was fairly simple. Simple, and terrible beyond belief.

Don't think about it, she told herself. Just go.

She tried to listen to music on the drive, but finally, she had to turn it off. Everything seemed banal and inappropriate in light of the reason for her trip, and Blair felt the need to think without distraction.

For so long, she had focused all her efforts on trying to find a physician who might have a cure for Celeste's condition. Working closely as she did with doctors and surgical teams in Philly, she called in every favor she could think of to explore the latest treatment options. But some cures were still beyond the reach of even the most skilled physicians. Celeste was not going to recover. As unbelievable as it seemed, Blair was going to lose her sister to this cancer.

To Blair it seemed that Celeste had been trapped by her life in the mountains. She had tried to escape, enrolling in a community college and moving into an apartment when she was eighteen, with her best friend, Amanda, as a roommate. The arrangement didn't last. Amanda ended up marrying her high school sweetheart, Peter, and moved out. Celeste spent a lot of lonely evenings in the bars, and became pregnant after a one-night stand.

Broke and unemployed, Celeste had been forced to return to her Uncle's house. She had fled at eighteen and, at twenty, she was back, pregnant and without options. From then on, she never managed to leave. Celeste gave birth to Malcolm ten years ago. As Blair moved out into the world, climbing from one success to another, Celeste stayed behind in Yorkville in Ellis's house and raised her son on a shoestring budget. Now, Malcolm, already fatherless, would be orphaned, just as Celeste and Blair had once been.

Blair noticed the traffic thinning as she crossed through the suburbs and began to climb into the Poconos. The day was gray and cloudy, and the deep woods made the November day seem dark, even though it was only early afternoon. Blair passed few cars on the way. It was a weekday and the high season in the mountains had not yet begun. It would be another month before the skiers and snowboarders clogged up the streets of Yorkville, contributing to a lively bar and restaurant scene.

Now it will be like a ghost town, Blair thought. Then again, for her, Yorkville would always be a ghost town.

She and Celeste had arrived there as children, haunted by the memory of their mother, who was lost to them forever. Soon, the specter of Celeste would also inhabit these woods. And, of course, the unquiet spirit of Molly Sinclair would always linger here. In Blair's young life, that loss had been almost as terrible as the loss of her mother. Making friends with Molly had given her hope. It had provided an escape from her bleak life in Uncle Ellis's household and suggested a different world full of possibility. But her uncle had sent Molly out into the rainy, foggy night alone and Blair had lost her friend forever. It had not been Blair's choice to let Molly walk out into the gathering darkness by herself. It was her Uncle Ellis's fault, as she tried to explain to the police at the time. But, in the end, it didn't really matter whose choice it was.

Blair got off the highway and wound her way through town.
She passed the Apres Ski café on Main Street. Molly's parents still
ran the coffee house, eventually taking over the stationery store
beside it and doubling the space. Though Janet and Robbie Sinclair
had been kind, insisted to Blair that they understood and did not
blame her, Blair had never believed them. Of course they blamed
her. She blamed herself. She always would.

Blair's car bumped along the rutted road which led to Ellis Dietz's
house. The road had not changed in all these years. The same
trailers and barking dogs that were pacing behind chain-link
fences shared the streetscape. At the end of the road was Uncle
Ellis's house. It seemed to have reached a point of stasis in the
decaying process: the paint was almost gone from the shingles;
the yard was still piled with automotive detritus; the windows
had missing panes and had never been washed, it would seem.
The only difference from Blair's childhood was that the
Confederate Flag, which had hung until it was in tatters, had
been removed from the front of the house. She remembered the
keen sense of shame she always felt when she arrived home and
saw it hanging there. Its absence was something to be grateful
for, she thought.

Blair parked her Nissan beside a compact blue Toyota with
Colorado license plates and got out, hoisting her bag from the
back seat. The blue sedan had a decal of the cross, encircled by
flowers, on the rear window and there were bible verse bumper
stickers on the rear fender. Blair took a deep breath and trudged
up the steps.

She pulled open the ripped screen door and pushed in the
weather-beaten wooden front door.

'Hello,' she called out. 'Anybody here?'

'We're in here,' someone called back from the living room in
a sweet, high voice.

Blair went in. The room was gloomy except for the light on a
table beside the hospital bed. A thin, mild-eyed woman in her
fifties wearing a pale blue cardigan and glasses was seated in a
chair beside the bed. An IV bag on a pole dripped into a tube,
which snaked down and then up, ending under a patch of
tape which was fastened to Celeste's bony forearm.

'You must be Blair,' said the woman. 'I'm Darlene, from the hospice.'

Blair avoided looking at her sister. She had to work up her courage. She smiled at Darlene, who gave her a bright, encouraging smile in return.

'Hi,' she mumbled.

'How was the trip?' Darlene asked kindly.

'It was fine,' said Blair. She could not help herself. She glanced at Celeste's face. At every stage, it had been a shock to see it. Celeste's dry, dyed black hair was fanned out on the pillow around her face. Her cheeks were sunken and her lips were pale, coated with a dried, white crust. Her eyes were rimmed with dark, bruised-looking circles and, at this moment, they were closed.

Darlene observed her gaze. She looked tenderly at Celeste.

'She just fell off to sleep a few minutes ago.'

'Let her be,' said Blair. 'Let her sleep.'

Darlene nodded.

'My uncle told me to come. He said she's . . . not good.'

Darlene sighed. 'No, she's not got a lot of time left.'

Tears rose to Blair's eyes. She knew it was happening. That was why she was here. But the reality of it stubbornly refused to register. She knew it rationally, but the small child inside of her kept on hoping that this was all some big mistake. She wiped her eyes and sat down in a chair on the other side of the hospital bed.

'She sleeps a lot now,' said Darlene.

Blair nodded. She wrapped her hands around the top side rail of the bed and lowered her chin onto her own fists.

'Is she in pain?' Blair asked.

Darlene frowned at the emaciated figure on the bed.

'No. We make sure she's comfortable.'

Blair knew what that meant. They had explained it all to her before, a month ago, when Blair visited the hospice center to discuss the process. Morphine on demand was the end game. Blair wiped her eyes and sniffled.

Just then, Uncle Ellis ambled out from the kitchen at the back of the house, carrying a steaming mug.

'Hi there, Blair,' he said. He handed the mug to Darlene. Then he walked around to Blair and put an awkward arm around her shoulders and gave her a brief squeeze. He gazed down at Celeste.

'Poor kid,' he muttered.

Blair nodded. 'I just can't believe it.'

Ellis scratched his head self-consciously and sighed.

'Well, now that you're here, Blair,' said Darlene, 'I've got some errands to run, and then I'll be back.'

Ellis turned to Darlene.

'I'll go with you,' he mumbled. 'Keep you company.'

Blair expected Darlene to protest, but instead, Darlene smiled.

'That would be very nice,' she said. Blair could hardly conceal her surprise.

Ellis walked over to a hook by the front door and pulled his old, plaid jacket down and shrugged it on. Then he held out Darlene's puffy parka so that she could slip into it. Blair could not remember ever seeing Ellis do such a thing.

'Thank you very kindly,' said Darlene.

'Malcolm will be home soon,' said Ellis to Blair. 'Kid's taking it hard.'

'I can imagine,' said Blair.

Ellis opened the front door and, as he did so, a gray and white cat slipped inside, paused for a moment and then dashed past them toward the kitchen.

'Hey,' said Blair. 'Did you see that cat that just came in?'

Ellis looked sheepish.

'It's Malcolm's,' he said. 'Got her at the vet's. Somebody brought in a feral cat and she had a litter six weeks ago. They've been taking care of them over there.'

'You got Malcolm a cat?' Blair could scarcely believe her ears. She and Celeste were never allowed a pet.

'I suggested it,' said Darlene matter-of-factly. 'A pet can be a big help to a child at a time like this.'

'Right,' said Blair, staring at them. 'I'm sure that's true.' She watched in amazement as the two middle-aged people made their way out the front door, Darlene chatting in her lilting voice and Ellis grunting in assent.

A cat? Darlene had talked Uncle Ellis into getting a pet for Malcolm. What next? The two of them taking dancing lessons? Blair would not have expected this woman to catch Uncle Ellis's fancy. Blair could understand how it might happen with normal people. A situation like this was very . . . intimate. It would be easy to imagine how a man could become dependent, even tender, toward a woman who was always there, helping his loved one through the final passage of life. *But this was Ellis!*

There had been times, in the course of Celeste's illness, when Ellis had seemed genuinely troubled. Maybe he was, in fact, grieving. As families went, they were a sorry lot, but Blair, Celeste and Malcolm were all the family that Ellis had.

'Blair?' Celeste's voice was a whisper.

Blair looked up at her sister's face tenderly.

'Hey. You're awake.'

Celeste did not bother to answer. Blair gripped her hand.

'I just got here,' Blair said. 'Can I do anything? Get you anything?'

Celeste shook her head slightly. Blair reached out and brushed Celeste's hair back off of her forehead.

'Darlene and Ellis went out to do some errands. You know, I have to tell you this,' she said, in the conspiratorial tone she used to use, when they shared secrets as young girls. 'I think there might be something going on with those two. Ellis helped her on with her coat. I saw it with my own eyes!'

Celeste's gaze was foggy, but a mischievious light appeared in her eyes for a moment.

'Unbelievable, right?' asked Blair.

Celeste nodded slightly.

'Honestly,' said Blair, 'I am trying to imagine what she sees in him. Uncle Ellis? I mean, how hard up would you have to be?'

Celeste suddenly gripped Blair's fingers with more force than Blair could have imagined possible.

'Blair, listen,' she said. 'While they're gone . . .'

Blair frowned and leaned in close to her sister's face.

'I'm listening,' she said.

Celeste licked her cracked lips.

'We have to talk about Malcolm,' she said.

Blair's first thought was to deny this. To assure her sister that there was no urgency about it. But the words died on her lips. Celeste was dying and the thing foremost in her mind was her son. It would be wrong – cruel even – to pretend that she didn't understand.

At least Blair was ready for this. She had given it a lot of thought. It was not something she would ever have wished for and she still didn't know how she would manage, with her long hours and a ten-year-old who knew no one in Philly. But she would find a way. Whatever it took.

'I don't want him to grow up in this house without me,' said Celeste.

'I totally get that,' said Blair. 'We both know what that was like.'

Celeste nodded. 'I need you to stand up to Ellis for me. He might give you a hard time.'

'Just because he's Ellis. Don't worry,' Blair reassured her. 'I'm not some helpless kid anymore.'

'I know. I trust you,' Celeste whispered. She squeezed her sister's hand. 'Blair, I've given it a lot of thought.'

'I'm sure you have,' said Blair.

'The thing is, this is his home.'

'This house?' Blair asked, incredulous.

'Yorkville. These mountains,' said Celeste. 'Everyone he knows. He loves it here.'

Blair nodded. She could not imagine why anyone would love it here, but she knew that many people did.

'I want him to stay here. To live with Amanda and Peter. And Zach.'

Blair was too stunned to speak for a moment. 'Amanda?'

'She's been my best friend forever.'

'I know,' Blair stuttered, 'but I thought . . .'

'The Tuckers are like family. They love him. They want him there.'

'Celeste, he's my nephew. I want to . . . take care of him,' Blair cried, surprised by the sincerity with which the words sprang from her lips.

Celeste tried to smile, but there were tears in her eyes.

'Oh Blair, that's kind. But I know what your life is like. There's no room in it for a young boy.'

Blair turned her face away angrily, trying not to say anything to her dying sister that she would regret later.

'There are a lot of ways . . . you can help him,' Celeste said softly.

'Like what?' Blair asked gruffly, bruised by her sister's decision.

'Well, as you know, I have nothing to leave him. Maybe . . . if you could help him out from time to time . . .'

'You mean, like, financially?' Blair asked bluntly.

'Only if you want to . . .' said Celeste. 'I would never ask . . .'
Blair was both hurt . . . and relieved. Giving money was easy,
compared to raising a child. Part of her wanted to say something
mean, to hurt Celeste for her choice. But she reminded herself
that she had asked how she could help and Celeste had told her
honestly. This was no time to be petty.

'Of course I can do that,' Blair said. 'I'll gladly do that.'

'And you'll stay in his life, right? You'll come to see him.'

'Of course,' said Blair, even though she could scarcely imagine
coming back to this town for any reason.

'When he gets older, maybe he'll want to come to the big city,'
Celeste said hopefully.

Blair was tempted to say something brusque about Malcolm
never wanting to leave these hills. And then she looked into her
sister's weary, pain-filled eyes. She'll never see him grow up, Blair
thought. It was hard to imagine how awful it must be for a mother,
to know that.

'Maybe he will,' Blair agreed gently. 'Maybe he'll . . . go to
school there. He'll always have a home with me, if he wants it.'

Celeste closed her eyes.

'Thanks for understanding, Blair.'

Blair nodded. She did not really understand. She was hurt and
. . . insulted, in a way. But she knew she had to try and see it from
Celeste's point of view. She didn't want to take everything familiar
away from her son. The front door slammed and Blair jumped. She
looked around and saw Malcolm trudging in, his backpack slung
over his shoulder. His narrow shoulders were slumped and he looked
weary, his school clothes dingy and disheveled.

'Malcolm,' she exclaimed.

Malcolm stopped short, alarmed at the sight of his aunt at his
mother's bedside.

'Hey Aunt Blair. What are you doing here?'

Blair hesitated. How much did the boy know? Children had a
way of avoiding the obvious. She remembered that from her own
mother's death.

'Uncle Ellis called me. So I came.'

'Why?' he demanded alarmed.

'Because I missed her,' said Celeste, in a weak, but determinedly
cheerful voice. 'Come here and give me a kiss.'

Warily, he approached his mother's bed, bent down and gave her a quick kiss on the forehead.

Celeste smiled. 'How was school?'

'Lame,' he said, shifting his backpack from one shoulder to the other. 'Did my cat come in?'

'I don't know. I may have been asleep,' said Celeste.

'He came in. He went back toward the kitchen,' said Blair.

'It's a she,' said Malcolm. 'Her name's Dusty.'

Blair smiled. 'That's a cute name.'

Malcolm shrugged. 'I woulda rather had a dog, but the vet had this cat. So I took it. I like her. She's pretty cool.' Malcolm started to walk back toward the kitchen.

'Malcolm. Stay a minute,' said Celeste.

Blair looked at the deathly pallor of Celeste's complexion, the almost imperceptible movement of her chest. She was emitting a dry, halting whistle with each breath.

'I'll come back,' he promised. 'Later.'

Blair could remember, as if it were yesterday, being in his shoes. He didn't want to see his mother like this. He was thinking that if he avoided going near her, maybe she would stop all this, get well and come back to their life. Come back to him.

'Ok,' Celeste whispered. 'Love you.'

'Love you too,' he mumbled.

Blair gazed helplessly at her sister's face. 'Don't worry, Malcolm. I'll stay with her.'

TWO

When Blair looked back on the next few days, they seemed to meld into one long, miserable day. The ancient curtains were pulled shut and the living room seemed to be in a constant twilight. Other people came and went, visiting and speaking in hushed voices. A few of the guys, whom Ellis drank with at the VFW, showed up with their wives. The women each sat a few helpless moments with Celeste, while their husbands drank beer in the kitchen with Ellis.

Darlene was often there and she and Blair would have desultory conversations. Blair wanted to ask her about Uncle Ellis, but it seemed disrespectful somehow. She settled for asking Darlene about her life.

'Well, I'm divorced,' said Darlene. 'My son still lives in Colorado.'

'I noticed your Colorado license plate. How do you like living here?' Blair asked her.

Darlene shrugged. 'It's ok. I'm living with my brother, Joseph. His wife of many years died, so I came here to try to help him out. They lived on a farm that used to be her family's place. It's very peaceful there.'

'That would not be my idea of a good time,' Blair admitted. Then, realizing how judgmental that sounded, she tried to mitigate the harshness. 'I guess I'm just too used to being on my own.'

'Well, Joseph's my twin,' said Darlene. 'I can practically read his mind. I could tell that it was too much for him to handle all alone.'

'Was his wife sick for a long time before she died?' Blair asked.

'No, it was sudden. He tried to be stoic after Eileen died, but the shock of it was awful.'

'It was good of you to come here to be with him. Leaving your other life behind that way couldn't have been easy.'

'Well, there wasn't that much to leave behind. Besides, that's what you do for family, right?' Then she looked kindly at Blair. 'You've been a very good sister to Celeste.'

Blair could not help blushing.

'Thank you,' she said, inordinately grateful for the woman's kind words. She often felt that no one understood how much this was tearing her up, but, of course, there were people who did. Several people.

Amanda came by often. Sometimes she came with her son, Zach, and sometimes with Zach and her husband, Peter. They would pick Malcolm up for dinner and the two boys would rough-house or tease one another as they left the house. Amanda was always tearful as she stopped in the living room to see Celeste. Peter would remain in the doorway, but Amanda would lean over to brush Celeste's hair back and kiss her forehead.

'How are you holding up?' Amanda asked Blair one evening as she arrived.

'I'm stiff in muscles I didn't know I had,' Blair admitted. 'I'd kill for a yoga class.'

'They have one at the Rec Center. Why don't you go? Take a break. I'll stay with her.'

Blair looked at Celeste's face.

'No. I need to be here,' she said.

'I understand. She's been my best friend forever,' Amanda said. 'I always thought we would spend our whole lives together.' She stifled a sob. 'What will I do without her . . .?'

Blair thanked Amanda for taking Malcolm away from the gloomy house for the evening. The woman nodded.

'Maybe it will get his mind off it,' she said, and then she shook her head sadly. 'As if . . .'

'Celeste told me,' Blair said, 'that Malcolm is going to live with you . . . after . . .'

Amanda nodded and began to weep. 'It's all that I can do for her.' Then a thought suddenly seemed to occur to Amanda. 'You don't mind, do you?'

Blair swallowed hard and shook her head.

'No. I think it's very good of you.'

'She wants him to live here, where everything is comfortable for him and familiar. And she said that you would explain it all to Ellis.'

'Oh I will,' said Blair grimly.

'We went to an attorney and everything. Celeste didn't want to leave it to chance.'

'That was wise,' said Blair. She glanced at Celeste, still breathing and felt terribly awkward to even be mentioning what was going to happen after . . . 'I don't think we should . . .'

Amanda glanced tearfully at Celeste's face.

'No. You're right . . .'

They never discussed the details. It was just too final a conversation to have while Celeste still lived.

The hours dragged but the days seemed to pass in a twinkling. Celeste rarely opened her eyes and when she did, she seemed to look upon the room and the friends and family members gathered there, as if she were already far, far away. Once in a great while she would utter a few words, but they were often garbled, and made no sense.

Sometimes Malcolm would come and stand beside the bed, staring silently at his mother. Blair tried to talk to him, but he mostly ignored her attempts, retreating to his room. One night, as Blair was sitting beside Celeste's bed, all her muscles cramped, longing for the peace and release of a long yoga class, she suddenly saw Celeste's eyes open and stare at her.

'Hi sweetie,' she said, glad she was here, rather than off in some class contorting herself into the downward dog. Here she was needed. Though, in truth, she was no longer sure if Celeste was aware of anyone or anything around her.

Celeste frowned, the parchment-colored skin of her forehead rippling slightly. She spoke in a whisper and Blair had to lean over to hear her.

'I have to tell you something,' she said quite clearly.

Blair's heart jumped. 'Anything,' said Blair.

There was a painful silence.

'I did something bad,' Celeste whispered.

'Oh Celeste. There's nothing bad that you did,' Blair said urgently. 'Nothing that matters now. You've always been the best mother and the best sister . . .'

'Blair . . .' Celeste said, a note of impatience in her scratchy voice.

Blair was shocked by her sister's insistence. She acquiesced immediately.

'I'm sorry,' said Blair. 'Tell me what you were going to say.'

Celeste closed her eyes and, for a moment, Blair thought she was going back to sleep. And then she seemed to marshal her forces. She opened her eyes and looked straight at Blair.

'Adrian Jones,' she whispered.

The name surged through Blair like a jolt of electricity. It was about the last thing she had expected to hear. No one had mentioned that name in years. Adrian Jones. Blair understood that he had another name now. Something Muhammed. He had become a Muslim in prison. He was in the state penitentiary at Greenwood. He was serving a life sentence for the murder of Molly Sinclair.

Blair frowned at her sister. 'What about him?' she asked.

Celeste stared at Blair for what seemed like a long time. She licked her lips a few times, as if she was going to speak and then she didn't.

'You're talking about the guy that killed Molly,' Blair prodded her.

Celeste looked relieved, as if she was not sure that Blair had understood who Adrian Jones was.

'He didn't,' she whispered. 'I was there.'

'You were where?' Blair demanded. 'I don't . . .'

'That night. In his car. Like he said.'

Blair stared at her dying sister, trying to grasp what she was hearing. On the evening that Molly was killed, after she left Blair's house, it had begun to rain. Blair could remember looking out at the rain and worrying about her friend. Chased away by Uncle Ellis, Molly had set out walking without even an umbrella or a raincoat. During the trial, the prosecution produced a witness; a delivery truck driver who had seen a car pull up beside Molly that rainy evening, on the road leading into the woods and saw Molly get in. From the man's description, they were able to trace the car to Adrian Jones.

Adrian Jones, a young African-American man who had been picked up a few times for possession of marijuana and shoplifting, knew Molly. His mother made pies and pastries for the Apres Ski café. When he was questioned, Adrian insisted indignantly at first that it was not him, not his car. When the police searched his car and found Molly's cell phone, wedged in the back seat, Adrian changed his story. He admitted picking Molly up, but insisted that he was not alone when he stopped for her. Celeste was with him and recognized the girl as Blair's friend. They offered Molly a ride because of the rain.

Uncle Ellis had been apoplectic when he heard this incredible lie. Blair could remember the raised voices, the accusations, the word 'nigger kid' spat repeatedly from Uncle Ellis's lips. Celeste had been steadfast, insisted that she was nowhere near that car. That she didn't even know Adrian Jones. Without an alibi, Adrian Jones became the obvious, the only suspect. At his trial, the jury convicted him in less than two hours.

'Celeste, that can't be. He went to jail for that. Adrian Jones. He's been in jail for . . . years.'

'Yes,' Celeste croaked. 'I lied.'

'But why?' Blair demanded, shocked by her sister's treachery. 'What were you thinking? Didn't you know what kind of trouble you were getting him into? You were sixteen. You had to know what would happen.'

'I didn't . . .' Celeste protested, and Blair saw tears form in her fever bright eyes.

Celeste held Blair's fingers in a surprisingly strong grip. Blair could see that it was taking every ounce of her will to explain this.

'Uncle Ellis. Me with Adrian . . . He would have killed me. Put us out in the street. You were so young,' Celeste said. She closed her eyes.

Oh no, thought Blair. Wait, just a minute. She had to stifle the impulse to tear her fingers from Celeste's grip. To push her away. You didn't do this for me, she wanted to say, don't use me as your excuse.

'I've been gone from this house for years,' she cried. 'But Adrian's still in jail. And you're saying now that he's innocent. How could you . . .?'

'I was a coward,' Celeste whispered.

'Celeste, my God . . .'

'I'm sorry,' Celeste whimpered. 'Sorry.'

But even as she reeled with disbelief, Blair knew that Celeste was right about one thing. Uncle Ellis never made any secret of the fact that having to raise his nieces had ruined his life. It would have seemed like all the rationale he needed to pitch them out. To expect a teenager to stand up to her bitter guardian, to defy those fascist rantings which were almost his religion, was the unforgivable thing.

'Tell them,' Celeste whispered.

'I'm sorry. What?' Blair asked.

'Tell them. Tell someone,' Celeste pleaded. 'He didn't kill her.'

Blair shook her head, as if she could not process the information all at once.

'Please,' Celeste whispered.

'Yes. Yes, I understand,' said Blair. 'I will. Don't worry. I will.'

Celeste sighed. Having rid herself of her terrible secret, she seemed to relax. Celeste's eyes closed and her ragged breathing became shallow. Her grip on Blair's fingers loosened and then her hand fell away.

'Celeste,' Blair whispered. 'Can you hear me?'

Celeste seemed to be receding in front of her eyes. Blair stared at her sister's waxy face, while her brain went into overdrive. My God, she thought. That man is in prison for a crime he didn't commit and now I know it for a fact. I have to do something about this. Celeste, freed of her guilty burden, began to breathe more slowly, with greater difficulty. Blair watched her helplessly. Her head was pounding and she was overcome with the exhaustion of sitting beside that bed, waiting. How long had it been? Her heart felt as if it were being torn and twisted in her body as she watched her sister start to disappear. Although she did not feel the least bit tired, she lay her head down on the bed, near Celeste's face. She could smell her sister's breath, foul as a pit. She closed her eyes, just for a moment, against the pain.

The next thing she knew, someone was shaking her by the shoulder. She opened her eyes and looked up. Ellis, unshaven, stood beside the bed in his work pants and thermal undershirt, the boots on his feet unfastened. He was staring down at Celeste's face.

Blair blinked at her uncle, frowning. She was halfway between sleep and waking, trying to take it in.

'What?' she mumbled.

'It's over,' he said. 'She's gone.'

THREE

Snow flurries began on the morning of Celeste's funeral and, by the end of the day, Yorkville was veiled in white. The service for Celeste was held in the unfamiliar sanctuary of Darlene's church, where Darlene's brother was a deacon. Darlene suggested that the service might be held there and Celeste's family, belonging to no congregation, gratefully accepted. The pastor, though he had not known Celeste, led a moving service, inspired by the loss of a young mother in the prime of her life. Blair wept frequently during the service; even Uncle Ellis's eyes glittered and reddened. Malcolm was stoic throughout. The effort he made was heroic, but pointless. No one expected him to remain composed at the funeral of his only parent . . .

After the service and the burial in a hillside cemetery beside the church, a small reception was held in the Church Rectory. Malcolm and Blair shuffled along the slippery sidewalk with the other mourners. Malcolm allowed Blair to hold his arm as they mounted the stairs to enter the Rectory, while Uncle Ellis walked behind them. The spacious, slightly shabby old house quickly filled up with people. Darlene bustled around setting out punch, trays of sandwiches and bowls of potato salad on doilies on the dining room table. Darlene's brother, a man with gray, thinning hair and wire-rimmed glasses just like hers, did as he was bidden by his twin, unwrapping paper cups and Styrofoam plates for the mourners. Darlene approached the family as they came in and introduced them.

'This is my brother, Joseph Reese,' said Darlene. Everyone shook hands. Ellis had clearly not met Darlene's brother before and he tried his best to be sociable. It was painful to watch Ellis's awkward efforts, while Reese peered at him suspiciously.

'Thank you for arranging this with your Pastor,' said Blair, when she was introduced.

'Oh, he was happy to do it. Very sad about your sister,' said Reese. His hand, when Blair shook it, felt cool and clammy. 'Terrible,' he said, 'when it's someone so young.'

'We really appreciate your help,' Blair said.

Reese sniffed.

'Well, when Darlene gets a bee in her bonnet . . . I did have to take the day off from work,' he admitted.

'Where do you work?' Blair asked politely.

'I'm a Greyhound driver. I do the regular route to Philadelphia.' Reese turned to Malcolm, who shook his hand as well. 'Sorry for your loss, son. We lost our father when we were young and then my mother had a breakdown,' Reese intoned, intending to be sympathetic. Blair could see that Malcolm was not comforted. 'Took me and Darlene years to get over it,' Reese recalled with a certain relish.

There were quite a few mourners. As antisocial as Ellis was, the Dietz family had been in this town for generations. People who had known not only Celeste, but also their mother, Tina, came up and introduced themselves to Blair. Blair went numbly through the motions, thanking everyone she met for coming. Although she had spent a lot of time in Yorkville since Celeste fell ill, she had not spent any of it socializing. She had not seen most of these people in many years.

Malcolm, on the other hand, seemed to know a lot of people. Blair watched as several kids his age in the crowd, accompanied by adults, greeted Malcolm awkwardly.

'Your mother would be proud of you,' Blair whispered to him, as Malcolm shook hands gravely with the adults.

Zach, Amanda and Peter were among the mourners. Blair thought that the Tuckers made an attractive family. Amanda was still trim, her coppery hair pulled up in a swinging pony tail. She kept one hand firmly on Zach's shoulder. The seven-year-old seemed a little frightened by the proceedings. Peter, who was a forest ranger, had thick hair that was sun-streaked and a complexion which was permanently bronzed from working outside. Blair felt a pang of loneliness, watching them. Zach was younger than Malcolm, but seemed to treat him like a big brother already. Amanda and Peter watched over both boys protectively. Blair could see how faithfully Amanda intended to fulfill her promise to Celeste. It will be fine, Blair thought. He'll have a good life with them.

Just then a middle-aged couple approached Blair.

'Blair, I'm so sorry about your sister,' said the woman. It took Blair a moment to place her, and then, when she did, her eyes filled again with tears. Molly's parents.

'Mrs Sinclair, Mr Sinclair.'

The woman smiled. She had aged a lot since Blair had seen her last. Her long, dark hair was shot through with gray and her face was deeply lined.

'Oh, call us Janet and Robbie,' the woman said kindly. 'We're all grown-ups now. What are you doing these days?'

Blair had been so preoccupied with Celeste's funeral, that she had not been able to concentrate on her sister's deathbed confession. Seeing Robbie and Janet Sinclair brought it all back to her in a rush. As she stumbled over a few details of her life in Philadelphia, Blair wondered if these nice people would still be speaking to her once they found out what she had learned about Adrian Jones, now Yusef Muhammed. But surely they would want the truth to come out. Wouldn't they?

'How about you?' she asked. 'You still own the Apres Ski?'

Robbie Sinclair nodded. He had a round, still youthful face, but his hair was graying and his eyes had a weary cast to them.

'Oh sure. Keeps us busy.'

Blair hesitated.

'I'm going to need to come and talk to you while I'm here. Do you still live in the same house?'

Janet Sinclair nodded. 'Same house. The neighborhood's changed a lot. A lot of big new houses where it used to be all woods. But we're right in the same place. Come by anytime. We'd love a chance to visit. We just wanted to be here to offer our condolences.'

'Thanks,' said Blair, squeezing Janet's hands in her own, cold hands. 'It was kind of you to come.'

People continued to stream through offering hugs and words of comfort. The whole day was exhausting and, when the last guests had said their goodbyes, Darlene urged Ellis, Blair and Malcolm to return to the house while she stayed behind to help tidy up the Rectory.

'Joseph will help me here,' she said. Darlene's brother was sitting by the window, looking worriedly out at the lowering skies, as if anxious to get out of there before the storm worsened. Blair pretended not to notice his impatience. She wanted to take the opportunity to leave. Everyone was drained and weary. They rode home in silence in Ellis's truck, entered the house and turned on a few lights against the gathering gloom of the afternoon.

'Malcolm, do you want anything to . . .' Malcolm shook his head miserably before Blair could finish the sentence and went up to his room. Blair went into the living room to turn on the lights there and saw that the hospital bed, and all the equipment that had been there for Celeste, had been removed while they were at the funeral.

'Wow,' she said.

'Wow what?' asked Ellis.

'What happened to all the stuff? The bed. Everything?'

'The hospice people.'

'That's an efficient organization,' Blair said. 'Did you know they were coming to pick up everything while we were gone?'

Ellis nodded. 'We had it all worked out beforehand.'

'You and Darlene?' said Blair.

'Yup.'

Blair looked around the living room, now emptied of the medical equipment. She noticed that the Nazi memorabilia which Ellis always displayed in the bookcase by the brick hearth was not in its customary place.

'How come you took down your Nazi stuff?'

'When I found out the hospice was coming, I hid it in that cupboard above the washing machine,' said Ellis. 'I was afraid someone of these strangers coming and going might help themselves to it.'

'Are you kidding? Nobody wants that vile crap.' It felt good – bracing almost – to call it what it was. Ellis couldn't threaten her any longer. She had her own life, far away from here.

'That's what you know. That collection is valuable.'

Blair shrugged. 'I can't picture Darlene coveting your swastikas. In fact, she'd probably be horrified if she knew you had them.'

'Not Darlene,' he scoffed. 'She's good people. But I knew all Celeste's lowlife friends would be coming around.'

Blair shook her head and did not respond. There was no point.

'So,' said Ellis, changing the subject. 'I guess you'll be leaving soon.'

Immediately, Blair thought of Adrian Jones.

'The fact is, I was planning to leave right away,' she said, 'but my plans have changed. Something has come up.' She was going to have to tell him about Celeste's confession eventually. She wondered if this was the moment.

But Ellis did not leave her an opening.

'Well, you can stay if you want. This is your home,' he said flatly.

Blair stared at her uncle. Her home? She despised this place, but she could see that he meant it sincerely.

'Well, I thought I would stick around a little while. Sort through Celeste's things. Maybe help Malcolm get adjusted to the new situation. It's a lot of changes for him.'

'What new situation?' Ellis demanded.

'Well, you know. His new home.'

Ellis peered at her. 'New home?'

Blair suddenly realized, with a sinking feeling, that Ellis knew nothing about it. Celeste had never told her uncle about her plans for Malcolm. Blair shook her head. Had Celeste ever dealt with a single uncomfortable truth head on? Had she avoided every single difficult admission?

'I thought Celeste would have told you,' said Blair.

'Told me what?'

'Malcolm is going to be living with Amanda and Peter Tucker, and their son, Zach.'

'The hell he is,' said Ellis. 'That kid's not going anywhere.'

'Frankly, I would have thought you'd be relieved to be rid of him,' she said coldly.

'I never said that,' Ellis protested, glowering. 'He can just stay put.'

'Look, I don't want to argue with you about this,' said Blair. 'Those were Celeste's wishes. As I understand it, she went to an attorney and made it all legal.'

'That's ridiculous,' said Ellis. 'She didn't have no money for a lawyer, unless you gave it to her.'

'This has absolutely nothing to do with me,' Blair protested.

'She didn't ask you to take him?' Ellis demanded.

'No, in fact, she didn't,' said Blair.

'Shows you what she thought of you,' he said unkindly. 'Taking her kid from family and giving him to strangers,' Ellis muttered. 'Who does that? It's wrong. It's just wrong.'

'It's what she thought would be best,' said Blair.

'Your sister was dumb,' he grumbled, 'But even she—'

'Do you mind?' Blair said icily. 'We've just come from her funeral. Do you think you could avoid trashing Celeste on the day we buried her?'

'I'm not trashing her,' Ellis insisted stubbornly. 'I'm telling it like it is. She lived under my roof for all these years. I guess I know a few things about her that you don't.'

'Look, she should have told you what her plan was. I assumed she had.'

'Didn't tell me nothing. In fact, I don't believe it. This sounds like something you cooked up.'

Blair sighed and shook her head. 'There's no use talking to you. I'm going upstairs.'

'We'll just see about this,' Ellis called after her.

Blair turned her back on him and headed for the stairs. She climbed up to the second floor and stopped at the door to Malcolm's room which was closed. She could see the light was on, but when she tapped on the door, he did not answer.

'Malcolm, it's me,' she said.

The boy did not reply.

Blair waited at the door for a few minutes and tapped again. Finally, the door opened. Malcolm stared out at her with desolate eyes.

'Oh Malcolm,' said Blair. 'It's been such a horrible day. I'm so sorry.'

Malcolm did not reply.

'Are you hungry? There's still lots of food in the fridge. Or I can take you out somewhere if you'd like.'

'I don't want to go anywhere,' the boy said.

'Do you want to talk?'

Malcolm shrugged. 'Not really.'

'Malcolm, I just want you to know that I understand. I really do. I know how terrible it is.'

The cat meowed and slid out around his legs and through the open door. She headed for the staircase.

'Can I come in for a minute?' Blair asked.

Malcolm hesitated and then stepped back from the door just far enough for Blair to enter the room. Blair looked around. The room was small and claustrophobic, with the bed, the chair and the floor near the closet piled with dirty clothes. Every inch of wall space was decorated with menacing-looking posters of zombies, vampires and heavy metal rock groups fastened to the wall with pushpins. A smiling photo of Malcolm and Celeste sat atop a bookcase that seemed to be exploding with disorganized books, papers and miscellaneous junk.

'I just want you to know,' Blair said. 'I'm going to stick around for a while and help you get everything sorted out. Did your Mom talk to you about what's going to happen?'

'What do you mean?' he demanded.

There it was again. She could see in his eyes that he had no idea of what she was talking about. How could you not have told him, Celeste, she wondered?

'Well,' Blair said, and she could feel herself backtracking. 'I mean, in your future.'

'What do you mean? Like going to college?' he demanded. 'Cause I don't want to go.'

Blair had to smile. 'Well, that's a long way away. I was thinking of other, more immediate things.'

'What other things?' he cried.

Blair licked her lips and tried again. 'Did Amanda and Peter talk to you about what your Mom wanted for you?'

'No,' he said. 'Why would they?'

'Malcolm, you know how much your mom loved Amanda, right? They were best friends.'

'I know,' he said. 'She said Amanda was like a real sister.'

Blair wondered what that meant about her. She couldn't help feeling a little hurt, but she reminded herself that her own feelings weren't important right now.

'And you and Zach are very close.'

'Yeah,' said Malcolm suspiciously.

'Well, your Mom wanted you to stay here in Yorkville and the Tuckers are a part of that plan.'

Malcolm was peering at her suspiciously. 'What plan?'

Blair hesitated. This might not be the moment, but she didn't want Malcolm to hear about it from Uncle Ellis.

'Look, your Mom thought it might be best for you to live where you'd have more of a regular family life. That's why she thought of the Tuckers and they want to take care of you.'

'Live with the Tuckers? But I live here,' Malcolm protested. 'With Uncle Ellis. Is he going away somewhere?'

'No, no. But your Uncle Ellis is getting . . . pretty old. Your Mom was worried about the future. She had to think about that for you.'

'Doesn't he want to keep me?'

Blair felt like this conversation was going awry and Malcolm was getting upset. She decided to speak in generalities. There would be time for specifics tomorrow.

'Of course. Of course he does. He loves you. And so do the Tuckers. A lot of people are on your side, and want to take care of you. Do you know that? I mean, it's not the same as having your mother, but the important thing is that you are definitely not alone.'

Malcolm shrugged. 'I guess.'

'With a loss like this, it can leave you feeling . . . adrift in the world. But you are absolutely not alone. Uncle Ellis. Amanda and Peter. And me. We all want to do anything and everything we can for you.'

'What about my cat?' he asked.

'What about your cat?' she asked.

'If I lived at the Tuckers, would my cat come with me?'

'Oh sure. Of course,' said Blair, encouraged that he was considering the idea and she hoped that no one had allergies to cat dander at the Tuckers.

'When would I go there?' he asked.

'Listen, sweetie, I don't want you to worry about it. There's so much that still has to be discussed and decided. There's no big rush. I just thought you . . . would want to know what's going on.'

'I guess,' he said.

'And Malcolm. I mean, just speaking for myself, you can always depend on me. You can call me, day or night. I'll always be there for you. You're my only nephew and I love you.'

'Ok,' he muttered, and then he yawned.

Blair sighed. Enough for one night, she thought.

'Look, we're all tired tonight. It's been a terrible day. The worst day ever. We can talk more about this tomorrow. Why don't we go downstairs and get something to eat?'

'Not hungry,' he said.

'I can't help worrying about you,' she said.

Suddenly, to Blair's amazement, Malcolm hurled himself at her and wrapped his arms around her waist. She smoothed his hair with her hand.

'It's ok. It's ok. Everything will be all right,' she whispered.

'Thanks, Aunt Blair,' he mumbled.

He let her go and flung himself on his bed. Blair looked at him sadly, wishing she could take the sorrow away, but there was no avoiding it. In the book of his life, this would always be the chapter on unbearable pain. Accepting the unacceptable.

'If you need me, I'm right down the hall,' she said.

Malcolm stared at the wall and did not reply.

Blair went down the hall to her room and sat down on the twin bed. She drew her knees up to her chest, pulling the old flowered quilt around her, looking out the window at the faraway moon. I'll help him, she vowed to herself. I will help him get through it. Blair shook her head. Celeste had lived her life avoiding confrontation and departed her life leaving huge issues unresolved. It wasn't just her nephew who was suffering, Blair reminded herself. Thanks to a lie from Celeste, an innocent man sat in his prison, as he had for fifteen years, his life stolen from him. Malcolm was not the only one who needed her attention. Tomorrow, first thing, Blair had to set the wheels in motion. She had to fulfill her promise to Celeste and begin seeking justice for Adrian Jones.

FOUR

The house was freezing, as usual. It seemed to rattle with every gust of wind and cold air leaked through the warped window frames. Wrapped in an old wool bathrobe, Blair sat at the kitchen table and ate cereal from an ancient melamine bowl, so scratched she could barely determine what color it had once been. She was grateful to be alone. Ellis had gone off to work and Malcolm was still sleeping. He needed to rest. Blair's only company was the cat, who had curled up on the extra kitchen chair in the corner.

As Blair munched on her cereal, she contemplated the problem of Adrian Jones. It seemed logical to go to the police first. She wondered, briefly, if they would resent any implication that they had not done their job sufficiently well all those years ago. It wasn't their fault Celeste had lied. They would probably be as eager as Blair to make this situation right. A great injustice had been done to Adrian Jones. The sooner it was rectified, the better.

Just then, her cell phone rang and Blair pulled it out of her bathrobe pocket.

'Blair?'

'Yes.'

'It's Amanda.'

'Hi Amanda. How are you?'

Amanda sighed. 'Hanging in there. Look, I think we need to discuss the details of how we're going to get Malcolm moved in with us. I'm at work, but you could meet me for lunch.'

Blair grimaced. 'Amanda, we're going to have to take this slowly.'

'Why?' Amanda asked.

'Well, I mentioned it to my Uncle last night, that Celeste wanted Malcolm to live with you and your family, and he was not happy.'

'What do you mean? Celeste didn't tell him?'

'No, she didn't. She didn't tell Malcolm either.'

'Oh my God.'

'I know,' said Blair. 'She was hopeless that way. Anything to avoid a confrontation.'

'I just assumed . . .' said Amanda.

'Listen, it could be worse,' said Blair. 'At least she took care of it legally. If she hadn't, there's no way my uncle would agree to it.'

'But he doesn't even want Malcolm.'

Blair sighed. 'It's as if Celeste planned to give away property that belonged to Ellis, without telling him. Look, there's no use in arguing with my uncle. It's impossible to reason with him. I thought I would get a copy of the legal agreement from the attorney to show him.'

'Well, you can get a copy from Brooks Whitman. He's the one we went to see,' said Amanda. 'I'd meet you there, but I can't miss any more work right now. I might need to take some time off while Malcolm is settling in.'

Blair could picture Amanda in her teller's cubicle at the bank. She was probably violating the rules by talking on the phone.

'Of course,' said Blair. 'Don't worry. I'll take care of it. Let me give this attorney a call. The sooner we get started, the better.'

Just then, Blair heard the front door open and a voice called out, 'Anybody home?'

Blair went out into the hallway and saw Darlene coming into the house, a grocery bag in either hand.

'Hi,' said Blair. 'What are you doing here?'

'Well, I brought over a few things. I thought I'd . . . clean up a little bit around here. Run the vacuum. You don't mind, do you?'

'Mind?' Blair yelped. 'Are you kidding? I'd be grateful. In fact, I need to go out for a while and Malcolm's upstairs asleep.'

Darlene hung her coat on a hook and waved off Blair's anxious question.

'Go on ahead. I'll stay here with him. I'll make him some breakfast when he wakes up.'

Blair had the impulse to embrace the older woman, but she hesitated.

'I can't thank you enough.'

'Get on with your business. We'll be fine.'

Brooks Whitman's office was located just past the town center in a small, two-story wooden building – once a private home – which was painted a sober, forest green with bronze and black trim. The house had a handicapped ramp as well as steps to the front porch. There was a sign at the roadside, painted in the same colors as the house, announcing the law practice of Whitman, Ferguson and Toll. A small, gravel parking lot in front of the building took up most of what had once been a front lawn. Blair parked her car and went inside.

The first floor was a wide, narrow reception area, blandly outfitted. Functional, not too comfortable chairs were separated by glass end tables and a large reception desk took up most of the room. Blair identified herself to the receptionist and sat down. She had barely thumbed through the pile of *Forbes* and *Business Week* magazines, when the door to the inner office opened and a silver-haired man wearing a gray suit and a wedding ring emerged. He spoke quietly to the receptionist and then he turned to Blair.

'Miss Butler, do you want to come in?'

'Yes, sure,' said Blair, jumping up from the chair.

'I'm Brooks Whitman,' he said, offering his hand. Blair shook it, and followed the attorney into his office.

'Thanks for seeing me today,' said Blair.

'I'm glad you called,' said the attorney.

He sat down behind his large desk and smiled. He was surrounded by an array of framed photos. There were family pictures all over the room: wedding pictures, smiling skiing shots, grandchildren, Brooks Whitman and his amiable-looking wife in formal attire. It was the story of generations of a family, captured in happy memories. Blair looked at them and felt a pang of envy. There was little from her own past that bore memorializing. Since she left Yorkville, she had been so busy with her education and her career that her single state never really bothered her. She thought of her life as streamlined. But there were some days, like lately, when she would have been most grateful to be half of a pair, part of a family.

'Now,' said the attorney. He straightened the papers on his desk, as if to get his thoughts in order and then folded his hands in front of him. 'First of all, let me say, I'm very sorry for your loss.'

'Thank you,' said Blair.

'Amanda Tucker called and said you needed a copy of that custody agreement she signed with your sister.'

'That would be hugely helpful to me,' said Blair. 'You see, my sister made these arrangements with Amanda, but never told my uncle. Right now, he is protesting the idea of my nephew moving away from the family home.'

Brooks Whitman grimaced. 'Well, Celeste was very concerned about her son. She wanted to protect him. I advised her strongly to discuss this with your uncle.'

Blair shook her head. 'Well, she didn't do it.'

'I'm sorry,' he said. 'These matters are rarely simple.' He pressed a button on his intercom and spoke to his assistant, ordering her to make a copy of the agreement between Amanda and Peter Tucker and Celeste. Then he folded his hands on his desk and smiled at Blair. 'This should take care of it.'

'And if my uncle tries to block it . . .'

'He can try all he likes. It's a legal agreement, witnessed, nota-rized and expressing the final wishes of your sister about the custody of her son.'

Blair nodded. 'Good.'

'Is there anything else I can help you with?'

Blair hesitated. 'Actually, Mr Whitman, while I'm talking to you,' said Blair. 'There is one other thing . . .'

He looked at her with raised eyebrows.

'Just before she died,' said Blair, 'Celeste said she had to tell me something.'

The attorney waited.

Blair hesitated and then launched into an abbreviated story of Molly's murder, and Adrian Jones's alibi. Brooks Whitman listened intently.

'You see,' she said, wrapping it up, 'there was a witness who saw Molly getting into Adrian Jones's car. Molly was found dead the next day, in the woods, not too far from where he picked her up. Celeste told me that Adrian Jones was not alone when he picked up Molly. She herself was in that car with him. She said that all they did was to give Molly a ride home, but when the police confronted her, she denied it. Adrian Jones was convicted of Molly's murder and has been in prison ever since. But Celeste knew, all that time, that Molly was fine when she got out of the car.'

Brooks Whitman grimaced. 'I see . . .'

'Do you remember when that happened? It was big news around here.'

'Of course,' he said. 'But it was a long time ago.'

'Fifteen years,' said Blair.

'So, you are saying that your sister could have exonerated this man, but she didn't.'

'Correct,' said Blair.

'May I ask why she didn't?'

Blair sighed. 'As she may have told you, when she had you draw up this custody agreement, my sister and I were raised by a man who is, not to put too fine a point on it, a bigot and a racist. Celeste was afraid, if she admitted she was with Adrian Jones, that Uncle Ellis would put us out on the street.'

Brooks frowned.

'Mr Whitman . . . I understand that this does not in any way excuse what she did. But you asked why and that's why . . .'

'Did you . . . by any chance . . . record what she said to you? Or write it down and have her sign it?'

Blair shook her head. 'She kind of blindsided me with this. I know I should have . . .'

'Were there any other witnesses?' he asked.

Blair shook her head. 'It was too late when I realized what she was telling me. She was dying. She was too weak and disoriented to repeat it again. But she said it, as sure as I'm sitting here. Isn't there some . . . law about what people say on their deathbeds being accepted as the truth?'

'Dying declarations,' he said.

'Yes, exactly,' said Blair. 'That.'

'It's considered trustworthy evidence based on the belief that people who know that they are dying will not lie. It's an exception to the hearsay rule.'

'That's what I thought,' Blair exclaimed. 'Well, I will swear to what she told me on any stack of Bibles. She gave Adrian Jones the alibi he needed. She admitted that she lied. With that kind of testimony, we should be able to get him released from jail.' She could see the attorney's frown deepen into a pained grimace. 'Why are you frowning?' she said.

'There's a problem,' he replied.

FIVE

Blair stared at him. 'What? What's the problem?'

Brooks Whitman rubbed his eyes and forehead with the tips of his fingers. 'I'm not a criminal attorney. I deal mainly with people's estates. I've never actually encountered a dying declaration before. But I've read about them and I know that the use of them is severely limited, mainly because the court is reluctant to depart from the general rule regarding hearsay. You know what hearsay is?'

Blair shrugged. 'Well, sort of. Not exactly . . .'

'The report of another person's words by a witness is not admissible as evidence.'

'Oh, ok,' said Blair. 'But with a dying declaration . . .'

'It has to be given when that person is at death's door.'

'Which Celeste was . . .'

'And it can only be used in homicide trials . . .'

'This *was* a homicide trial,' Blair insisted.

'And . . . if I'm not mistaken . . . the circumstance must be that the accused is charged with the death of the declarant. Celeste being the declarant.'

Blair shook her head. 'What? You're kidding.'

'I'm afraid not. Generally, these cases are about people who are dying as the result of an assault. When they are asked to identify their assailant, their reply is considered irrefutable because it is their dying declaration. It's about whoever they accuse, at the point of death.'

'And that's it? That's the only circumstance?'

'For the declaration to be entered into evidence in court . . .'

'But that's ridiculous,' Blair protested. 'Celeste could have given this man an alibi, but she lied and because of her lie, he was convicted of Molly Sinclair's murder. And now, after these years, she admits it and it's of no use to him? This man has been in jail for fifteen years!'

Brooks held up his hands. 'This case has already been decided. If you were to take this information to the police, they might be unwilling to reopen it.'

'Why?' Blair demanded. 'When they know this man is innocent.'

'They don't know that. They only have your word for it and it's not really in their interest to pursue it,' said Brooks.

'That's unbelievable,' Blair declared. 'They'll do nothing? Even if the wrong man went to prison?'

Brooks frowned. 'Look, I can't say for certain what they will do, but I do know something about how the police operate. Getting them to reopen this case will be an uphill battle. If you were expecting that you would tell your story and the prison doors would swing open . . .'

'I'm not that naive,' said Blair coolly.

'You're right. I apologize,' said Brooks. 'But I want to be sure you understand. The law doesn't work like that.'

Blair, who was sitting with one leg crossed over the other, tapped her sneakered foot impatiently.

'Well, that may be, but I can't pretend that I didn't hear this. That I don't know it. This man's life is in my hands. I have to do something. Celeste made me promise I would.'

'I understand.'

'And that's what you think. That the police won't be interested,' said Blair.

'I think it's highly likely,' said Brooks.

Blair pondered this a moment. 'Well, I have to try.'

'I'm just saying that this could prove to be a very long and frustrating process.'

'This is a question of what's right,' said Blair.

Brooks Whitman smiled ruefully. 'I do agree with you. If what Celeste told you was true, this man has been incarcerated for a long time, probably for a crime he did not commit. Have you spoken to Mr Jones yet?'

'Actually, Mr Jones is now called Mr Muhammed. He became a Muslim in prison. And no, not yet. I have not.'

'You might want to tell him the good news,' said Brooks.

'Suddenly it doesn't feel like such good news,' said Blair.

'Well,' said the attorney cautiously. 'It could be.'

On her way out of the office, Blair was handed her copy of the agreement between Amanda and Celeste. Once she was in her car, she called Darlene to ask if she could stay a little longer with Malcolm.

'Oh, heaven's yes,' said Darlene. 'We're playing Rummikub.'

Blair thanked the older woman. 'I have a few more errands to do,' she said.

'Take your time,' said Darlene.

Blair googled Greenwood prison and called the number which came up. A recorded announcement came on, detailing rules and regulations for the families of prisoners. No one was to bring any gifts, packages or money to the prison. Donations to the commissary could be made on inmates' behalf. Inmates could have Skype visits during regular visiting hours – from one to four – which had to be arranged in advance. There was a list of numbers and contacts for families and law enforcement. Blair listened briefly and then ran out of patience. If people were too busy or lazy to go and see their loved ones, Skype visits made sense. But the discussion which she needed to have with Yusef Muhammed was something that had to be said face-to-face. She looked at the time on the car's dashboard. She could still make it before four o'clock. She stuffed her phone in her pocket and turned on the ignition.

'On my way,' she said.

SIX

I t took about thirty minutes to drive there, but with the help of her GPS she had no trouble finding the prison. The sight of its blank brick walls and loops of barbed wire was both depressing and a little bit frightening. The guard at the front desk – a balding man with salt and pepper fringe, who wore a name tag which read: Selenski – seemed bemused when she said that she wanted to see Yusef Muhammed. Blair could see a second guard smirking as he sat at his desk, doctoring his coffee.

'You've wasted your time coming out here,' said Selenski.

'Why? It's visiting hours,' Blair protested.

'You can only talk to him on Skype,' he said.

'On Skype?' Blair protested. 'But I'm here in person!'

'Doesn't matter. You can't do face-to-face. Not on a weekday. Not unless you're an attorney or a priest.'

'That's ridiculous.'

'Those are the rules. In fact, technically you're supposed to set up Skype visits in advance, but since this is your first time . . .'

'I came all the way out here so I could see him.'

'If you listened to the tape, it specifically said that you had to visit the inmate on Skype.'

'It didn't say "only on Skype",' Blair protested.

'You weren't listening,' said the guard flatly.

'I don't understand. Why can't we meet face-to-face?' Blair persisted.

'We only have face-to-face on weekends.' He pointed to a list that was posted outside the office. 'Sometimes Saturday, sometimes Sunday.'

Blair read the posted information sheet. Sure enough, face-to-face meetings were severely limited.

'I'm sorry,' Blair insisted. 'I don't understand that. I'd like you to explain to me why that is.'

Selenski rolled his eyes. 'Security is expensive,' said the guard, in a condescending tone which suggested that Blair was mentally challenged. 'It costs money to escort prisoners and visitors in and out. You gotta worry about weapons. Contraband. This way, there's none of that.'

'But, it seems . . . cruel,' Blair protested.

'So write a letter to the governor.'

'And unfair,' said Blair.

Selenski's expression hardened. 'Do you want to talk to him or don't you?'

Blair hesitated, but finally acquiesced. 'Yes. I need to talk to him.'

'Sit down over there,' said Selenski, pointing to a cubicle with a desktop PC on the surface.

Blair frowned at the cubicle indicated. 'It's not very private,' she said.

'This is prison,' said the guard flatly. 'Not the country club. Next time, save yourself the trip. You can Skype him from home.'

Blair could see that she was going to get nowhere with the guard. She sat down.

The guard pushed a few keys on his computer.

'When they bring him to the visiting room, he'll appear on the screen. Then you can talk. Fifteen minutes. That's it. Then it will be shut off.'

Fifteen minutes, Blair thought. To explain to Yusef Muhammed, why he had needlessly spent fifteen years in prison. But fifteen minutes was what she had. It was not as if they were giving her a choice.

'All right,' she said.

She sat down in front of the monitor and waited. A timekeeper in the corner of the screen let her know that her call would begin in a matter of seconds. Blair felt her heart pounding in her chest. She licked her lips nervously. The screen was suddenly illuminated and a man in an orange jumpsuit settled himself on a molded plastic chair. The backdrop was a dingy beige wall. The prisoner looked into the screen.

His head was shaven and he had broad, symmetrical features. He was wearing black, horn-rimmed glasses. His eyes were dark, calm and cold. He said nothing. He didn't even ask who she was.

'Mr . . . Muhammed?' Blair asked.

The man nodded curtly.

'My name is Blair Butler.'

The man blinked at her slowly, like a lizard, and waited.

'I'm here because . . . um . . .' Blair cleared her throat. 'I believe you knew my sister. Her name was . . . that is, my sister was Celeste Butler.'

The man looked at her impassively, and made no reply.

'Do you . . . remember Celeste?'

Yusef Muhammed narrowed his eyes. 'I won't soon forget her,' he drawled.

The icy tone of his voice gave Blair a chill. 'I guess you and Celeste were friends back in high school.'

'She was no friend of mine,' he said.

This man has every reason to hate Celeste, she reminded herself. What she did to this man was unforgivable.

'Well, I'll get to the point. The reason I'm here is . . . Celeste died recently. She had a particularly deadly kind of cancer.'

'Good,' said Muhammed.

Blair grimaced at the cruel remark, but did not protest. Keep your cool, she thought. You can't blame him for being bitter.

'The thing is,' she said, 'before she died, Celeste told me something. She told me that she was with you when Molly Sinclair was killed, but that she lied to the police, to everyone, and said she wasn't.'

Yusef stared at Blair, his gaze cold and implacable, the muscles in his cheeks flexing as he maintained his silence. Blair hesitated, and then continued.

'She felt that she had done you a terrible injustice and she wanted me to promise her to try to make it right.'

She could see his mind working as he continued to stare at her. His body was coiled and tense, and he fairly oozed hostility, but there was an undeniable curiosity in his narrowed eyes.

'She told you that?' he said.

Blair nodded. 'She did. She knew she was dying. She wanted to tell me before she died.'

Yusef smiled, but there was no mirth in his eyes.

'I been in this hole for fifteen years for something I didn't do. And now she decided to tell the truth. Why? Afraid she wouldn't get to heaven?'

'Well, I guess . . . because she was dying . . .' Blair said helplessly.

'She could have lived to be ninety,' he said.

Blair nodded, embarrassed by the truth of what he said.

'Well, yes. I know. She should have spoken up before. But now, at least, we can try to bring this to an end . . .'

Yusef shook his head and put one large hand over his eyes, resting on the frame of his glasses.

Blair waited a few seconds. 'Mr Muhammed . . .?'

'She stole my life from me,' he whispered.

'I'm sorry . . .?' Blair asked.

'*She stole my life!*' he shouted.

Blair flinched and pressed her lips together. She glanced up at the guards, but they were involved in their own conversation. She spoke quietly.

'I don't blame you for being angry.'

'Oh, you don't?' he said sarcastically.

Blair held up her hands as if in surrender. 'Look, Mr . . . Muhammed, I'm sorry for what happened to you. I'd like to try to help you. This was the first I knew of it. I mean, you were the one convicted of Molly's murder. I just assumed, like everybody else, that you did it and that you were where you belonged. I was stunned when my sister told me this. Celeste was in hospice care and she could barely speak, but she told me that she lied. She said that she was with you at the time that Molly was murdered. That you and she picked Molly up in your car that evening . . .'

'It was raining,' he said.

'Right. And you . . . took her home?'

'We took her home,' Yusef agreed.

'That's what she told me. It was just as you said.'

'Did she tell the cops that?' he demanded.

Blair frowned. 'What do you mean? You mean, back then? You know she didn't.'

'I mean now. Did she tell the D.A.? The judge? Anybody who matters?'

'She just told me,' said Blair evenly.

'Did she write it down? Have it notarized? Swear to it on a Bible?'

'No,' said Blair apologetically. 'I wish I could have gotten her to do that but she was too far gone . . .'

Yusef pushed up his glasses and rubbed his eyes with his long, shapely fingers. Then he shook his head.

'That bitch.'

Blair flinched, but did not protest. 'At least she said something before it was too late.'

Yusef Muhammed glared at her through the monitor. 'Why don't you spend fifteen years in this hellhole and then you can talk about what is or is not too late.'

Blair flinched. 'I'm trying to help.'

'Yeah. You're a big help.'

Blair took a deep breath. She could see that he was trying to intimidate her. Probably out of frustration, she told herself, and tried again.

'All right. Maybe I said it wrong. But I promised Celeste and I'm going to see it through. I'm not going to let this drop . . .'

'Who is going to believe you? Why should they?' he cried. 'You claim she said this. That's proof of nothing. I can see you don't know too much about how things work in this legal system.'

'I can see that you do,' said Blair.

'Damn right, I do. I've had plenty of time to study it.'

'Do you have an attorney that you'd like me to talk to?' Blair asked.

'I have had several attorneys from legal aid over the years. One worse than the other. Ain't none of 'em any use. Why do you think I started reading the law?'

'Well, the next thing I'm going to do is to go to the police and tell them everything I know.'

Muhammed shook his head. 'The police got no interest in reopening this case. They got a little dead white girl and they got their killer. They don't give a good God damn about the truth,' he said coldly.

'Look, I don't blame you for being bitter, but that little dead white girl was my best friend,' said Blair indignantly. 'She did nothing to deserve what happened to her.'

Muhammed gazed at her through narrowed eyes. 'No, she didn't,' he conceded. 'And neither did I.'

'I think the police will be interested,' Blair said stoutly.

'We'll see about that,' he said.

'It may take a few tries,' she admitted. 'I don't know. I've never had any dealings with the justice system before.'

'The injustice system,' he snorted.

'Look, I know you have every reason to be angry . . .'

Muhammed peered at her. 'We done here?'

Blair looked at the digital clock in the corner of the screen. Her time was almost up. She had expected that this man might thank her for her efforts, but clearly, thanks were not in the cards.

'I guess so. I'll be in touch with you soon.'

Yusef shook his head and muttered something Blair could not understand.

'What did you say?' she asked.

'I hope there's a hell,' he said, 'and I hope she's in it. Your sister.'

'I'm sorry,' said Blair, just as the screen went dark.

SEVEN

Dinner that night, as it had been since Celeste's funeral, was a matter of microwaving a serving of one of the casseroles in the refrigerator, which had been made for them by kindly local people and left at the house. Malcolm accepted a plate from his aunt and said he was going to eat in his room.

'Are you allowed to do that?' Blair asked.

'Sure, I do it all the time,' the boy said.

'Well, please be sure to bring your dirty dishes back downstairs after you eat,' said Blair.

'I will,' said the boy.

'You trying to get him civilized for life at the Tuckers'?' Ellis asked bitterly.

Blair gazed at him coldly. 'It wouldn't hurt,' she said.

Ellis took his plate into the living room and parked himself in front of the television, turning on a NASCAR event to watch while he ate. Blair sat alone at the kitchen table, picking at her food.

Ever since she left the prison, she had been undecided about what to do next. On the one hand, she knew that she had to go to the police, but then she had to consider the Sinclairs. She certainly didn't want Molly's parents to find out about Yusef Muhammed's alibi from some policeman arriving at their door. After much debate with herself, she finally made up her mind. She would go and see the Sinclairs first. Next to Muhammed himself, no one had a stronger right to know. Besides, she was hoping that the Sinclairs might point her in the direction of the police detective who had worked on Molly's case. It might be helpful if she was able to talk with the person who had been in charge of the investigation, especially if she could cite the Sinclairs' support. Of course, that presumed that they would be supportive. Well, she thought, as she dumped the uneaten portion of her dinner into the garbage, there was no avoiding it. She had to find out.

Ellis came back into the kitchen with his empty plate and rinsed it off at the sink before sticking it in the ancient dishwasher.

'We got invited to dinner tomorrow,' he said.

'Really? Where?'

'Darlene wants to make us dinner at her house.'

'All of us?'

Blair thought she saw a little self-conscious flush in his cheeks.

'It was her idea,' Ellis said defensively.

'Well, that's awfully nice of her,' said Blair.

'I said we'd come,' said Ellis.

She wanted to remind her uncle not to speak for her. Not to make plans without asking her. But her objections seemed petty in the face of Darlene's generosity.

'Ok,' said Blair.

Ellis opened the refrigerator and looked inside. He took out a slab of bread pudding from a plate on the second shelf.

'I have to go out tonight, Uncle Ellis,' Blair said.

Ellis turned and frowned. 'Where you going?'

'I have an errand to do,' said Blair. She had not yet told him about Celeste's confession. She did not relish that prospect at all. She thought she would let him find out as it unfolded, when there was no way he could prevent it or object to the consequences.

'Just paying a visit to Molly's parents,' she said.

Ellis was not interested. 'Get some milk while you're out,' he said. 'For the kid's cereal.'

*   *   *

A number of the shops in downtown Yorkville were open, thanks to the Christmas shopping season which had already begun, but there were precious few pedestrians on the streets. Blair parked right outside of the Apres Ski café, locked her car and went inside. A bell jingled as she entered.

The place was almost twice as big as it had been in her youth. It had an inviting, lodge-like atmosphere, with a wood-burning stove at the center and weathered beams across the ceiling. There were patrons seated at a couple of the candlelit tables covered with checkered tablecloths and a smattering of drinkers along the bar, but the place was not what you would call busy. There was no hostess on the door. Blair walked up to the bar and waited for the bartender – a slim young woman in jeans and a fitted flannel shirt – to be free to speak to her. At the moment, the bartender was dealing with a patron who had already had one too many.

'Sorry, Randy,' she said to the middle-aged, bearded man who was wobbling on his barstool. Her voice had the light but firm tone of long experience. 'Time to hit the road.'

The man peered at her through bloodshot eyes, his face red with anger. 'You refusing to serve me?'

'Yup. And I just called your daughter. She's on her way. So you best pay up.' She dangled his car keys in front of him. 'You can come get these tomorrow.'

'Give me those keys . . .' Randy demanded.

'Can't. If you get in an accident, they'll blame me.'

'You're not my keeper. Give me those goddam keys.'

'All right, that's enough,' said a guy on a neighboring stool, standing up and grabbing the obstreperous drunk by the back of his shirt. 'That's no way to talk to this nice lady. Now get out or I'll throw you out.'

The bartender flicked her towel in the direction of the young man who had come to her defense.

'Thanks, Cary,' she said, smiling, and turned to Blair without missing a beat, her demeanor calm and unruffled, as her two customers began an argument. The older man was raving in protest. Cary was quiet, but clearly had the situation in hand.

'What can I get you?' the bartender said to Blair.

'Nothing. Actually,' said Blair, 'I'm here to see the Sinclairs.'

'Sorry,' said the girl. 'They aren't working tonight.'

'Neither one of them?'

'Nope,' said the bartender.

'Oh, ok,' said Blair. She started to turn away. 'Are they home, do you know?'

The bartender was circumspect. 'Maybe. I can't say.'

Blair could see, to her mild surprise, that the girl was reluctant to give out any information about the Sinclairs. As if she had been instructed to keep that information to herself. Was this a normal way to do business, or was this what happened when a violent crime tore through people's lives? Every stranger was to be mistrusted. In an effort to reassure the bartender, Blair said, 'Janet told me to stop by anytime. Molly was my childhood best friend.'

'Oh,' said the bartender. 'So you know where they live.'

For a moment Blair's mind was blank, and then she suddenly remembered. 'Fulling Mill Road,' she said.

The inebriated customer stopped in mid-argument and turned on Blair, his gaze menacing, his breath a blowtorch of alcohol.

'That's where my house is. Or it was my house, till the judge gave it to that bitch,' he muttered.

The bartender shook her head. 'Randy, get out of here. Go back to Arborside. Don't be bothering my customers.'

A young woman with long, dark curls had come in and was stomping across the restaurant toward the bar, shaking her head.

'Don't call me anymore. I mean it. Call the police. I'm not coming for him again. He should be in jail.'

The bartender shrugged. 'Sorry, Jenna. But he's too drunk to drive.' She turned her attention back to Blair. 'Yeah. Fulling Mill Road. Shall I call them and tell them you're on your way?'

Blair shook her head. 'I'll surprise them,' she said.

For years, even after Adrian Jones was convicted of Molly's murder and safely locked away, Blair had avoided the road that ran through the woods, even in the safety of a vehicle. Maybe she had sensed somehow that Molly's killer was not really behind bars at all, although she could never remember entertaining that thought. Now she knew that it was true. But tonight, as she left Main Street and turned onto the road that crossed through the woods, it seemed necessary to her to stop at the spot where Molly's body had been found.

Blair drove slowly down the road, but all she could see were the bare trees caught in her headlights, their dry leaves whipped up by the night wind. Now that she was on that road, she had no sense of how far she had to go, or where that fateful spot actually was. At one time, there had been a makeshift memorial there of balloons and teddy bears, but all of that was long gone. It was somehow painful to realize that the spot, which she was once sure she could never forget, was now lost to time and change.

A couple of times she thought she had recognized it. She glimpsed a boulder, or a break in the trees that might have seemed familiar, but, in truth, she had no idea. Somewhere in these woods, not far off this road, her twelve-year-old best friend had met her death. Now that she knew that Adrian – she corrected herself – Yusef, along with Celeste, had picked Molly up at the entrance to the woods, a question occurred to her. Those two drove the girl home. That's what Celeste said. So, if they drove her to her house, how did Molly end up back in the woods, in the rain? Suddenly, it seemed as if everything Blair knew about that day needed to be re-examined. Was the answer about Molly's killer there, in one of those questions?

Blair felt positively relieved when she drove out of the woods and rolled to a stop at the corner of Fulling Mill Road. The houses along this road used to be few and set apart from one another by forest, as far as the eye could see. Now much of the forest was gone, and handsome new homes were built far back from the road. In many cases, tall trees had given way to perfect lawns. Blair knew that to get to Molly's house you had to turn left. She made the turn and drove slowly down the winding road. She could see house lights far back from the road, some through a cluster of tree branches, warmly beckoning. But which house was it? She peered at the mailboxes in her headlights until one, which said Sinclair, caught her eye. Got it, Blair thought. She knew it was not far. She turned into the driveway and slowly rolled up to the house at the end of the drive.

The Sinclair's house was built in the style of a log cabin. It had a porch which ran the length of the simple structure and the lamp beside the front door was lit. Its glow illuminated the wide planks and railing of the porch. Blair parked her car and got out. It was still peaceful here, as it had seemed to her when she was a girl.

In those days, she loved to come over to Molly's house. It had seemed rustic and enchanted, tucked into a clearing surrounded by woods. It was the kind of place which inspired a child's imagination, until murder brought an abrupt end to her innocence.

Blair looked back at the road. It wasn't far from here to the turnoff which led into the woods. But why would Molly have taken a ride home, and then deliberately gone back there in the rain? Blair shivered. After so many years, how could you ever know? Or find out?

Blair walked up on the porch and knocked. Robbie Sinclair was silhouetted at the window looking out, as if he had gotten up when he heard a car in the drive. He opened the door right away. He frowned at Blair for a moment and then his face broke into an expression of happy surprise.

'Blair. How nice to see you!'

'Hi, Mr Sinclair.'

'Robbie,' he said firmly.

'Robbie,' Blair repeated, though it was difficult for her to address Molly's Dad as an equal. He had always been a grown-up to her.

'Come on in.'

'Thanks.' As Blair entered the house, she saw Janet coming in from the direction of the kitchen, wiping her hands on her apron. She, too, smiled when she recognized their visitor.

Wordlessly she opened her arms, and Blair awkwardly, gratefully, embraced her.

'Hi Janet,' she said.

'I'm so glad you came over,' said Janet, taking off her apron and laying it over one of the dining chairs by their long table. She led Blair to an old leather armchair by the stone hearth. A Hudson Bay blanket had been thrown over the back of the chair to disguise some wear or tear in the leather. Blair sat down and both Janet and Robbie sat down on the sofa at the other side of the low coffee table. A small but lively fire burned in the fireplace. A big golden retriever, now turning gray, was snoozing on a plaid dog bed at the edge of a hooked rug. He barely lifted an eyebrow when Blair settled herself in the chair.

'Is that . . . Molly's pup?' Blair asked.

Robbie reached down and scratched the dog behind her ears. 'Yup. Pippa. She's a pretty old girl now.'

'God, how I envied her that dog. I wasn't allowed to have a pet.' Blair sighed and looked around the cozy living room. 'I always loved coming over here when I was a kid. Your cabin in the woods. It always seemed magical to me.'

'Can I get you anything?' said Janet. 'Have you eaten?'

'Thanks, but I did have something,' said Blair. 'Everyone kindly brought us casseroles. Uncle Ellis may never cook again, which would be a mercy.'

'How's your uncle doing? He seemed very upset at the funeral.'

Blair thought about it. 'I guess he was. Hard to tell with him.'

'Well, you and Celeste were like his children,' said Janet.

'Before the funeral, I hadn't seen him for years,' said Robbie. 'Is he still . . . the same?'

Blair knew what Robbie was referring to. 'Still a nut job? Yup. Though he might be mellowing. He actually took the confederate flag down!'

'Thank God,' Janet exclaimed.

'Actually, I think it just finally disintegrated,' said Blair. She could feel herself settling in for a long conversation with these people and she knew that she couldn't allow it to go any farther without being truthful with them. But how to begin? Her smile faded and she sighed again.

Robbie frowned at her. 'You ok?'

'Well, I can't be in this house without thinking about . . . Molly.' To her own surprise, Blair choked up, and tears came to her eyes. She could see the pain in their faces, but also their gratitude. Obviously it was comforting to them that the thought of their daughter could still bring tears to the eyes of someone beside themselves. Janet reached over and squeezed Blair's hand.

'Look, I haven't been up front with you. I'm here because there's something I have to tell you both.'

'What about?' Robbie asked warily.

'I'm afraid it's going to come as a terrible shock,' said Blair.

The Sinclairs looked at one another and then back at Blair.

'After all these years,' said Janet, 'What could you have to tell us now?'

Blair cleared her throat. 'Well, just before Celeste died, she said that she had something she wanted to tell me. A confession, if you will.'

The room was utterly silent. The Sinclairs stared at Blair, but did not speak.

'Obviously, we all know that Adrian Jones, well, Yusef Muhammed now, was convicted of Molly's murder.' Blair hesitated. 'But according to Celeste, Muhammed was not the one who . . . killed Molly.'

'How would Celeste know that?' Robbie protested angrily.

'It seems that . . . on the day that Molly was . . . killed, Celeste was in that car with Muhammed. Celeste was with him when he picked up Molly. She said they stopped to pick her up because it was raining. They drove her home.'

'That's not true,' said Robbie coldly.

'I'm afraid it is,' said Blair.

'But, your sister swore she was not with him,' Janet cried. 'He tried to use her as an alibi, but she swore she was never in his car. Why would she lie?'

Blair kneaded her hands together and nodded. 'I asked her the same question. She said she was terrified that Uncle Ellis would throw her, and me, out on the street for good if she admitted she was with a black guy. So she lied.'

Janet shook her head. 'No.'

'I'm so sorry,' said Blair. 'I know this is the last thing you want. To have the past dredged up like this. I've been dreading coming to tell you this. But I promised Celeste that I would try to help Muhammed. It seems as if he has spent many years in prison for something . . . well, that he didn't do.'

'He did it,' Janet cried. 'They said so. The police. The jury . . .'

'I know how difficult this must be . . .' said Blair.

Robbie's eyes were wide, and horrified.

'No, you don't,' he said. 'You have absolutely no idea . . . What you're saying . . . Why should we take your word for this?'

Blair opened her hands. 'Why would I lie about it?'

Janet began to weep.

'That's not a reason,' Robbie insisted.

'My sister was dying,' said Blair. 'It was on her conscience. She wanted to tell the truth before she died.'

Robbie stood up. 'I want you to leave,' he said.

Blair was shocked by his abrupt command. 'I was hoping that we could . . .'

'Now,' Robbie cried. 'Get out of our house.'

Blair had expected them to be shocked, and upset. But not this. It was as if they blamed her. She reminded herself that she could not really imagine how they felt. She nodded and stood up. 'I'm so sorry about this. I'm so sorry that my sister lied about it.'

'Just go,' said Robbie, through gritted teeth.

Blair started toward the front door. Then she turned back. Robbie had his arm around his weeping wife, trying to console her.

'I'm going to have to see this through,' said Blair. 'I'm going to the police. It's only fair.'

The two of them ignored her. They were huddled together as if against a marauder's onslaught. Blair took a last regretful look at them and then slipped quietly out, pulling the door shut behind her.

EIGHT

Blair drove home, barely aware of being behind the wheel. She realized that she had never expected the Sinclairs, no matter how shocked they were, to be angry with her. They had always been kind to her and, when she and Molly became friends, Blair had often thought that they saw her as almost a second daughter. She sometimes fantasized that one day they might ask her uncle if she could come and live with them.

Blair knew that her own terrible grief at Molly's death was a solace to the Sinclairs, and no matter how often Blair apologized for letting Molly leave the house alone on that fateful night, they had never blamed her. They urged her not to blame herself. There was only one person to blame, they often said, and that was the man who had taken Molly to the woods, who had killed her.

So it unsettled her deeply to see that anger in their eyes. Even after all these years, their opinion mattered. And now, just because she was trying to do the right thing, she was banished. Banished and blamed. The unfairness of it made her indignant, but most of all, it was just painful. Blair barely spoke to her uncle when she returned to the house. She went directly to her old bedroom and closed the door. She checked her phone for messages and saw that there were a few work-related texts, but she did not have the strength to answer them. She just wanted to close her eyes and blot out the world. Blair got into the narrow bed, still in her clothes, and pulled up the covers. Before she knew it, she was asleep.

Several hours later she sat up in the bed, her heart hammering, jolted awake by a nightmare she could not remember. She was filled with a disturbing sense that she had forgotten something important. The house was dark and silent and Blair was aware that everyone had long since gone to bed. Whatever she had been dreaming about eluded her, it had been replaced by the realization that she had failed to ask the Sinclairs the names of the detectives who had investigated Molly's murder. Well, she certainly couldn't ask them now. They had made it clear that they didn't want to hear from her again.

Blair turned on the lamp on the bedside table and picked up her phone. She googled Molly's name and any number of combinations of words pertaining to the murder, but the references she found were only a few lines and there was no in-depth information about the police investigation. The archives of the county paper online only went back ten years. There was one article from five years ago about Yusef Muhammed, when he received his college degree and began his law studies. In it, he complained about the injustice of his incarceration and never even mentioned Molly.

She wondered if perhaps her uncle had kept any clippings about the crime, but she immediately dismissed that idea. The only reason he took the paper was for the hunting and fishing report. But she wanted to go to the police tomorrow armed with all the relevant information. I can stop at the newspaper office tomorrow, she thought, on my way to the police station. The office was where it had always been, right off of Main Street. Surely they would have every issue accounted for in their own archives. It was an outdated way to get information, but it might still be possible to find what she wanted. Somehow it seemed appropriate for this out of the way hamlet in the mountains and she found the thought strangely calming. She switched off the light and lay back down. As she began to drift off to sleep, she suddenly remembered. She was supposed to buy milk for Malcolm. She would run and get it in the morning, before Uncle Ellis had a chance to complain.

* * *

The offices of the Yorkville County Clarion were not exactly bustling. Even so, Blair had to wait for several minutes at the front desk to attract the attention of the pudgy, bespectacled, sweatshirt-clad girl who was intently staring at her computer screen.

'Yeah, can I help you?' she asked at last, when it became clear that Blair was not going away.

'I'm trying to find information about a crime that was committed in Yorkville fifteen years ago. I was wondering if you had archives I can search. I looked online and you've only got articles going back ten years.'

'It's not my fault,' the girl insisted defensively. 'If they want it done, they need to hire somebody to put it online. I can barely keep up with my own work. They'd have me delivering the damn paper if they could. My Dad told me this was a dying business and I should get into some other line of work, but I had all these ideals about the free press. I mean, come on—'

'Archives?' Blair interrupted her.

'Oh. Right. Well, they're not very organized.' She pointed to a doorway at the back of the office. 'Go through there. You're looking for something from fifteen years ago?'

'About that,' said Blair.

'Well, call me if you need a hand,' said the girl, but Blair did not think this was a sincere offer.

She walked down to the back door, turned the knob and went inside. The room seemed to be a general storage area filled with boxes of Styrofoam cups, a crate containing sports equipment and a line of old jackets and hats hung along the wall. There were also piles of newspapers everywhere, some labeled as to the year and others just piled haphazardly, with no apparent rhyme or reason. She waded into the towers of newspapers and began to search.

It took her a lot less time than she would have thought to find the correct year. The papers were – it turned out – grouped together in order by year, even if they weren't all labeled. She hunted through them until she found the month and weeks of, and after, the crime. She thought she was only going to look for the name of the detectives who worked on the case, but, in fact, she ended up sitting at a table in the corner, reading all the accounts of what had happened.

There were no gruesome pictures of Molly's body, but there

were pictures of the spot where the body was found. Grim-faced detectives in topcoats conferred in the wooded clearing while uniformed officers searched the area. There was one heartbreaking photo of Molly's parents being whisked into the police station, Robbie's face stony and Janet covering her mouth with one hand. Blair and Uncle Ellis were not mentioned. The earliest accounts said that Molly had visited a friend after school and then was walking home when she encountered her killer. The police were talking to an eyewitness who saw Molly getting into a gray sedan. Police were looking for that car and its owner. The body was being examined for signs of sexual assault, but preliminary indications were that Molly Sinclair was not raped.

'Can I help you?' a voice asked.

Blair jumped, and looked up. A tall, tired-looking young woman with greasy blond hair and the profile of a beauty queen poked her head into the room. She was wearing jeans, a faded gray T-shirt and a ripped, down vest. Blair peered at her. She looked somehow familiar but Blair couldn't put a name to the face.

'Oh, no thanks,' she said. 'I think I've found what I'm looking for. Although it would be a lot easier if these papers were archived online.'

'Probably a good idea,' the woman said.

Blair frowned at her slightly. 'You look familiar to me,' she said.

'I've got one of those faces,' she said dismissively.

'I thought maybe we went to school together,' she said. She gazed at the grungy clothes and elegant features. They made a jarring contrast. She wore no makeup and her skin was sallow over her drab clothes. This woman wasn't fashionably comfortable. She was unkempt.

'Couldn't tell you,' said the woman. 'Gotta run.'

Blair mentally ran through some of the people she had known in school. And then, suddenly, it clicked, and she saw the woman as she once was.

'Wait a minute,' said Blair. 'Aren't you Rebecca Moore?'

The other woman reacted defensively. 'Should I know you?'

Blair shook her head. 'No. No. I was sort of . . . You were a few years ahead of me. You were kind of a legend.' She could remember her clearly now. She was one of those girls who was always trailed by a gaggle of boys. Her clothes casually preppy. Perfect nails. Perfect hair.

'Ah yes,' she said sarcastically. 'Big fish. Small pond.'

'After college, didn't you end up as an anchor on the TV news in some big city?' she asked.

Rebecca sighed. 'Yes. L.A.,' she admitted.

Blair nodded. 'I remember now. Your success was the talk of the town,' said Blair. 'You were like a shooting star around here.'

Rebecca shrugged. 'It was another life. So, what about you? Never left this place?' she asked.

Rebecca's assumption reminded Blair of why she had always wanted to get away from Yorkville. In this town she would always be seen as what she was in high school: an unpopular kid from a family that was down on its luck.

'As a matter of fact, I live in Philly,' she said archly. 'I have my own company there.'

'Well,' said Rebecca briskly, 'good for you.' She started to walk out of the room.

Blair was irked by the other woman's dismissive tone. Was it so onerous for her to be remembered for her success?

'How come you're back here?' she asked. She was aware that it sounded as if she were asking Rebecca what became of that big career of hers. The question hung in the air.

'Shit happens,' Rebecca said, terminating the conversation.

Never mind, Blair thought. Just another high school hotshot who flamed out before she really made her mark. Blair thanked her stars that she was established elsewhere and would not be staying in this town for long. Then she shrugged, glanced at her watch and went back to her research.

Half an hour later she walked into the Yorkville Police Station and approached the uniformed young man seated at a desk behind a Plexiglass window.

'Can I help you?' he asked.

Blair looked at the paper in her hand. 'I'm here to see Detective Henry Dreyer,' she said.

The desk sergeant nodded. 'Do you have an appointment with the Chief?' he asked pointedly.

The Chief, Blair thought! He had moved up in the ranks but he was clearly still here. After fifteen years, she was afraid that Detective Dreyer might have retired, or moved on.

'No,' she said. 'But I'd appreciate a few minutes of his time.'

The desk sergeant started to enter the extension and then hesitated. 'Your name?'

'My name is Blair Butler.'

'And this is about . . .?'

'This is about . . . an old case. The murder of Molly Sinclair.'

The desk sergeant nodded, and repeated that information into the phone. Then he looked back at Blair.

'Chief Dreyer will be right with you,' he said. 'Have a seat.'

There was a line of chairs between the Plexiglass window and a bank of flags. Blair was too anxious to sit. She began to pace. A man came in and approached the desk. Blair rocked on the balls of her sneakered feet. In a few minutes, a door opened and a silver-haired man in a dress uniform adorned with stars and bars came out and looked around the waiting area.

'Ms Butler?' he said.

Blair went up to him, introduced herself and shook Chief Dreyer's hand.

'Thank you for seeing me,' she said.

'Right this way,' he said.

He led her in through a warren of desks to his roomy office and closed the door. He indicated a seat for Blair and sat down behind his desk. The phone was ringing and he picked up the receiver, indicating to Blair that it would only be a minute. She looked around while she waited. The walls of his office boasted many framed photos of the Chief receiving awards and shaking hands with local dignitaries. But there was also a large bulletin board that had row after row of Missing Persons posters, some of which were yellow with age. Many of them were young and female, and Blair felt an overwhelming sadness as she looked at them. Some looked world-weary and some had young, fresh faces, their photos now faded with time. All of their disappearances remained unsolved, unavenged.

'So,' he said hanging up the phone, 'I'm intrigued. The desk sergeant said you were here about the Molly Sinclair case.'

'That's right,' said Blair. 'Molly was my best friend. She was visiting me at my house that night, before she started to walk home. I was questioned by a number of officers at the time. You may have been one of them.'

'Oh, you're Ellis Dietz's niece.'

'I am,' said Blair.

'I remember you,' he said. 'So what brings you here today?'

'I may have some new information about the case.'

'Really? That case has been closed for quite a while,' he said.

'Nonetheless,' said Blair. She told him, briefly, about what Celeste had confessed on her deathbed. 'So, it seems that my sister could have given Mr Muhammed an alibi, but she didn't. She failed to do that. According to my sister, he has spent fifteen years in jail for a crime he didn't commit.'

The Chief's expression did not give away his feelings. He remained calm and detached.

'You say your sister was near death when she told you this. I'm not a medical man, but I think she may have been suffering some kind of . . . hallucinations from her condition when she told you that. Mr Muhammed was convicted of Molly's murder, based on a preponderance of evidence.'

Blair tried to mirror his calm demeanor. 'Look, I understand this is coming out of left field. But my sister was very adamant that she wanted me to try and do something about this . . . injustice.'

'Let me get this straight.' Henry Dreyer grimaced and shook his head. 'Her crisis of conscience only arose after fifteen years?'

'I know it seems strange. But my sister and I lived with my uncle, who is – not to put too fine a point on it – a bit of a racist. She didn't say anything about being with Yusef Muhammed for fear my uncle would toss us out on the street.'

'Well, I could understand that. But it's been fifteen years. She had plenty of opportunity since.'

'That's true,' said Blair. 'But my uncle never changed and Celeste never really . . . got on her feet. She and her son were still living with my uncle until she died.'

Dreyer shrugged. 'Well, that's unfortunate. It seems to me that most people would speak up if they knew something that important.'

'Look, I'm not defending her choices,' said Blair. 'I agree with you. She should have spoken up. Long ago. But she was not a . . . very strong person in some ways. Just before she died though, she decided to tell me her secret. She trusted me to do something about it.'

'This isn't really evidence, Ms Butler. It's just hearsay.'

'It was her dying declaration,' Blair insisted, glad she knew the accurate term, even though it did not apply in this case.

'That's an awfully broad interpretation,' he said.

'Don't you even want to look into it?' Blair asked. 'You may have sent an innocent man to prison for life.'

The Chief leaned forward to speak emphatically. 'I'm sorry, Miss Butler, but I don't believe that. Yusef Muhammed is not an innocent man. I remember this case very well. That little girl. Her poor parents. We who worked on this case had children of our own. We were determined to get it right. As it happened, we had an eyewitness. And we found Molly's cell phone wedged between the seats in Muhammed's car. We did not make a mistake. We got the right man. I'm sorry, but, some scrap of hearsay evidence after fifteen years . . .? That wouldn't even make it to court. It just wouldn't. This case is closed.'

Blair's heart was beating hard in her chest. It was just as the attorney, Brooks Whitman, had predicted. The police were not going to want to hear about anything that contradicted their findings.

'This is exactly what the lawyer said would happen,' said Blair, angry now and incredulous.

'Which lawyer said that?' Dreyer demanded.

'Never mind,' said Blair.

'Ms Butler, I have spent my whole career on this police force. And I admit that I have certain cases that still haunt me, but this is not one of them. I'm sure what your sister told you is upsetting to you, but what you heard may well have been the ravings of a cancer and drug-riddled mind. In any event, it's not relevant to this case or how it turned out. Now, I need to get back to work. Can you see yourself out?' he asked.

'If Yusef Muhammed did not kill Molly Sinclair, then someone else did,' Blair insisted. 'Don't you even want to know if there's a murderer out there who got away with it?'

'If there is, that murderer hasn't exactly been on a crime spree all these years.'

'Isn't one murder enough? Whoever killed Molly needs to be

punished for it. The man you have in prison for the crime could be innocent.'

'Any murder is one murder too many and Yusef Muhammed is not innocent,' said Chief Dreyer. 'Good day, Miss Butler.'

NINE

Henry Dreyer was convinced that he was right and he was not interested in revisiting this case. And yet, Blair was certain that what Celeste had told her was the truth. She reviewed what the chief had said as she walked across the parking lot to her car. Just as she was opening the car door, she sensed someone coming up behind her. She glared over her shoulder, as if daring them to approach.

'Well, what do you know,' said Rebecca Moore equably. 'We meet again.'

Blair was feeling surly after her meeting in the police station.

'Surprise,' she said.

'Sorry,' said Rebecca, holding up her hands in an exaggerated gesture of surrender. 'What's got you in such a mood?'

'Nothing. Never mind. What brings you here?' Blair asked to make up for her rudeness.

Rebecca sighed. 'The police blotter. I have to see if there's any interesting crime going on here in Small Town, USA, that I can use for the paper. Unfortunately for me, if it weren't for traffic violations and drug abuse, we'd have no criminals at all around here. I think of my visit here as a pointless weekly penance . . .'

Blair nodded and slipped into the car. 'Well, good luck with that.'

She watched the reporter as she started to walk away. The crimes in this small town probably did seem awfully pedestrian compared to those in a big city like Los Angeles. Then, suddenly, she had an idea. Maybe there was another way to approach her own problem. A way that might interest Rebecca Moore. She scrambled back out of her car and called out across the parking lot.

'Hey, Rebecca . . .'

She stopped and turned around, frowning at her. 'I'm at a disadvantage here. You know me, but I don't know you. What's your name?'

'Blair Butler,' she said.

Rebecca frowned. 'Butler?'

'You might have known my sister, Celeste. She was a few years ahead of me in school.'

Rebecca shrugged. 'Nope. Don't remember her.'

'Well, would you . . . do you have a few minutes to talk? I have something that I think might interest you.'

Rebecca immediately turned wary. 'Look, I don't know what you're after. But I don't want to read your short story, or speak to your ladies group about TV news in the big time. I'm just here to work,' she said.

'What I'm after?' Blair said, offended. She realized that Rebecca had not absorbed one word Blair had told her about herself. 'As I already told you, I don't even live here. I live in Philly. And I don't have a ladies group. Here or there. And even if I did, I'm sure no one would be interested in TV news in the so-called big time anyway. What I'm after is for someone in the news media to give a damn about a miscarriage of justice.'

Rebecca did not reply, but she did not walk away either.

Blair hesitated for a moment, trying to think how best to express it. 'I have new information about an old case. A murder. And the police don't want to know about it.'

Rebecca frowned and hesitated. Then she began to walk back in the direction of Blair's car.

'I'm listening,' she said.

Blair suggested that they talk over a cup of coffee. There was a diner, which had seen better days, on the corner.

'Let's go there,' she said. They took a booth near the back of the place.

Before the waitress could even ask, Rebecca said, 'Two coffees'. Then she turned to Blair. 'So. Spill. What is this murder story you are talking about?'

Blair took a deep breath. 'You may actually remember when this happened. Fifteen years ago, Molly Sinclair was murdered and her body was left in the woods. She was twelve.'

Rebecca frowned and thought for a moment, then she nodded. 'Oh, sure,' she said. 'That was big news around here. Her parents own the . . .'

'The Apres Ski,' said Blair. 'They were the first people I talked to about this new information. They did not want to hear it.'

'Her parents weren't interested? That seems a little . . . odd.'

'Well, the information I have could exonerate the man who went to prison for Molly's murder.'

Rebecca peered at her as if trying to recall an old song she hadn't heard in years. 'Some black guy killed that girl, didn't he? He's been in jail for years.'

'Only he didn't kill her,' said Blair.

Rebecca inhaled deeply and shifted around in her seat. Blair saw a veiled look come over her eyes, as if she was suddenly wondering if she was having coffee with a crackpot. 'Ok,' she said slowly. 'And you know this . . . how?'

Blair filled her in. Rebecca's body language continually gave the impression of impatience, so Blair boiled it down into a concise summary. She concluded with Celeste's deathbed confession.

Rebecca looked at her narrowly. 'So Celeste was your sister?' she said.

'I told you that,' said Blair.

'Right,' she said. 'She and I went to high school together. So you told the police about her confession?'

Blair nodded. 'They weren't interested.'

'Well, they wouldn't want anything turning up that proves they cocked up that investigation. That's characteristic of most police departments, in my experience.'

'No, they don't,' said Blair. She watched Rebecca curiously. It was almost as if she could see the wheels turning in her head. 'But it occurred to me that it might interest you to look into it, as a journalist.'

Rebecca frowned. 'You don't have much to go on,' she observed.

'Isn't that where you journalists come in?' said Blair. 'To dig up the truth?'

'Well, this newspaper operates on a shoestring. It has no budget for an in-depth investigation,' she mused aloud. 'There are expenses. It's time consuming.'

'I might be able to help with that,' said Blair. 'As I said, I have a successful company. I promised this to my sister. I intend to see it through.'

'It can take time,' she protested.

'I make my own schedule,' said Blair.

Rebecca looked at her with raised eyebrows. 'How nice for you.'

'Will you look into it?' Blair asked.

Rebecca hesitated and then she nodded. 'Yeah. I'll take a whack at it.'

Blair felt undeniably better after she left Rebecca Moore. That reporter was experienced and knowledgeable and had worked in a big city. If anyone knew how to dig into this story, it was Rebecca. It must have been fate, she thought, that they had crossed paths this morning. Still, she was curious as to how Rebecca ended up back here when her star had formerly been on the rise. She thought she would go in the house and google her when she got home.

But as she got out of the car at Uncle Ellis's house, she was greeted by her uncle waiting impatiently for her by his truck.

'Where have you been?' Ellis demanded.

'Errands? Why?' said Blair.

'Hurry up and get in the truck. Did you forget about it? The dinner at Darlene's?'

Blair glanced at her watch. 'No, I didn't forget about it, but isn't it a little early for dinner? The sun isn't even down yet.'

'That's what time she asked us for,' said Ellis. 'Malcolm's already in the truck.'

'Ok,' said Blair, stifling a sigh. 'I'll follow you in the car.'

Ellis took off out of the driveway, throwing up gravel with his squealing tires. He barely stopped to look before turning off out the dirt road and his rattletrap truck bumped over the mountain roads much faster than it should have been going. She almost had the feeling he was trying to lose her, but her Nissan had no trouble keeping up. Besides, why would he try to lose her? He was probably just worried about making Darlene unhappy by being late. The idea was so foreign to Blair that she could hardly absorb it. Ellis, worried about this woman's feelings? Blair shook her head at the wonder of it.

They took one of several roads that cut through the forest and, when they emerged from the forest, Ellis turned right without bothering to signal. Her uncle seemed to be disinclined to give her any warning when a turn was coming. The truck traveled up the mountain, wheeled around a few curves past the reservoir and turned right into a long driveway, which meandered through pastures to an old shingle-style house built into a hill. The house was surrounded by trees, untended fields and, across an overgrown field, a barn. Blair thought this must be one of the last farms left in town. Ellis stopped the truck and got out and Malcolm followed suit. The boy looked less than thrilled to be dragged to this dinner. That makes two of us, Blair thought.

Darlene ushered them in. There were no preliminaries like a house tour or a cocktail hour. Joseph Reese, still dressed in his Greyhound uniform, offered them each a beer, which Ellis declined and Blair took gratefully. Darlene directed them to the scarred dining table and Blair offered to help her serve. Darlene beckoned to her to come into the kitchen, while Ellis sat at the table with Joe and Malcolm, and the men talked spasmodically about the weather and local politics.

The kitchen was woefully out of date, as it was at Ellis's house, but Darlene had filled it with the appealing smell of pound cake and a pot roast cooking.

'This smells delicious,' Blair said sincerely.

'I hope you all will like it,' Darlene said.

'Can I help?' Blair asked.

'I'll fill these plates and you bring 'em in,' said Darlene.

'Ok,' said Blair. She watched Darlene bustling around the kitchen. Was Ellis, she wondered, thinking of making this kindly, competent woman his wife? It was hard to imagine. Blair took the plates in and set them around the table. Then she sat down next to Malcolm.

Malcolm picked up his fork and looked hungrily at his plate. Blair followed suit. Joe cleared his throat noisily and folded his hands. Darlene bowed her head. Ellis conspicuously followed her example. Blair waited as Joe intoned a blessing over the food.

'All right,' said Darlene. 'Let's eat.' Everyone eagerly began to tuck into their meal and murmurs of appreciation went around the table. Darlene asked Malcolm what he had done that day and

Malcolm's reply was monosyllabic. But he clearly didn't want to offend.

'This is really good,' he said.

Darlene thanked him, and turned to Blair. 'I was going to the grocery store and I saw you coming out of the police station, Blair,' Darlene said pleasantly. 'Don't tell me you got a parking ticket?'

Blair looked up, startled. 'No.'

Ellis glowered at her. 'Well what then?' Blair heard the curiosity beneath the irritation.

'Oh, it doesn't matter,' said Darlene, trying to avoid an argument between them. 'None of our business.'

Blair poked at her food with her fork. She didn't want to spoil the dinner, but all eyes seemed to be on her. Maybe this was as good a time as any, she thought. Uncle Ellis won't dare to go ballistic in front of Darlene and her brother. Blair felt instinctively that Darlene would find it perfectly reasonable. And it was only a matter of days before Rebecca Moore put it into the paper and everyone would know. She took a deep breath.

'Actually, I went there because I had something important to tell the police.'

'What was that?' Darlene asked pleasantly.

Blair glanced around the table. She could feel Ellis's gaze boring into her. It was as if he knew she was about to lob a grenade into the dinner party.

'Well, when Celeste was . . . at the very end, she told me that she wanted to make a kind of . . . confession. Get something off her chest.' The room was silent, all eyes on Blair. 'A long time ago, when we were twelve, my best friend from junior high, Molly Sinclair, was murdered in the woods. They convicted a local guy of the murder, Adrian Jones, and he's been in jail ever since.'

'Yes, we know. And what has this got to do with Celeste?' Ellis demanded.

'Well, it turns out that Celeste was with Adrian Jones, now called Yusef Muhammed, at the time when Molly was murdered. She could have given him an alibi, but she didn't say anything to the police.'

'She didn't say anything? Why ever not?' Darlene asked, looking shocked.

Blair looked across the table, straight at her uncle. Uncle Ellis was staring at Blair, all the color drained from his face. His fists were tightly clenched around his fork and knife. Blair chose her words carefully. 'It's a long story. She was afraid she'd get in trouble,' said Blair. 'She was only a teenager herself at the time.'

'In trouble how?' asked Darlene. 'Were they up to something?'

Blair hesitated. She knew this was her opportunity to blame Ellis and she was tempted, but at the last minute, for some reason, she decided to spare him. 'The kid had a reputation . . . as kind of a ne'er do well,' said Blair.

'What did the police say about all this?' asked Darlene.

'They weren't too interested,' said Blair.

Darlene put down her fork. 'Well, ne'er do well or not, that doesn't seem right.'

'That's not all he was,' Ellis blurted out.

Blair looked at her uncle defiantly. 'What else was he, Uncle Ellis?'

Ellis glowered at his plate.

'Go ahead,' said Blair. 'Tell us what you were going to say.'

Darlene looked at Ellis curiously.

'He was a troublemaker,' muttered Ellis.

'Even so,' said Darlene. 'Do you remember when that happened, Joe?'

Joe looked up from his food and blinked, as if he had been half-asleep. 'Eileen and I were away when it happened,' he said. 'Church retreat. But we sure did hear about it when we got back. That was big news in this town. The Sinclair girl was only a youngster.'

Suddenly Malcolm, who had been sitting silently, frowning, spoke up. 'Does that mean the guy will get out of jail now, since he didn't do it?'

'I hope so,' said Blair. 'I certainly do hope so. I have a reporter from the local paper, a girl named Rebecca Moore, who's taking an interest in the whole thing. We hope to get the whole case reopened.'

'Well, let's hope you succeed,' said Darlene. 'You did have something important to do today.'

Blair glanced again at Ellis, who was staring down into his plate. 'Yes, I really did,' she said.

* * *

The evening ended as soon as the pound cake was served and eaten. As Blair was getting into her car, to head back to Ellis's house, her phone rang. Eric, from the office, was apologetic, but explained that he had no choice but to call. The administrative and surgical staff from Hahnemann Hospital were interested in their product, but had questions and wanted to meet with the partners tomorrow afternoon. No one understood the 3D printing process the way that Blair did. Eric was all apologies, but said that they needed Blair to be there.

Blair reassured him. 'I understand. Of course I'll be there,' she said. 'Tell the others they can count on me.' Blair ended the call and started toward the house. When she walked into the front door of the house, she could hear Ellis yelling at Malcolm.

'Go upstairs.'

'But I want to hear about the murder,' Malcolm protested. 'When Aunt Blair gets here.'

'You do as I say,' Ellis insisted.

Blair heard Malcolm's footsteps dragging up the stairs as she entered the kitchen.

'When were you going to tell me about all this?' Ellis demanded.

'About what?' asked Blair, enjoying his indignation.

'About Celeste and her so-called confession.'

'I did tell you,' said Blair. 'Tonight.'

'Did you make it up?' Ellis accused her.

'No. Of course not.'

'So now you're saying that Celeste was involved, was having relations, with that nig—'

Blair raised a hand as if to say *stop*. 'Just don't . . .'

'She was sleeping with that worthless . . .'

'I didn't say that,' said Blair. 'I don't know anything about their . . . friendship. But she was in his car with him at the time, that she told me for sure. And the fact that she never admitted it is your fault. She was too afraid to tell the truth about Adrian because she knew what a . . . how prejudiced you were. Instead of yelling at me, you should be ashamed of yourself.'

'You're blaming me?' Ellis thundered.

'Yes, I do blame you,' Blair retorted. 'Celeste let a man go to prison for something he didn't do, rather than admit to you that she had a black friend.' Blair shook her head. 'It's just sick.'

Uncle Ellis shook his head. 'You went and told this pack of lies to some newspaper reporter? We're going to have our whole lives plastered all over this town.'

'An innocent man is sitting in prison because of what went on in this household. It's time for the truth to come out.'

Ellis narrowed his eyes and peered at her. 'I don't believe Celeste said any such thing to you. I think you're lying.'

'Why would I make it up?' Blair demanded.

'Why do you do anything? To try and get attention . . .' Ellis accused her.

Blair flinched as if he had thrown a bucket of water at her. 'To get attention? When did I ever get your attention for anything?'

Suddenly the landline rang and both of them looked at it in surprise. Blair was closest to it and picked up the phone.

Rebecca Moore was on the other end. 'Blair, this is Rebecca.'

'How did you get this number?' Blair asked.

'It's listed. I'm a reporter.'

'Of course. Sorry. Well, what's up?'

'I called Yusef Muhammed. I'm going up to the prison to talk to him tomorrow. I thought you might want to be there.'

'No point in going there. You have to Skype with him,' said Blair.

'No. I have permission. I've already cleared it. I will see him face-to-face.'

'Does it have to be tomorrow?' Blair asked. 'I've got to go to Philly.'

'I'm jumping on this,' said Rebecca. 'No time to waste.'

Blair debated with herself for a minute, truly torn. 'I can't do it tomorrow. I have to go to this meeting for my company. It's very important.'

'Well, I don't need you there to do my job,' said Rebecca. 'This is just a courtesy call.'

'I'm glad you're not wasting any time,' Blair said. 'How was Muhammed when you talked to him?'

'Cranky. Suspicious,' said Rebecca.

'Sounds like him,' said Blair.

'I need the phone,' Ellis demanded, interrupting her.

Blair rolled her eyes. 'I've got to go. I'll talk to you when I get back. Thanks, Rebecca.'

The minute Blair hung up, Ellis demanded to know who that was on the phone.

'That was the reporter whom I told about Celeste's confession. She is trying to get this information together, to get Yusef Muhammed out of jail.

Ellis glared at her. 'I don't want her calling here,' he said.

Blair returned his gaze without flinching. 'I know. There's a lot you don't want. Welcome to the new world, old man.' Blair turned her back on him and left the room.

TEN

By the time she got back to Yorkville, Blair was weary. The meeting with the doctors at Hahnemann had been, on the whole, productive, but not conclusive. Everyone agreed that there was much more to discuss, more questions to be answered. Still, it had felt exhilarating to Blair to be back at her office, back working with her partners, back to being taken seriously for her very specialized skills and ideas. Returning to Yorkville filled her with her unfinished grief over Celeste and a feeling that she was disliked and unappreciated here. She climbed the steps to the house and passed by the door to the living room. Uncle Ellis did not look up from the television when she said hello.

'Good to see you too,' Blair muttered.

She went down the hall to the kitchen. There was no sign of Malcolm anywhere. She thought of asking Uncle Ellis where he might be, but she decided against it. It might set him off. No, she just wanted to eat something quickly and get to bed. She opened the door to the refrigerator and looked inside. There were still the remains of a few dishes from friends and neighbors, but by now they were about ready to be dumped into the trash. Otherwise, there was nothing much beside peanut butter. She wished she had eaten in Philly. She thought of going to bed without dinner, but that seemed like punishing herself. The hell with it, she thought. I'll go out.

For a few minutes she sat in her car, trying to decide where to go. She often ate alone in the city and there it seemed normal. But she felt as if all eyes would be on her here in Yorkville, speculating about a woman alone. She hesitated and then picked up her phone and texted Rebecca Moore.

'Back from the city. On my way to grab a bite at . . .' She hesitated. She didn't want to have to avoid Molly's parents forever. She had done nothing wrong. '. . . the Apres Ski. How did the meeting go with Muhammed?' She sent the text, and turned on the engine. She hoped Rebecca would be interested in coming out for a drink at least. They might not be friends under other circumstances, but Rebecca seemed to be a woman alone in this town too. Blair put the car in gear and headed downtown.

The Apres Ski was doing a desultory business. Blair was led to a table near the front window. She did not see either of the Sinclairs as she glanced back toward the kitchen. Blair settled into a chair facing the door of the café and ordered a beer from the waitress. She took out her phone to see if she had received any texts.

Nothing. She tapped the phone gently on the tabletop. What had Rebecca accomplished today, she wondered, while she was gone? She wanted details, but it might have to wait until tomorrow. Blair glanced around the room. There were couples at scattered tables and several young people at the bar. People having fun.

Sometimes it seemed to Blair that she almost never had any fun. It was either work or solitude these days. Her life was productive and well organized, but fun . . .?

The waitress brought her beer and took Blair's order. Blair sat staring at the front door, sipping from her glass. Then she had an idea. She pulled up the screen on her phone and entered Rebecca's name into the search engine. She had meant to google her earlier, but she forgot. She was certainly curious about her unlikely ally.

The first thing to come up was a line of photos. They were clearly Rebecca, but it was a different Rebecca, sleekly dressed and camera-ready, her smile wide and appealing. Instead of uncombed hair and no makeup, she was perfectly groomed. She was pictured in form-fitting dresses and even an evening gown. Her presentation was sleek. Sexy. Chic. What happened here, Blair wondered? What made Rebecca go from high profile TV anchor to a reporter working at a sleepy, local paper?

A tapping on the window beside her made her jump. She turned and looked out. Rebecca Moore was pressed against the window, pointing toward the door and giving her a questioning look? She could feel her face redden, wondering if Rebecca could see that she was looking at her pictures on her phone screen. She quickly swiped away the screen and nodded, pointing at the door, as if to say, come on in.

By the time Rebecca arrived at the table, Blair was cool and composed. Rebecca sank into the chair opposite hers as Blair slipped her phone back into her pocket.

Without bothering to greet Blair, Rebecca looked around for the waitress. When she caught her eye, she beckoned her over, and ordered a beer.

Blair said, 'Make that two.'

Rebecca sat back. 'So, how was Philly?'

Blair could see that she was only asking to be polite. 'Fine,' she said. 'How was the interview with Muhammed?'

Rebecca was instantly happy to have the focus back on herself. She launched into a long-winded description of their meeting. Luckily, Blair was vitally interested.

'What it boils down to,' Rebecca said, 'is that if we take Celeste's word for this . . .'

'And we do,' said Blair.

'Then someone else had to have killed little Molly Sinclair.'

She hated the way Rebecca said: 'little Molly Sinclair.' It sounded condescending and dismissive, but she decided not to make an issue of it.

'I think it's important that we develop an alternate theory of what happened. I decided to investigate any similar incidents or crimes in this area at the time of her death; incidents involving young girls who were murdered, or who disappeared. I wanted to show Muhammed that I was serious about this, seriously taking his side.'

'That was probably a good idea,' Blair admitted.

Rebecca nodded. 'I could see that he liked that. He has studied the law on his own and he's done quite a bit to plead his case. Filed motions. Petitioned the court multiple times. But he has lacked a champion on the outside all these years. That's a pretty lonely, hopeless spot to be in.'

Blair nodded. Rebecca seemed to have a certain understanding of what motivated people. She liked that about her. It must have contributed to her original, speedy ascent to the top of her profession.

'Makes sense,' Blair said. 'So what did you come up with?'

Rebecca rummaged in her backpack and pulled out some papers that she set on the table. 'I printed these out cause I knew they wouldn't let me take the phone in when I went in to see him. Have a look.'

'I don't get why they let you have a face-to-face, and not me. They said only priests and lawyers were allowed access to prisoners on demand.'

Rebecca smiled and shrugged. 'Truthfully? My uncle's the warden there. He still thinks of me as a TV star. A lot of people do around here. Anyway I called him.' She accepted a beer from the waitress, who took Blair's empty and set her beer down beside her. Blair pored over the printed clippings.

'Molly's murder was unlike any other crime in this area. There just weren't any others that mirrored it.'

Blair frowned. 'You're right. There's not a great resemblance between these crimes and Molly's murder. A teenage girl who claimed that she was raped by her neighbor, although his wife swore he was asleep beside her at the time. A schoolgirl who was having an "affair" with her swim coach. He wasn't charged but he lost his job. A runaway who hasn't been seen in fifteen years; her older brother came home from the service and found that she was gone. He finally raised the alarm. Her mother said she threw the girl out because she insisted that this kid was trying to steal her boyfriend from her. More like the kid was the boyfriend's victim. God, people are sick,' Blair shook her head. 'But I still don't really see a correlation.'

Rebecca shrugged. 'I was looking for a pattern, looking for someone who preyed on young girls.'

'But as I recall it,' said Blair, 'Molly was not sexually assaulted.'

'I know. It's odd,' Rebecca said. 'I would have expected there to be a sexual component to Molly's murder.'

'I don't think there was,' said Blair. She could not help

remembering the innocent young girls that she and Molly were at the time. Boys were alien creatures whom they had romantic fantasies about. Sex was something that looked kind of exciting, but also weird and scary on the internet.

'None,' said Rebecca. 'No indication of a sexual assault. And yet, she was killed by a violent blow delivered by someone powerful. It was no accident.'

Blair forced herself to be objective, distant. 'That's true. She wasn't robbed. She wasn't raped. So why was she killed?'

'And what was she even doing there? According to Yusef Muhammed, he and your sister picked her up, took her home that day and left her at her house.'

'He has no reason to lie about that,' said Blair.

'None that we know of,' Rebecca said.

'He definitely said that? That they left her at her house?'

Rebecca nodded and took a swig of her beer. 'So, if that's true, what happened to Molly?' she asked.

'Does he have a theory?' Blair asked.

'Who? Muhammed?' Rebecca shook her head. 'If he does, it's all about how everybody was out to get him. He's a pain in the ass that way.'

'Wouldn't you be?' said Blair.

'I suppose,' said Rebecca. 'Poor bastard's been in jail for fifteen years for something he didn't do. One word from your dear, departed sister and his whole life might have been different. How could she have left him there to rot like that, all those years . . .?'

Blair was embarrassed by the question. There was no good answer to it. 'The question now is Molly . . .' Blair said. 'If he didn't kill her, who did?'

Just then Blair became aware of someone standing by the back of her chair.

Rebecca looked up at the person standing there. 'Can I help you? This is a private conversation,' she said.

'Blair, I'm surprised to see you here.'

Blair turned around and saw Janet Sinclair looking down at her. She was unsmiling. Blair tried not to betray any anxiety at the sight of Molly's mother.

'Janet,' she said. 'I'd like you to meet Rebecca Moore. She's a reporter at the paper. Rebecca, this is Molly's mother, Janet.'

Rebecca, unruffled, extended a hand. 'Nice to meet you. Sorry about . . . you know . . .'

Janet stared at the outstretched hand.

Blair sighed. 'Look, if you want us to leave . . .'

'No,' said Janet. 'On the contrary, I want you to stay.'

ELEVEN

Janet looked at Blair with a troubled gaze. She rubbed her forehead as if it were aching.

'I've thought about a lot of things since the other night, Blair. It's very hard for me to consider another explanation, after all these years. But, I keep asking myself, why would Celeste lie?'

Blair felt a wave of relief wash over her. Janet had heard her. She had listened.

'That's what I was trying to say,' Blair said earnestly. 'Celeste had no reason to lie. Not at that point. So what we thought all these years was the truth . . .'

'Was not,' said Janet.

'After I saw you, I went to the police,' said Blair. 'When I told them what Celeste told me, they didn't want to hear it. They refused to reopen the case. I didn't know where else to turn so I decided to go to the press. Rebecca offered to help.'

Janet was shaking. Blair pulled out a chair and gestured for her to sit down.

'Please, Janet,' Blair said. 'It would be such a help to have your version of what happened.'

Janet sighed and wiped her eyes. She hesitated, and then she sat down in the chair between them. Rebecca shot Blair a triumphant glance. Blair recoiled at her sense of victory and concentrated on the bereaved mother beside her.

'You just caught us off guard the other night, Blair. I did not want to hear it. At least, before you came along with that story of your sister's confession, I had some sense that justice for my daughter had been done. Now, I don't know what to think,' she said.

Rebecca opened her mouth to speak and Blair shot her a warning glance that was impossible to misinterpret.

'Look,' said Blair gently. 'Celeste did a terrible thing by keeping this a secret for so long.'

'Why didn't she just tell the truth when it happened?' Janet wailed.

'We'll never really know,' said Blair.

Janet pulled a Kleenex from her pocket and sniffled into it. 'You know, his mother, Lucille, still makes our pies.'

'Yusef's mother. Yes, I know Lucille,' said Blair. 'Molly and I stayed at her house after school one time, when you were called into work. She gave us pies.' Blair could still conjure up in her mind the face of the tired-looking black woman who, in later years, she had always believed, was the mother of Molly's killer. 'She must have always associated me with my sister, who destroyed her son's alibi. Although she still says hello to me if I run into her when I'm home.'

Janet nodded. 'Lucille is a good woman. Yusef – he was Adrian then – used to deliver our order sometimes, when Lucille was too busy to come herself. We knew him. He would stop and talk. He knew Molly. That only made it seem like more of a betrayal.' Janet was quiet for a moment and her gaze was far away, as if she were looking back in time. Janet sighed. 'Lucille tried to quit, back then, when her son was arrested for our daughter's murder. She said she could never face us again. We did consider it, but we didn't think that was right. We didn't blame Lucille. We told her we still wanted to work with her.'

'That's the way I remember the two of you,' said Blair. 'You always gave everybody the benefit of the doubt.'

Janet wiped her eyes and nodded. 'You wouldn't say that if you saw me this afternoon. Lucille came by with the pies for the week and she was walking on air. She was praising the Lord that Yusef was gonna get justice at last, and it was all I could do . . .' Janet shook her head and staunched her tears. 'I just wanted to scream at her. I knew it wrong of me . . . I mean, of course she was happy and full of hope for her son. But it just made me furious . . .'

'That had to be very difficult,' said Blair. 'But Janet, look, all we want is justice too. For Molly. And for Yusef. We want Molly's actual killer to be punished. That's the important thing now. That's what matters now.'

'It's too late,' Janet wailed. 'Whoever did it is long gone. The evidence is long gone. He got away with it and there's nothing to be done about it.'

'You can't be sure of that,' Rebecca corrected her. 'Sometimes, if you go back and look at a case again with new information, you see things differently.'

Janet shrugged slightly, but the look in her eyes was one of hopelessness.

'Let's just. . . revisit that day. Now according to Mr Muhammed,' said Rebecca, 'he and Celeste picked up your daughter, because they saw her walking in the rain and they drove her all the way home. Yet, somehow your daughter ended up back in the woods. So we are wondering why she would have gone back into the woods after she had been safely deposited at home, when the day was so rainy?'

Janet shook her head miserably. 'I have no idea.'

Blair shook her head and turned to Janet. 'I'm sorry, Janet. I know you're hurting . . .'

Janet shook her head. 'No, that's ok. For Lucille's son there's no time to waste. What do you want to know?'

'I want to know everything,' Rebecca said, leaning toward her. 'Molly's routine. What she usually did. What happened that day that was different?'

'Well, I can tell you one thing,' said Blair. 'She was not supposed to be home that afternoon. She came home from school on my bus with me and was supposed to stay for dinner at my house, cause her parents were in Philadelphia. As I remember, you didn't want her staying alone. Some trouble in the neighborhood . . .'

Janet frowned, as if trying to remember. 'Oh, you mean the guy who lived in the next house up the road. Knoedler. I forget his first name. He used to get drunk and beat up his wife and kids. I don't think he was dangerous to anyone but his family, but sometimes you could hear a terrible commotion from over there. The police came several times. I thought Molly might be scared if it started up again and she was all alone.'

'She and I were having fun together,' Blair remembered, 'until my uncle came home. Speaking of commotion, my uncle was mad at me for something and started yelling. I forget what. He never did need much of a reason. Molly stuck up for me.'

'That was Molly,' said Janet. 'She was like that. I never knew where she got that self-possession.'

'She was fearless,' Blair agreed. 'I used to wish I could be more like her.'

Janet warmed to the memory of her daughter. 'It seemed like she was born with it,' Janet said. 'Most girls her age are shy but not Molly . . . She always stood her ground.'

'She did,' Blair agreed, nodding. 'I admired her so much for that.'

Rebecca seemed impatient with their reminiscing about Molly. 'So, then . . .?'

'Well, Molly let my uncle know that he was being unfair to me. That's when he told her to leave. So Molly gathered up her stuff and headed for the door. I wanted to go with her but . . . I wasn't as brave as Molly. I was afraid of him. Of his anger,' said Blair.

'You lived there,' Janet said kindly. 'You had no choice.'

'So she left your uncle's house,' Rebecca continued, 'and we now know that Muhammed stopped and offered her a ride home. He and Celeste. And after she got home, we know that Molly left the house and went back out into the woods. Why? When you came home, were her things inside? Her backpack or whatever?'

Janet frowned. 'No. No. At the time he said that he brought her home. But no one believed him because she never entered the house and they found her backpack on the ground in the woods, not far from her . . . body . . .'

'But now we know that he did, indeed, bring her home. So why didn't she go into the house?' said Rebecca. 'That seems very strange.'

Janet shook her head hopelessly. 'I don't know.'

'Someone called her, perhaps?' Rebecca offered. 'Asked her to come and meet them?'

Janet shook her head slowly. 'No. Her phone was found in Muhammed's car, between the seats. It must have fallen out of her backpack while they were driving her home.'

'Could she have gone looking for her phone?' Blair asked.

'Why would she?' Rebecca pointed out. 'She hadn't been anywhere but in Muhammed's car.'

'True,' said Blair. 'Maybe she thought she left her phone at my house. Maybe she was walking back to get it.'

Rebecca frowned. 'She could have just called you on the land line and asked. Do you have a land line?' she asked Janet.

'We did in those days,' said Janet.

'Ok, so that rules out walking back to Blair's house. Normally, what would Molly do when she came home from school?' asked Rebecca.

'Come inside,' said Janet. 'Take her coat off. Probably have a drink or a snack, but there were no dishes in the sink . . .'

Blair tried to think back. Back to that fateful day when she and her best friend were chatting and applying new nail polish. Blissfully unaware of what was to come. What had they chatted about? Their schoolwork, boys they liked, something about camp. Then Blair had a moment of clarity. 'Her dog,' Blair said.

'Yes,' Janet exclaimed, remembering. 'You're right. That's how we knew for certain that Molly was never in the house. When we left in the morning, we left the puppy in the basement. She wasn't trained yet. So, we put her in the basement and closed the door. But if Molly had come in, she would have let her out right away. Would have put on her leash and taken her out for a walk. First thing. And she would have kept her upstairs, with her. But that evening, when we got back, Pippa was still in the basement, barking frantically.'

Blair and Rebecca exchanged a glance.

'At the time, I hardly thought about it,' said Janet sadly, shaking her head. 'It didn't seem to matter, after they found . . . Molly . . . in the woods.'

Blair looked up at Rebecca. 'But if he drove her up the driveway . . .'

Rebecca shook her head. 'I think he said he left her at the foot of the driveway.'

'I think we need to ask,' said Blair. 'Because somewhere between the time he dropped Molly off, but before she could walk into the house . . .'

'She was lost,' her mother wailed. 'She was lost.'

TWELVE

For a moment Blair and Rebecca sat in silence, humbled by a mother's fresh grief after so many years.

Finally, Rebecca spoke. 'So what we need to know is where exactly did he leave her and what happened in the time it took for Molly to walk up the driveway?'

Janet shook her head. 'That's impossible to know. It was fifteen years ago.'

Rebecca and Blair exchanged a glance. Blair could tell what Rebecca was thinking. It was not impossible. But they were wasting time sitting here. Suddenly Blair felt extremely grateful to Rebecca for her involvement in this.

Janet reached out and took Blair's hand in her own. Blair was surprised at the softness and warmth of her touch.

'I appreciate this, Blair. I really do. I'm sorry Robbie and I were so cold to you the other day. I know that you really do care about this for Molly's sake.'

Blair squeezed the older woman's hand back. 'I won't give up on her.'

Janet held Blair's hand for a moment and then she sighed, and stood up. 'All right. I'd better get back to the kitchen. Listen, if there is anything I can do to help . . .'

'We'll ask you. Don't worry,' said Blair.

'Whoever killed my girl . . .' Janet began, and then bit her lip as her eyes glistened. 'I thought I knew. But now . . . well, I still need to know.'

'Tell the police that,' said Rebecca.

Janet frowned. 'What do you mean?'

'It might help if Molly's mother wanted the investigation reopened.'

'All of those policemen. They worked day and night. They did everything they could for us,' Janet protested.

'They helped convict the wrong man,' said Rebecca flatly.

'I can't be the one to say that. Not without proof,' said Janet.

Blair shook her head. 'Janet, never mind. Don't worry. We'll take it from here.'

'I'm sorry. I do want the truth . . .' Janet's voice faded away. Her head down, she started to make her way back toward the kitchen.

Blair turned back to Rebecca. 'What's the matter with you?'

'What?' she demanded. 'If she were to go to the police, we might get a little cooperation. That wouldn't hurt anything.'

Blair shook her head. 'All we have is Celeste's admission, which they've already discounted, and a raft of questions. They are not going to care.'

'You're right about that. They won't cooperate,' Rebecca said.

'So how do we find out what happened in those crucial few minutes it took for Molly to walk up the driveway?'

'We keep asking questions,' Rebecca said, draining her beer glass and setting it down on the table. 'Until we find someone who knows the answer.'

Blair frowned. 'Someone must know.'

Rebecca looked at her coolly. 'The killer knows.'

Blair nodded and finished her beer. 'That's true. Just tell me where we begin.'

It was late when Blair got back to the house. Ellis and Malcolm had both retired for the night. Blair did not want to wake either of them up. She tiptoed upstairs to take her shower and managed to slide, unnoticed, into her room and under the covers. After the long day she fell instantly asleep.

She was awakened by the sound of knocking at the front door and was surprised to see that it was morning. A gray morning, but morning all the same. Blair looked at the clock and realized she had failed to set it.

'Coming,' she hollered as she pulled on her robe and ran her hands over her disheveled mass of hair. She slid into her slippers and descended the steps.

Amanda, Peter and Zach stood at the front door. Amanda looked stricken when she saw Blair.

'I'm sorry. We woke you up.'

'That's ok,' said Blair.

Amanda looked ruefully at her husband. 'I told you we should have called.'

'No, no,' said Blair. 'It's fine. I was just so tired. A lot's been going on. Come on in. What's up?'

'Well,' said Amanda, 'we're going to rent ATVs and ride through the mountains. We thought Malcolm might want to join us.'

'That sounds like something he'd enjoy,' said Blair. She looked out in front of the house. Ellis's truck was gone. 'Let me call upstairs.' She pulled her robe closed and stood at the foot of the staircase.

'Malcolm,' she called out.

Malcolm came out of his room and looked over the railing with sleepy eyes.

'What?'

'The Tuckers are here. They want to rent ATV's today. They thought you might enjoy going with them. Is that something you'd like to do?'

'Cool,' said Malcolm. 'That would be awesome.'

'Ok. Well, get dressed. You need to have some breakfast before you go.'

Malcolm rushed off into his room and Blair invited the Tuckers to sit down in the living room. 'He just needs to get dressed and have some breakfast.'

'We thought we'd stop for breakfast on the way,' said Amanda.

'Can I go up to Malcolm's room?' Zach asked, who was jiggling impatiently from one foot to the other.

Amanda looked at Blair.

'Sure. Knock on his door,' said Blair.

She indicated towards the battered-looking sofa and Peter and Amanda sat down. Blair sat down on the edge of Ellis's chair.

'This is really nice of you,' she said.

'Well, we thought it might be fun for him,' said Amanda. 'You know, get his mind off things.'

'I'm sure it will be.'

An awkward silence descended.

'How are you doing?' Amanda asked.

'I'm ok,' said Blair. 'How about you?'

Amanda hesitated and then grimaced a little. 'I've been thinking that we probably should talk about when we're going to . . . you know, move Malcolm and his things in with us.'

Blair pushed her hair back out of her eyes and nodded. She

fumbled in the pocket of the robe and found a coated elastic band. She pulled her hair up into a ponytail. 'I have to give my uncle some warning.'

Peter and Amanda exchanged a worried glance.

'Is he going to oppose this move?' Peter asked. 'Because all the legalities are in order . . .'

'I know,' said Blair. 'And he's going to have to adjust to the idea. I mean, this is a done deal.'

Amanda shook her head. 'I wish it didn't have to be like this,' she said. 'Malcolm doesn't need to have people arguing about him. It's going to be hard enough of an adjustment . . .'

'I will talk to Ellis again today,' said Blair. 'He's been avoiding me, I think. And I've had . . . other matters to attend to. But I am going to lay this all out for him. Do you have a . . . a date for when you want Malcolm to move in with you?'

Amanda looked at Blair apologetically. 'We were thinking maybe . . . Thanksgiving weekend. It would give him the long weekend to adjust, and the holiday is a happy time. I was thinking we might invite Ellis to our family's Thanksgiving.'

Blair frowned. 'That is beyond the call of duty.'

'And you too, Blair,' said Amanda. 'Really. I want us all to be family.'

Blair realized that her first impulse was to say no. Other people's holidays made her anxious. There had not been much celebrating in Ellis's house. She didn't really know how. But then she remembered her promise to Celeste – that she would be present in Malcolm's life. This first holiday in his new home might be a time when he really needed his family around.

'Of course,' she said. 'Thank you.'

'Everybody brings something,' said Amanda eagerly.

'I don't really cook,' Blair demurred.

'Bring wine,' said Peter.

Blair smiled at Amanda's husband. He was such a nice guy. 'Done,' said Blair.

There was the thunder of boys' footsteps on the stairs and Malcolm came in, trailed by Zach. He suddenly seemed to have a sudden attack of shyness.

'Hi Aunt Manda. Uncle Pete,' he muttered.

'You got everything you need?' Blair asked him.

Malcolm seemed relieved to be answering a familiar question. 'Yup,' he said. 'Ready to go.'

Blair felt a sudden, piercing affection for her nephew. 'Come here,' she said. 'Give me a hug.'

Malcolm's eyes widened in surprise, but he stepped close to where she was seated on Ellis's chair and draped an arm around Blair's neck.

'Have fun today,' Blair whispered.

'Let me get a picture,' said Amanda. 'Smile, you two.'

Blair was about to protest, but Malcolm turned his head to look at Amanda's phone and Blair followed suit. Amanda took a couple of shots. Blair noticed that Malcolm kept his arm around her neck for all of the photos. She felt self-conscious being photographed wearing a bathrobe, but she decided not to fuss. She didn't have a recent picture of herself with Malcolm. What difference did it make what she was wearing?

'Will you send those to my phone?' she asked Amanda.

'Sending them now,' said Amanda.

Peter clapped his hands on his knees and stood up. 'You ready for some trail riding?' he asked.

Malcolm nodded.

'Good. Let's get going then.'

'Race ya,' said Zach and headed for the door. Malcolm was hot on his heels.

Amanda and Blair got up and embraced awkwardly.

'Thank you for this,' said Blair.

Amanda smiled. 'Now you can go back to bed and catch up on your sleep,' she said.

'Not me,' Blair said. 'Not today.'

'What are you up to?' Amanda asked pleasantly.

Blair hesitated. She did not want to go into it. She opened the front door and stepped out onto the porch, shivering in her bathrobe and slippers. Amanda and Peter followed her out. Blair inhaled deeply of the chilly, gray morning.

'I have some errands,' she said.

The newspaper lay on the front porch in a plastic bag. Blair bent down to pick it up and tucked it under her arm. Then she waved as Amanda and Peter descended the steps and climbed into their SUV. The two boys were already in the back seat, ready to go.

Blair kept waving. 'Have fun,' she called out.

As Amanda and Peter pulled out of the driveway, Blair removed the paper from its plastic bag and glanced at the front page. In the middle columns below the fold was Molly's school picture: **WHO KILLED MOLLY SINCLAIR?** read the headline above Rebecca's byline. Below Molly's picture was another headline in smaller type: *A deathbed confession to a sister throws doubt on the guilt of a local man. Has he spent fifteen years in prison for a crime he didn't commit?* Her own picture appeared just under that headline. It was a picture that had appeared in the local paper, sent by the University when she got her graduate degree.

Seeing her face on the front page was jarring. Wait a minute, Blair thought. Even though she knew Rebecca was a reporter and it would all end up in the paper, she felt somehow betrayed. Blindsided. It was too soon. They had too few facts. She pulled her robe more tightly around her and went back into the house to read the story. As she closed the door behind her, the phone started ringing off the hook.

'Hello,' she said.

'Hello, am I speaking to Blair Butler?'

'Yes,' said Blair.

'This is radio station WRYV news. Could you comment on the story in the *Yorkville Gazette* this morning . . .?'

'No, I can't,' said Blair. 'Not now.'

Startled by the call, she slammed the receiver back down on the hook and fished for her cell in her bathrobe pocket. She started to compose a text to Rebecca. Somehow it all seemed too speculative. Precipitous.

'The front page? We need to talk,' she wrote. 'We need some ground rules, ASAP.'

The dismissive answer was back in seconds. 'Meet later. Busy making those calls.'

Rebecca doesn't feel a shred of guilt or regret, Blair thought. And why should she? Last night they had discussed the people they needed to talk to, to try and explain those missing minutes of Molly's life. Rebecca was already working on it. She's right, Blair thought. Why should Rebecca be apologetic? You couldn't ask a newspaper reporter not to write a story. Ready or not, it was in the public domain now. Blair hurried up the stairs to get dressed.

She had her own part to do in this investigation and now, with
Malcolm safely in the hands of the Tuckers, she had the whole
day to do it.

THIRTEEN

'The foot of the driveway,' Yusef Muhammed growled.
'That's where she told me to leave her.'

Blair glanced at him on the screen of her iPad and
made a note in her notebook.

'You didn't offer her a ride to the door?' Blair asked. 'It was
raining.'

'She said she didn't want one,' he said. 'Why you asking me
this? Are you accusin' me again?'

'No,' said Blair. 'I just need an accurate picture of what happened
that day. Timing seems to be crucial.'

Muhammed was silent.

'You'll hear from us soon,' said Blair. 'Really. Try to be patient.'

'Awright,' he muttered. 'But hurry.'

Last night, she and Rebecca had tried to imagine the people
who might have been at Molly's house on a weekday afternoon.
People who might have seen something or known something, even
if they weren't aware of it. At the top of her list was Muhammed,
whom she had just contacted via Skype. Her next stop was the
post office. When she arrived there, Blair asked to see the
Postmaster, who turned out to be a squat, middle-aged woman
named Rose. She had tightly curled brunette hair and was wearing
a shirt which gaped between the buttons. Blair inquired about the
mailman for the route which faced the woods. Rose was able to
tell her that the mail carrier, who had been on that route fifteen
years ago, was still on that same route.

'Is he here?' Blair asked eagerly. 'Can I talk to him?'

'No, he's out on the route,' said Rose. 'He won't be back in
until around 2:30 or three.'

'So you're saying that he's done with his route by three?'

'Oh yeah. Except on rainy days,' said Rose.

Blair's heart leapt in her chest. 'Is it later, on rainy days?'

'No, earlier,' said Rose. ''Cause he doesn't stop to chat with people.'

'Oh,' said Blair, 'ok.' Not him, then, she thought. 'Well, I'll keep an eye out for him.'

'Salt and pepper hair. Has a limp,' Rose offered. 'His name's Jim Fox.'

'Thanks,' said Blair. She got back into her car and drove the road which cut through the woods, to the Sinclair's neighborhood. On one side of the Sinclair's lot, overgrown with mature trees, was a large, landscaped lot with a well-tended lawn surrounding a sprawling, brick Colonial-style house set in the middle, like an island. She drove up the winding drive and parked behind a pristine Land Rover. Blair went up to the front door and knocked. As she waited, she looked over toward the next home up the street. It also was large and impressive. Prosperity had come to Yorkville since she was a kid. After a few minutes, the door was opened by a rumpled-looking man wearing an MIT sweatshirt.

'Can I help you?' he asked. He looked almost like a recent graduate.

'I'm looking for the owner of this house,' Blair said doubtfully.

'I'm the owner,' he said proudly. 'My wife and I.'

A young girl of eight or nine, with gray eyes, blonde, wispy hair, and long legs, wiggled past the man in the doorway and leaned against him, staring out at Blair.

'Who is this, Dad?' she asked.

Blair smiled at her. 'Well, my name is Blair Butler. I . . . have some questions about something that happened at the house next door to this one some years ago.'

'How long ago?' asked the man abruptly.

'Fifteen years ago,' said Blair.

'Can't help you. We only bought the house five years ago.'

'Do you know who lived here before you?'

'I don't,' said the homeowner. 'You can ask the realtor.'

'Who did you use?' Blair asked.

'Cronin's,' he said. 'On Main Street. They're owned by Christie's now.'

Blair nodded. 'Oh, ok, I will. Thanks.'

As she turned to leave, the man said, 'What happened?'

Blair turned and looked at him questioningly. 'Excuse me?'

'All those years ago. You said something happened?' he asked.

Obviously he did not read the local paper or he would have read about his next door neighbors this very morning. Probably subscribed to the New York Times and steered clear of the locals. Blair looked at the small girl, her father's hand protective on her shoulder. No need to give her nightmares.

'Nothing,' she said. 'It was a . . . property issue.'

The man shrugged and closed the door.

Blair got back in her car and drove out to the road. She passed the Sinclair house and kept driving. The next property was so heavily wooded that Blair nearly missed the driveway. At the last minute, she recognized it and she turned and pulled slowly in.

The driveway wound between the trees of the wooded property. There was a small, wooden shed on the left with a door standing open and what looked like bikes, rakes and a jumble of other equipment inside. The shed appeared to be the only building on the property. But as she went farther up the drive, the main house came into view. It was clapboard-sided Colonial which had seen better days. The Sinclair's log cabin style house, was older, but not dilapidated. Robbie and Janet had maintained it scrupulously all these years. This house hadn't been painted in decades. There were large patches of clapboard that were worn down to the primed wood, with sizable flakes of paint hanging off, or lying in the untended bushes which ringed the house. There was a twig wreath with pine cones hanging on the front door.

Blair parked and got out. She went up to the door and knocked. The lights were on inside, and she could hear a TV running. She waited patiently until she heard someone talking under their breath and fiddling with the doorknob.

The door opened and the woman standing there blinked at Blair over her half glasses. It was hard to tell her age. Probably late fifties, Blair thought. She was a trim woman and her chin-length hair was tinted an unnatural brunette color. She was wearing a cardigan, stretchy waist pants and furry slippers. Her complexion was sallow.

'Can I help you?' she asked.

'Mrs Knoedler?' asked Blair.

'Yes,' said the woman.

Blair introduced herself and explained her purpose.

'Is this about that story in the morning paper? About the Sinclair's daughter?'

'It is,' said Blair. 'Mrs Knoedler, I—'

'Carol,' she said. 'Come on in.'

The woman gestured for Blair to follow her back into the cheerful, cluttered kitchen. A newspaper on the table was opened to the crossword puzzle that was partly filled in. A TV was running in another room. A pale young man with a bony, sculpted face, wearing sweatpants and a faded T-shirt, was seated at the table, pensively smoking. He was barefoot and his feet looked grimy. Blair couldn't remember the last time she'd seen someone smoking inside the house. The smoke in the air was suffocating.

'Connor, can't you go outside and smoke?' asked Carol.

The young man smashed the butt into an overflowing ashtray on the kitchen table, which indicated to Blair that this was a regular habit of his.

'Who's this?' he asked.

'This woman is asking about Molly Sinclair's murder,' Carol said.

'Why? That was years ago.' Connor protested.

'She just wants to talk to me,' said Carol. 'Now go turn that TV off in there if you're not watching it.'

'I'm watching it,' he said, unfolding himself from the chair. Without a look back at either of them, he shuffled off in the direction of the TV noise.

The woman put a kettle on one of the stove burners. Through the kitchen windows, Blair could see nothing but trees. The Sinclairs' log cabin style home was somewhere over in that direction, Blair thought, but not a board of it was visible.

'I'd love to help you,' said the woman, 'but honestly I don't remember much about that day. Fifteen years ago I had four kids under ten years old. I was running in four directions at once.'

'I'm specifically interested in Molly walking up that driveway that day. I had hoped that you might be able to see the Sinclairs' driveway from your house.'

Carol shook her head. 'Oh no. This house is so secluded. All the trees. I always liked that feeling of being out in the woods. You could sometimes hear things.' She frowned in thought, one hand on her hip. 'I do remember that dog of theirs yapping. My son, Connor,' she said, cocking her head to indicate the young man who had just left the room, 'was always after me. "Can we have a dog? Please mom?" I'd hear that yapping and think, "That's all I need. More commotion."'

'Do you remember Molly?' Blair asked.

Carol turned around and leaned back against the countertop, one hand covering her lips. She shook her head. 'Oh, sure. I mean, we knew our neighbors. We knew who they were. What a wonderful child she was. The parents never did get over it. I wouldn't have either.'

For some reason, Blair felt the desire to confide in this woman. 'She was my best friend,' said Blair.

Carol shook her head and her face seemed to pucker with sadness. 'Just terrible. Is it true now that they don't think the right guy went to jail for it?'

'Yes, it's true,' said Blair. 'That's why I'm here. We're trying to determine what really happened.'

'Well, she was killed in the woods down the street and on the other side, wasn't she?'

'That's where they found her,' Blair admitted. 'But it turns out that she had a ride home that day. Something happened to her before she ever made it into the house.'

'So how did she end up over in the woods?'

'That's what we need to know.'

'Hmm,' said Carol shaking her head. 'I wish I could help you. It was a rainy day. I know that. I can remember the sirens, all the police cars. You could see their lights flashing through the trees, long into the night. But honestly, I don't recall much else. On a rainy day, my kids would have been running around, tearing the place apart, like wild Indians.'

'What about Mr Knoedler?' asked Blair innocently. 'Do you think your husband might remember something?'

'Why are you asking about him?' Carol asked defensively.

'I'm curious about anyone who might have seen or heard something.'

'No, he'd be no help to you.'

'Are you sure? I mean, he may have . . .'

'By that time of day he was already in his cups. He wouldn't notice anything.'

There was a stirring at the back door as it opened and closed and a voice yelled out,

'Ma. It's me.'

'We're in the kitchen, honey,' Carol called back.

A nice-looking girl in her late twenties, with long, brunette curls, a blue moto jacket and high boots over her jeans, came into the warmth of the kitchen and set a white paper bag with a Walgreen's logo on the table. She looked familiar to Blair.

'I stopped and got your shampoo,' the girl said. She took off her jacket and hung it on a crowded clothes tree just outside the kitchen door.

'Thank you, honey,' said Carol. 'This is . . .' Carol Knoedler peered at Blair. 'Tell me your name again.'

'Blair Butler.'

'Miss Butler. Blair. Blair, this is my eldest daughter, Jenna. She works as an aide at the high school,' Carol said proudly.

Jenna smiled and nodded. 'Nice to meet you.'

'I feel like we've met before,' said Blair.

'How was the store?' asked Carol.

'It was easy. No line,' said Jenna, glancing curiously at Blair.

'She's asking about your father,' Carol said frowning.

'My father? What about him?' Jenna's face was instantly stormy.

In that moment, Blair remembered where she had seen this girl. She had come to the bar, to drive home her inebriated father; the abusive guy with the beard.

'I'm not actually here about your father,' said Blair. 'I'm here because of Molly Sinclair. She was one of my best friends. It's beginning to look like the wrong man went to jail for her murder.'

'What's that got to do with my father?' asked Jenna defensively.

'Nothing that I know of,' said Blair. 'I'm just trying to piece together what happened on the day Molly was killed.'

'My father was probably at work,' said Jenna.

Carol Knoedler snorted, as if that was a laughable idea.

'Well,' said Blair to the girl. 'Is there anything you remember?'

Jenna shrugged. 'I remember when we heard all the sirens, of course.'

'Your brothers all wanted to go over there,' Carol said, 'but I told them to stay put. The police didn't need them underfoot. They sneaked out anyway. Boys aren't capable of resisting the police sirens and the lights.'

Jenna nodded, as she went to the refrigerator, opened the door and pulled out a bottle of apple juice.

'We all wanted to know what happened.'

'Were you friends with Molly?' Blair asked.

Jenna shrugged. 'She was a few years older than me. At that age, a few years are a big gap. Besides, I wasn't looking for playmates. I had my brothers and my sister to play with.'

'Do you remember anything about that day? The day Molly was . . . killed. Anything before the police showed up?' Blair asked, without a lot of hope.

Jenna grimaced as she twisted off the lid of the apple juice bottle. 'Actually,' she said, 'I do remember something.'

'What's that, honey?' Carol asked, surprised.

Jenna's eyes widened, recalling the day. 'Well, of course you don't forget a day when a girl was murdered who lived next door. You don't forget that.'

'No, of course not,' said Blair.

'But now that I think about it . . .' She was pensive for a moment, taking a swig of her apple juice. She set the bottle down on the kitchen table. 'We were playing hide and seek. It was raining, but I sneaked out the front door and ran down the driveway to the shed. I figured they would never find me there.'

'It's no wonder you were always getting a cold. Did you even wear a coat?' asked Carol, shaking her head.

'I remember,' Jenna mused, 'that Connor was looking for us, just yelling all over the house. I was out there in the shed, crouched down behind two bicycles, trying to be real quiet, so he wouldn't find me. But while I was in there hiding, I did hear something from next door, over where the Sinclairs lived.'

'What did you see?' Blair demanded.

'Well, I didn't actually see anything,' Jenna corrected her. 'I didn't want to get up or look out the window of the shed, cause Connor might find me and I'd be "it". But I could hear something. Somebody was banging on the door of the Sinclairs' house and making these terrible sounds, like crying and pleading.'

'Somebody like . . . a man, a woman, a child?'

'A woman, I think. But it was faint. I couldn't hear the words. Just the sounds. But they sounded . . . desperate.'

'You didn't look out?' Blair cried, incredulous.

'No, cause of the game. I was hiding. But Connor found me anyway. I could hear him coming down the drive and then he came in and began tossing stuff around, until he spotted me. Then I was it. So I ran back up to the house with him chasing me.'

'And you never went next door?' asked Blair. 'To find out why somebody was banging on the door like that?'

Jenna shook her head. 'Nope,' she said solemnly. 'I guess I forgot about it. I was only ten. All I was thinking about was the game.'

FOURTEEN

'W hat do you think?' Blair asked. 'Was it Molly?'

'Honestly,' said Jenna. 'I don't know. Connor came bursting in saying that I was "it", and I said "no fair" and he began to chase me up to the house. I didn't think any more about it. Not till all the police were there.'

'Did you tell the police?' Blair asked.

Jenna shook her head. 'We heard that they found Molly in the woods across the road. Why? Do you think it matters?'

'I don't know,' said Blair. 'At this point, anything I can find out about what happened could matter.'

'Well, that's what I heard,' said Jenna.

'Thanks,' said Blair. 'I guess I'll . . .' she rose from her chair at the kitchen table and pointed to the back door.

'If we think of anything . . .' said Carol, and then her voice drifted away.

Blair thanked them both and then went out to get in her car. She got a message from Rebecca as she was buckling her seat belt.

'Made some progress. Let's meet,' she wrote.

For a minute Blair couldn't help feeling excited. Maybe they were getting close. It was like a treasure hunt and then she reminded herself of Molly, who had been murdered. This was not a party game.

'Sure. Where?' she wrote.

'How about Cascade?'

It was a new restaurant that was one of those farm to table places, very trendy. Maybe Rebecca was trying to impress upon her that despite the fact that she lived back in the old home town, she had once been in the big time.

'Sure,' Blair said. 'Half an hour?'

'See you then,' Rebecca said.

Blair put the car in gear and headed for Cascade and, despite her resolve to focus on the seriousness of her task, she felt undeniably excited and hopeful.

From the outside, Cascade was a combination of wood and glass perched above a waterfall, nestled in the trees. Blair had passed by it often, but never actually been inside, and she wondered, for a moment, if she was properly dressed. She reminded herself that she was a modern entrepreneur. People her age never dressed up for the occasion. It was almost a religious tenet that jeans and running shoes went everywhere. She walked in and glanced over at the bar which ran the length of the front windows. She didn't see Rebecca there. Could she have gotten a table already? She thought uncertainly. She was about to ask the hostess, when she heard someone call her name from the direction of the bar. She turned around to look.

A woman in a business suit with a short skirt and silk shirt, her hair loose and coiffed in waves, was gesturing to her. It took Blair a moment to realize that this was Rebecca. Rebecca's perfect legs were crossed at the knee. She wore dark hose and high-heeled shoes. Blair walked over to the barstool where Rebecca sat and had to consciously close her mouth which was hanging open. Rebecca laughed at her reaction.

'Yes, it's me,' she said.

Blair shook her head. 'What happened?'

'Opportunity knocked,' she said. 'Here, sit down. What do you want to drink?'

Blair turned to the bartender and named a cocktail.

'I can still clean up well,' Rebecca said.

Blair stared at her. She looked like those pictures on her phone. Sophisticated and . . . sleek. Something about this transformation made Blair feel uneasy; her cocktail arrived and she began to sip it.

'So what does that mean?' she asked. 'Opportunity knocked?'

'Oh, just a phrase,' Rebecca said dismissively. 'Tell me what you've been up to today. We'll compare notes.'

'Well,' said Blair wryly, 'while you've been at the hairstylist and the boutique, I've been talking to people.'

'I've been talking to people too,' Rebecca protested. 'And what have you learned in your travels?'

'Not as much as I'd like,' Blair admitted. 'I spoke to Yusef and he definitely remembered leaving Molly at the foot of the driveway.'

'Ok, that answers that,' said Rebecca.

'The people who lived next door, on one side, have only been there a few years. I have to get the name of the people who lived there before them and track them down. He gave me the realtor's name. The people on the other side are the Knoedlers . . . one of their daughters was there. She remembered playing hide and seek with her brothers and sisters on the day that Molly died. She heard someone banging on the door to Molly's house that afternoon. Sounding frantic according to Jenna Knoedler.'

'Who was it?' Rebecca asked.

Blair shook her head. 'Don't know. The kid was hiding. She didn't look out.'

'Hmmm . . .' said Rebecca. 'Well, that might be important.'

'By the way, about your article in the paper. You were kind of jumping the gun, weren't you?' Blair chided her.

'You would be amazed at all the calls I got about that article today,' Rebecca said enthusiastically. 'People coming out of the woodwork.'

'Anything useful?'

'Yes. Did you go to the post office like we said?'

'I did. But the mailman was out on his route.'

'Yeah, well, it turns out that he read my article and he called me. He's a guy named Jim Fox. It seems that Jim was in the woods that afternoon, taking a catnap. He was working a double shift that day, cause it was getting close to Christmas. So he pulled the mail truck off the road through the woods, into a little clearing, just to catch forty winks in between shifts.'

'Did he see anything?' Blair asked.

'He said he was woken up by a thud, like something toppling over. But he was groggy. He wasn't sure if he dreamed it or not.

The rain was coming down so he couldn't see much. Anyway, he was getting ready to leave when he saw a vehicle leaving the woods. Not Yusef's car. It was a truck, a pickup truck.'

'The most common of all vehicles around here,' Blair observed. 'Why didn't he tell the police?'

'He was sleeping on the job,' said Rebecca. 'Besides, the police were only interested in Muhammed's sedan. He had been seen picking Molly up.'

'True,' said Blair.

'But I got to thinking,' said Rebecca, 'what if somebody killed Molly elsewhere, and brought her to the woods to dump her body. That would cause a thud.'

'That's true,' said Blair. 'But why would they . . .?'

'Well, there are still more questions than answers,' Rebecca admitted.

Blair nodded. 'So what is our next move?' she asked.

Rebecca hailed the bartender and asked for her tab. 'Well, my next move is to drive up to New York. But you might want to have dinner here. It's really very good.'

Blair looked at her in confusion. 'Aren't you . . .?'

'I can't stay, but I recommend it,' she said as she slid off the barstool and gave her a little salute. 'Enjoy it. We'll talk tomorrow,' she said.

'Yeah,' said Blair, facing another lonely dinner. 'Thanks.'

She waited until Rebecca pulled away before she left the bar. She wasn't going to eat an expensive meal alone in this trendy place. It made her feel stupid and friendless. She went out to the parking lot and got into her car. She drove back to Ellis's house and went inside. Ellis was sitting at the table, finishing off a plate of food.

'Is Malcolm back?' Blair asked, looking in the refrigerator.

'From where?' Ellis demanded.

'He went ATV riding with Amanda and Peter. I left you a note.'

'I didn't read it,' Ellis said.

The cat came up to her and mewed, brushing against the legs of Blair's jeans.

'This cat seems hungry.'

Ellis shrugged. 'Cat's always hungry.'

'Did Malcom feed Dusty before he left?' Blair asked, noticing the cat's empty bowl beside the counter.

'Don't know, don't care,' said Ellis, dumping his empty plate into the sink. 'Not my cat.'

Blair shook her head. This wailing cat was going to drive her crazy. She got out her phone and punched up Malcolm's number. The call went directly to voicemail.

'Malcolm, it's Aunt Blair. Did you feed Dusty? Cause the cat seems to be hungry. Call me back.'

She managed to put together something for dinner and then went into the living room where Ellis was seated in his stained, oversized chair, actually reading the newspaper.

Although he did not look up from the paper, he spoke up when Blair entered the room.

'I hope you're happy having our private business splashed all over the newspaper,' he said.

'You mean the article about Molly,' she said.

'This is that reporter that called here the other day,' Ellis said accusingly.

'Yes. She wants to find out the truth about what happened to Molly.'

'She doesn't seem that concerned with the truth to me,' Ellis said angrily, shaking out the paper between his hands.

Blair ignored him. She took out her phone and did something she had been meaning to do for several days. She googled Rebecca Moore a second time. And almost as soon as she did, she felt queasy.

There were a number of articles about Rebecca, dating back three years or so. They all told the same story. Rebecca had been a reporter at a network in L.A., her rise meteoric by all accounts. But it had seemingly not been fast enough to suit her. She had been reporting on an underage sex scandal with Hollywood connections. She interviewed a witness, seen only in a darkened profile, who named some big names in the entertainment business. When she was questioned about her sources, Rebecca cited her first amendment protections. But another reporter from the same network finally outed her with the truth: Rebecca had created the witness, enlisting an actor and scrambling his voice to name the names involved. Rebecca was fired and forced to leave town.

No station with a big demographic would hire her. Not in L.A. Not anywhere.

'What's the matter with you?' asked Ellis.

Blair looked up from her phone, startled that even Ellis had seen the dismay on her face.

'Nothing.' The cat continued to yowl and jumped up on the arm of her chair. Blair stood up abruptly and the cat leapt away.

'I'm going to go pick up Malcolm. He should be back by now.'

'He won't like you following him around,' said Ellis.

Blair ignored his advice. She just wanted to get out of the house and away from what she had just learned about Rebecca. She went out, got in her car, and drove to the Tuckers. Uncle Ellis was probably right, she admitted to herself. Malcolm wouldn't be happy about her showing up before he had summoned her, but she needed to get out and think.

The Tuckers lived in a recently built, single story house with a two-car garage, in a cul-de-sac only a short distance from where Ellis lived. The large yard was raked and the front porch had a seasonal display of pumpkins and mums, arranged on a bale of hay. Blair parked behind the SUV, slammed the car door and walked up to the front door of the tidy house. She knocked on the door. In a few minutes, Amanda answered the door.

'Hi Blair,' she said, surprised.

'I figured while I was out I'd come and pick up Malcolm. I know he could walk home but I thought I'd give him a ride.'

Amanda stared at her. 'He's not at your uncle's house?'

'No,' said Blair. Blair felt a shiver of alarm.

Amanda's forehead wrinkled into a frown. 'He left hours ago. He said he was going to walk home.'

Blair wondered if she had somehow misunderstood. 'Are you sure?'

'Oh, I'm sure. I wanted to drive him back. I offered to give him a ride. He wouldn't have it. He said he wasn't a baby and he didn't want to be treated like one. I mean, he's walked home from here a million times. But today he was angry . . .'

'Angry about what?' Blair asked.

Amanda's cheeks were pink. She shook her head. 'He and Zach had a little . . . argument. Here, come inside.'

Blair followed her into the tidy living room. She felt her heart start to hammer. Amanda indicated a chair. Blair sat down. Don't panic, she thought.

'An argument about what?' she asked.

Amanda sighed and squeezed her hands together anxiously. 'Well, everything was fine on the trail ride. Peter had to cut it short and go off to work unexpectedly. The boys were a little disappointed, but Peter said next time . . . Anyway, we came home, and while I was fixing lunch, Zach started talking about Malcolm and when he was coming to live with us. Before I knew it, they got into a fight over how it was gonna be and who was gonna have the better room. It was just stupid, kid stuff. But Malcolm suddenly decided that he wanted to leave.'

Blair tried to smile. 'Well, it doesn't sound terribly serious. Just a misunderstanding.'

'I probably shouldn't have let him go,' Amanda said anxiously, 'but . . . he doesn't live here yet. And he's always walked over here in the past. Not even any roads to cross. So I didn't want him to feel like a prisoner.'

Zach emerged from the back of the house and came up to stand beside his mother. He was a smaller, thinner boy than Malcolm, with an open expression on his face.

'What's up?' he said.

'Zach, Malcolm didn't go home this afternoon when he left here.'

Zach's eyes widened. 'Where did he go?'

Blair and Amanda exchanged a glance.

'I'm not sure,' said Blair.

A wary expression replaced Zach's normally guileless aspect. He suddenly, belatedly realized that they thought he was to blame.

'He started it. I didn't want him to go.'

Amanda adjusted her tone, dialing down the anxiety. 'We're not blaming you,' she insisted. 'But do you know where he might have gone? What did he say?'

Zach seemed to squirm from an internal debate. Blair held her tongue and waited, realizing it was no use pushing the boy. Finally, he shook his head.

'I don't know. He didn't tell me.'

'We should make some calls,' said Amanda.

'Yes,' said Blair, feeling helpless. 'I suppose. Although I don't know who to call.'

Amanda was already punching in a number. 'I do,' she said grimly.

FIFTEEN

Amanda called the mother of one of Malcolm's classmates, who knew nothing of Malcolm's whereabouts, but gave her another suggestion. Blair listened anxiously as one dead end led to another. She knew that she had to make a call as well. She dialed Uncle Ellis, explaining the situation and asking if Malcolm had arrived home since she went out. Ellis exploded at her on the phone, cursing at her and saying he was going out to look for the boy. He hung up on Blair before she could lodge the faintest protest.

'This is my fault,' said Amanda. 'I shouldn't have let him leave when he was angry like that. It just seemed to come out of the blue.'

'He's so . . . confused,' said Blair. 'He's just . . . weighed down, between his sorrow over Celeste and all these changes. Look, would Peter know anything?'

Amanda shook her head. 'He got a call and he had to go back to work. There was a fire on the mountain. We took the ATVs back and another ranger picked him up since we were already in the area.'

Blair looked at Zach. 'Is there anywhere you can think of that Malcolm might have gone? Might be hiding?' she asked.

Zach shrugged. 'He always wanted to go hunting. He could be out in the woods.'

Blair suddenly had an image of Molly, face down in the wet leaves. She looked helplessly at Amanda.

'I think I'm going to call the police,' she said. 'My uncle never would, but I think I will.'

Amanda's face was pale. 'It might be a good idea.'

That was all the encouragement that Blair needed. She called the police and made the report. They promised to send a squad car right away. Blair asked them to meet her at Uncle Ellis's house. She stood up and pulled on her scarf and jacket.

'You don't have to leave,' said Amanda.

'I do,' said Blair. 'What if he comes home? I don't want him to come back to an empty house, but thank you both for the help.'

'I'm sorry,' said Zach. 'I didn't mean to . . .'

'You didn't . . .' said Blair. 'It's not your fault.'

Amanda walked her to the door. 'I feel so terrible about this.'

'He's probably just cooling off somewhere,' said Blair, pretending to feel calm.

'I hope you're right. You'll let me know?' Amanda asked.

'I will.'

Frowning, Blair went out to her car. She drove back to Ellis's house as fast as she could. There was no one there when she arrived. Ellis had obviously taken his truck and gone looking for the boy. Blair went inside, calling Malcolm's name, but she was greeted with silence.

Before she even took off her jacket, a police car pulled up in front of the house. She went down to speak to the patrolman who got out. His partner remained seated in the car.

'Ma'am, are you the boy's mother?'

'I'm his aunt. His mother died recently.'

The patrolman looked up at the ramshackle house. 'You live here?'

'No. This is my uncle's house. They lived here. My uncle went out to look for Malcolm. I've been calling around.'

'Did the boy threaten to run away?' the cop asked.

Blair jammed her hands in her pockets and shook her head. 'No. But I did find out that he was mad about something.'

'Mad about what?' the cop asked.

Blair hesitated. 'It's just . . . it was just a misunderstanding.'

'It might be important,' said the officer.

'He and a friend had a quarrel,' said Blair. 'It wasn't anything serious, but the boy has been through a lot.'

The policeman looked at her kindly. 'Sometimes they just bolt. Boys especially are prone to this kind of thing. Have you got a photo?'

'In the house,' said Blair, leading the way up the porch steps.

She went inside and the cop followed her into the living room.
Malcolm's school picture, his face pale against the blue background, was sitting on the mantle. Blair took it down and handed
it to the cop. The cop removed it from the frame and handed the
frame back to Blair. Blair set it back on the mantle.

'Ok,' he said. 'We'll make copies.'

Blair nodded. She felt as if her stomach was clenched into a
knot.

'Thanks,' she said.

Just then there was the crunch of gravel as a vehicle pulled in
the driveway. Blair ran to the window and pulled back the curtain.
Uncle Ellis was getting out of his truck, alone. He came up the
stairs scowling at the patrol car and greeted Blair and the officer
with a snarl.

'Who called the cops?'

'I did,' said Blair. 'I'm worried. We need help.'

'You didn't need to go involving the cops.'

'Well, it looks like *you* didn't find him,' Blair cried.

'*I* didn't lose him!' Uncle Ellis bellowed.

'All right, all right,' said the patrolman. 'Let's just take it easy.
Tempers get frayed at a time like this.'

Ellis turned on him as if he was going to challenge him to a
fight when the phone rang. Ellis hesitated and then picked it up.
There was undeniable anxiety in his voice as he answered.

'Yeah. Hello. Oh, hi Darlene.'

Blair turned away, her slim hope that it might have been
Malcolm, dashed.

'What?' Ellis cried. 'Yeah, he's still missing. What? You're
kidding. Oh, wait till I get my hands on him.'

'What?' Blair demanded. 'Is it Malcolm?'

Ellis waved off her concern. 'Ok. Yeah. Ok. See you soon.' He
hung up the phone and turned to the cop. 'All right. You can leave
now. He's ok.'

'Where is he?' Blair demanded.

'With Darlene.' He turned to the officer and rolled his eyes in
Blair's direction. 'Sorry she bothered you.'

'No bother,' said the cop. 'You should always report a missing
child.'

'Are we going to pick him up?' Blair demanded.

'They're on their way here,' said Ellis.

Blair knew better than to ask any more. Ellis would only tell her exactly what he felt like saying.

'Ok,' said the cop. 'I'm glad it turned out all right. You folks have a nice evening.'

Blair walked him to the door. 'Thank you for coming.'

'No problem,' he said. 'That's what we're here for.'

She watched him go down the steps and then she turned back to Ellis, who was looking extremely satisfied with himself.

'Darlene found him?' Blair asked.

'He's fine. That's all you need to know,' said Ellis.

'Goddam it,' said Blair. 'Just tell me.'

'Your sister wanted him to live with Amanda,' Ellis said, shaking his head. 'And Amanda's the one who lost him. Figures.'

'Do you even care?' Blair cried. 'You told us about a million times what a burden Celeste and I were.'

Ellis lifted his chin defiantly. 'I took care of you, didn't I?'

'Is that what you call it?' Blair demanded. She shook her head.

'Couldn't have been all that bad. Your sister came back here and lived the rest of her days in this house, with her son.'

Blair sighed. 'I don't know how,' she said.

Just then they heard a car pulling up outside. Blair went to the door and hurried down the steps, as Darlene parked her blue Toyota in the driveway. Joseph was sitting in the passenger seat and Malcolm's small frame was visible, hunched over in the back seat. They all got out of the car.

'Malcolm . . .' said Blair, as the boy emerged, avoiding her gaze. She reached out to embrace him, but he flinched and evaded her. Blair looked at Darlene. 'Did he come to your house? Is that where he's been?'

'Joseph found him,' said Darlene. 'He was at the bus station.'

'I called the bus station earlier. They said he wasn't there,' Blair protested.

'Tell them,' said Darlene.

Joseph, still dressed in his bus driver's uniform, cheerfully obliged. 'You called the wrong station. He was at the Philly bus station.'

Blair looked at Malcolm in confusion. 'Philly? How in the world . . .'

'I took a bus,' said Malcolm bitterly. 'How else?'

Joseph nodded in agreement. 'I got off my bus and went into the Philly station to take a leak and get a cup of coffee. And I saw him there, huddled up in one of those waiting room chairs, shivering, looking lost. I know that look. The station is full of kids like that. Anyhow, I recognized him,' said Joseph. 'From that dinner the other night and the funeral.'

'Thank God,' said Blair.

'I went up to him asked him what he was doing there, didn't I?' Malcolm shrugged. 'Yeah.'

'He was pretty miserable by then,' Joseph explained. 'Ready to come home. So I offered him a ride back.'

'He took it,' Darlene said grimly.

'We just pulled in a few minutes ago.'

'You little fool,' said Ellis, almost fondly.

Malcolm kept his eyes lowered.

'Thank you so much,' said Blair, shaking Joe's hand. 'I'm so grateful to you.'

'Want to come in for a beer?' said Ellis.

'I think you all have some things to sort out,' said Darlene crisply. 'Come on, Joe. Let's get home.'

Ellis looked forlornly at Darlene, as Malcolm began to climb the porch steps. 'I didn't know he was going to do something like this.'

'Talk to him, Ellis,' Darlene admonished him, as she climbed back in her car. 'The boy is obviously confused.'

'Thank you both,' said Blair. Then, as they pulled away, she went up the steps and back into the house without a word to her uncle.

Malcolm was already climbing the stairs to his room when Blair called to him from the foyer. 'Malcolm, come back down here. I think we need to talk.'

The boy hesitated on the staircase.

Ellis came in, slamming the door behind him. 'Get down here, boy,' he called out. 'Right now.'

Slowly, reluctantly, the boy descended the staircase and walked into the living room. Blair had taken a seat in a chair, her arms folded over her chest. Ellis leaned against the empty fireplace, staring at the empty frame on the mantel which had held Malcolm's photo. He sighed wearily.

Malcolm slumped down on the sofa.

'What?' Malcolm asked. His defiant tone was undermined by the actions of his cat, which was purring and rubbing himself against Malcolm's legs.

'Why'd you do that?' Ellis demanded. 'Hop a bus to Philly? You don't know your way around the city.'

'I just wanted to get away. Somewhere far.'

'You're lucky Joe found you there. That was a stupid thing to do,' said Ellis.

Malcolm shrugged.

'Amanda said that you and Zach had an argument,' said Blair.

'It wasn't an argument,' Malcolm protested.

'What was it then?' asked Blair.

'I just got tired of it. Zach was going on like he was the one who decided everything. Like I was moving into his house and he was gonna be . . . the boss of me,' said Malcolm miserably, appealing to Ellis. 'Why do I have to live there? Why can't I stay here?'

'Don't blame me for it,' said Ellis.

'Actually . . .' said Blair.

'You said you were going to teach me to shoot. And this summer I want to get a boat and go fishing at the lake,' Malcolm reminded him.

'Steady on there, boy,' Ellis protested. 'Nobody said nothin' about a boat.'

'Do I have to leave here, Uncle Ellis?'

Ellis hesitated. 'Don't change the subject, boy. You should have just said something instead of running away.'

'This is where I live,' Malcolm cried.

Blair walked over to her nephew and sat down on the arm of the sofa. She wanted to reach out to him, but she could feel him bristle when she reached a hand toward him. She withdrew it, and folded her hands in her lap.

'Malcolm, this isn't Uncle Ellis's decision. Your Mom decided this before she died.'

'Why?' Malcolm protested. 'Why would she?'

'Well, for one thing,' said Blair carefully, 'your Uncle Ellis is . . . getting old. You understand that, right?'

'Is he gonna die too?' Malcolm cried.

'Not a thing wrong with me. Getting old,' Ellis scoffed.

Blair kept her focus on Malcolm. 'No, I'm not saying that. Ornery as he is, he'll probably live forever. But your Mom made these arrangements with the Tuckers because she thought they would be best for you. A young family like that. You're already close to them. And Zach looks up to you like a big brother.'

Malcolm shook his head. 'Zach's a jerk.'

'This will be a big change for both of you,' said Blair. 'You and Zach. There are things you both have to get used to. Suddenly, you'll both have a brother.'

'He ain't my brother,' Malcolm protested.

'He was awfully worried about you,' Blair said. 'He felt so bad about you leaving cause of what he said.'

Malcolm stared at his hands and was quiet. Finally he said, 'It wasn't just that.'

'What was it?' said Blair.

'I want things to be the way they used to be!' Malcolm cried.

'Before your Mom died,' said Blair.

Malcolm nodded miserably.

'Well, that would be nice. But we don't get a say in these things.'

'I know,' he said angrily, wiping his eyes.

'Amanda is missing Celeste almost as much as you,' Blair said. 'She promised your Mom that she would always take care of you. It's kind of her way of keeping their friendship alive. In fact,' said Blair, 'Before I do another thing, I need to call her and let them know you're safe.'

Blair quickly dialed the number. Amanda picked up before the first ring was over.

'Amanda, he's home. He's ok. Yes, he took a bus to Philly, but a friend found him there and brought him home.' Then Blair spoke to Malcolm. 'Amanda wants to talk to you.'

Malcolm looked like he was about to refuse, but then he reached for the phone and held it to his ear.

'Yeah,' he muttered. 'Yeah, I'm ok.' He got up and walked out into the foyer where his conversation would not be overheard.

Blair and Ellis waited in the living room.

'You happy now?' Ellis asked. 'The kid thinks nobody wants him.'

'*You* don't want him,' said Blair.

'But I'd keep him,' said Ellis.

Blair heard the truth in her uncle's words. She understood that, for whatever reason, he actually meant it. She gazed at him thoughtfully.

'I think you mean that,' she said.

Ellis curled his lip at her. 'Ha! More than I can say for you.'

Blair couldn't argue. She knew he was right. 'Celeste knew better than to leave him to me. I'm not much as an aunt,' she admitted.

At that moment Malcolm came back into the room and handed the phone back to Blair.

Blair thanked him and slipped the phone in her pocket. 'Everything ok?' she asked.

Malcolm shrugged, but he seemed less upset. 'Zach was crying.'

'Well, he was really scared.'

'I guess,' said Malcolm. 'I told him not to worry about it.'

'Good,' said Blair.

'He's not that bad,' Malcolm conceded.

'And Malcolm, you know, even if you don't live in this house, you can still see your Uncle Ellis. You'll be right around the corner. You can see him all the time. He's your uncle. He'll always be your family. Right, Uncle Ellis?'

Ellis looked at Blair contemptuously. But he nodded. 'I'm not going anywhere.'

'And all those plans you were talking about . . . the boat and the hunting. You can still do them with Uncle Ellis. Isn't that so, Ellis?' Blair asked.

'Not if you do crazy things like you did today,' said Ellis. 'I'm too old for it.'

'See? I told you,' said Blair. 'He's too old.'

'Sorry,' Malcolm muttered, but he smiled a little bit.

Blair could feel the tension ease. 'How about I make us some eggs?' she said.

'I hate eggs,' said Malcolm.

'We'll order a pizza,' she said.

SIXTEEN

The house was quiet and Blair was in her bedroom, trying to read, but her nerves were still buzzing from the events of the day. The evening had turned out pretty well, all things considered. The pizza was still hot when it arrived and the three of them ate together, for once, sitting around the kitchen table. Malcolm gave Blair a brief hug before he went up to bed, which lifted her heart.

Still, what a roller coaster of emotions today, she thought. She had been so frightened when Malcolm was missing. All she could think of was Molly and the fate she had met when she started to walk home alone from this house. Thank God, Blair thought, that Joseph noticed Malcolm in the Philly bus stop and this had a different ending.

The message beeped on her phone. It was a text from Rebecca.

'Still in NYC. Leaving soon. Back very late. Need to see you tomorrow, first thing. Please come over.' Rebecca included her address.

'I'll be there,' Blair texted back. 'Hope your meeting went well.'

'Absolutely did,' Rebecca wrote. 'See you tomorrow.'

What's this about, Blair wondered? Could she have come across some news about the investigation? Rebecca had, by her own admission, a lot of feelers out. Maybe one of them had come up with information. Blair could not help but hope. She tried to go back to her reading, but she couldn't concentrate. When she turned off the light, oblivion wouldn't come. It was four a.m. before she fell into a brief, deep sleep.

Despite her lack of rest, Blair was up and out of the house before either Ellis or Malcolm were awake. It wasn't until she was en route that she realized that she was jumping the gun a bit. Rebecca had said to come early, but this was too early. She stopped at the diner on Main Street and had a cup of coffee. Once the sky was more pink than grey, she went back out to her car. She put Rebecca's address in her GPS and headed for her house.

Rebecca lived far out of the town, deep in the woods. As she pulled into the driveway, she caught sight of the old house. It was sided in stucco and stained with age. The roof looked quite a bit worse for wear. Even at this early hour, smoke was curling out of the chimney. The house was in need of a lot of TLC, but its bones were good. She wondered if Rebecca owned or rented it. She parked beside her truck and went up to the front door.

She knocked once and waited for Rebecca to answer. Blair heard someone approaching the door and undoing the locks. The door opened and a skinny woman with gray hair, wearing a chenille bathrobe and scuffs, stood there blinking at her over her half glasses.

Blair frowned and shook her head. 'I'm sorry. My name is Blair Butler. I'm looking for Rebecca Moore. I must have the wrong house.'

The woman did not smile. 'No. You've got the right house. But it's kind of early to come visiting.'

'I got a text from Rebecca saying to be here first thing.'

The woman shrugged. 'Come on in.'

Blair stepped through the door and into the living room. She understood instantly, as soon as she saw the family pictures on display and the exhausted-looking décor, that this was Rebecca's childhood home. 'Are you . . .?'

'Her mother,' the woman said wearily.

At that a man's grumpy voice called out from another room, 'Who is it at this hour?'

'Some girl for Rebecca.'

Blair heard the gruff voice mutter something unintelligible.

'Upstairs on the right,' said the woman. 'Rebecca,' the woman yelled.

There was no answer.

Blair started through the house and looked back at the disheveled woman as if for permission. The woman gestured impatiently toward the steps.

'She's up there. Probably still asleep. She got in at all hours.'

Blair thought of leaving, and coming back later. But she reminded herself that Rebecca had indicated it was urgent in her texts.

'Thanks,' Blair said to Rebecca's mother. She climbed up the creaking steps. The top floor had sloped ceilings. All the doors were open but one. Blair knocked on it.

'Rebecca?' she whispered.

Before she could even step back, Rebecca flung the door open. She was wearing a form-fitting red dress and she was barefoot. Her hair was wet, but had been combed through. Her eyes were artfully made up.

'Blair. Glad you're here. Come in.'

Blair stepped inside and looked around. The room was a catastrophe. Every surface was piled with electronics or teetering piles of folded clothing. A few suitcases, half-packed, were open on the floor. Rebecca did not offer her a seat, but, if she had, it would have been academic. There was nowhere for her to sit.

'Sorry for the mess,' Rebecca said. 'I'm packing, as you can see.'

Blair stared at her. 'Packing? Where are you going?'

Rebecca's face brightened and she held out her arms as if inviting a hug.

'They hired me! They want me. Cable news. The story about Yusef Muhammed is what sold them on me. They want me to start right away.'

Blair avoided the hug. 'Based on that one article?' Blair said, frowning.

'Well, that, and the fact that I was a star reporter at a top network in L.A.,' Rebecca said airily.

'You mean before that time when you . . . manufactured a witness,' Blair reminded her. 'I googled you.'

'And I have paid for it a thousand times over. Believe me,' said Rebecca.

'I'm sure,' said Blair. 'So you finally found a way to get back in. Thanks to Yusef Muhammed.'

'Well, the story got me the interview and I took it from there.'

Blair looked around at the suitcases. 'And you're going right now?'

Rebecca nodded and sighed. 'Thank God. Can you imagine what it's been like for me, living here? In my childhood home? With them?' She gestured toward the door and Blair knew she was referring to her parents.

'But . . .'

'What? I thought you'd be happy for me.'

'Well, yes . . . of course,' said Blair.

'It's been a living hell here,' she said. 'Working at that two-bit paper, being under their roof.' Rebecca shuddered. 'Well, I guess I had it coming. But now I can close this chapter. I am outta here . . .'

Blair nodded, unable to speak for a moment. 'And this is what I needed to come out here first thing to hear?' she asked.

Rebecca stopped throwing things into her suitcase and sighed. She pushed it back on the bed and sat down. There was not enough space for Blair to sit beside her. Rebecca gazed at her own, inter-locked fingers. Then she leaned forward and pushed the books off her Sleeping Beauty desk chair and they thudded onto the wood floor.

'Here, sit,' she said.

Blair perched her butt on the edge of the chair.

Rebecca sighed. 'Look, I didn't want to do this to you . . . You have to believe me, Blair. I was excited about working on this story.'

'Well, it's not really me that you need to explain to. It's Yusef Muhammed. You promised him your help.'

'I never expected all this to happen so quickly,' said Rebecca. 'But, I'm constantly throwing out feelers and, like I said, when opportunity knocks . . .'

'I thought the feelers you were throwing out were about the investigation into Molly's murder,' said Blair coolly.

Rebecca grimaced. 'Blair, I know it's important to you.'

'To me? What about you?'

'Hey, I thought if anyone would understand about my career it would be you.'

'Well, I'm sorry, but this pisses me off a little,' said Blair.

'What? You expect me to stick around here, looking into this little case when I have a chance to go back to TV on a national network.'

'This case is not little to the people involved,' Blair said in an icy tone.

Rebecca ran her manicured fingers through her long, damp hair and avoided meeting Blair's eyes.

'Look, it's not going to be easy for me either. I'm going to have to move to Miami. They hired me for the Miami office. I have zero money for this move and if I'm not everything they want, I could make this whole relocation thing, and then be out of there in a heartbeat. I mean it's going to be sort of an ordeal. Trial by fire.'

Blair thought of Yusef Muhammed, spending years behind bars for something he didn't do.

'This is what you call an ordeal?' she said.

Rebecca ignored her sarcastic tone. 'Look, you're all bent out of shape, but, in fact, you're just here for a few days. You wouldn't give up your career to pursue this.'

'I'm not a reporter. I thought this is what you do.'

'Yes, but I'm used to a little bigger story, if you know what I mean. I could spend years on this. I haven't got years to waste.'

Blair nodded. 'I see.'

Rebecca sighed. 'This is not charity work I'm doing. I have to look out for myself, for my future. Who knows? Maybe sometime I might be able to interest the network in pursuing this story. After all, they did love the article. I mean, not right away. At first I have to do what they want me to do.'

Blair stood up from the desk chair. 'Well, I'll tell that to Yusef Muhammed. You're still interested, but not right away,' she said.

'Oh stop being such a drag,' Rebecca said wearily. 'What were the chances we would ever get him out of there? I mean, realistically.'

'Realistically . . .' Blair pursed her lips and looked up at the ceiling. 'How shall I phrase it? You are a selfish bitch.' She looked directly at Rebecca and gave her a sharp nod. 'Is that clear enough?'

Rebecca sighed. 'I guess you don't wish me well in my new job.'

Blair shook her head but did not reply. She picked her way through the debris and went down the stairs without looking back.

Rebecca came out of the room and gazed at her over the landing. 'I have to think about myself . . .' she said.

Blair did not look back at her as she left, though she raised her middle finger and jerked it in Rebecca's direction. Blair crossed the living room to the front door, just as Rebecca's mother shuffled into the room in her bathrobe and slippers, looking tired and bewildered. Blair offered no explanation. Mrs Moore would find out her daughter was heading for Miami when Rebecca walked out the door with all her baggage. Blair doubted she would get more warning than that. Good riddance, Blair thought angrily, and slammed the door behind her.

SEVENTEEN

Blair looked through the windshield at the bleak, wintry mountain landscape. I need to get away from here, she thought. I don't belong here. These people are like savages. She turned the key in the ignition and started back down the driveway.

The thought of leaving, of driving away from Yorkville, seemed undeniably appealing. Personally, she liked the idea of never coming back. Of course, as long as Malcolm lived here, she would always have a reason to come back.

There was still the problem of Yusef Muhammed. She had promised Celeste that she would try to correct the injustice that had been done and it had seemed like she was making progress, when Rebecca agreed to help her. Now, with Rebecca gone, Muhammed's case was back in her lap, and, as much as she wanted to help him, she was not an investigator. Plus, she had a life in Philly and a company to run. The thought of it gave her a headache. Would Muhammed ever get out? She dreaded having to tell him about Rebecca's new job. Rebecca had offered him hope, and then, just as suddenly, erased him from her concerns. Well, there was no escaping it. She had to explain the situation. It was really Rebecca's place to do it, but she knew that Rebecca would not.

She drove back to Ellis's house and slowly climbed the front steps to the porch. She let herself into the house and sat down heavily on the battered sofa in the front room. There was no use avoiding it, she thought. She had to give Muhammed a call. Blair exhaled a few times, to steady her voice, then dialed up the prison and asked to speak to the prisoner.

She expected a song and dance from the security guards and a series of hoops which she needed to jump through, but the man she spoke to was, if not pleasant, at least civil. He promised to connect her with Yusef Muhammed, and, in only a few minutes, she heard his deep voice at the other end of the phone.

'Yusef,' she said briskly. 'This is Blair Butler.'

'Yeah . . .' he said warily.

'Look, that article about your case in the local paper has stirred up some interest.' As she spoke to him, her gaze traveled across the room to the mantel, where Malcolm's photo had been replaced in the frame.

'Yeah. I heard that,' Yusef murmured. 'Rebecca told me.'

'So now we just have to see if we can turn that interest into a plan to get you out of there.'

'Who's we?' asked Yusef suspiciously.

Blair sighed. 'Well look, that's partly why I'm calling. Rebecca has to leave. She has . . . taken a job in Miami. But I haven't given up.'

There was a sharp intake of breath and then a long silence at Muhammed's end of the phone.

'Yusef?' she ventured.

There was no reply.

'I guess she has to,' she said into the silence 'to . . . attend to her own career, but she's not the only one who can help.'

Yusef snorted, a short, bitter laugh. 'No. Course not,' he said.

'I know this is disappointing, but I thought you would want to know. We ought to be clear about the situation going forward,' Blair said.

'Crystal,' said Yusef.

'Excuse me?' said Blair. 'Oh you mean like, "crystal clear".'

'No, I get it now,' said Yusef. 'The fucking liar.'

Blair, huddled in a crouch at the edge of the chair, did not correct him, or come to Rebecca's defense.

'I'm sorry this happened,' she said. 'But don't give up.'

'Give up?' he asked coldly. 'Why would I give up? No, no. This fills me with newfound hope. A reporter promises to help me, manages to make my situation into front page news after all these years and then she leaves town. Leaves me to rot. But hey,

I've still got you on my side. The sister of the woman who put me here fifteen years ago.'

'Now that's not fair. I tried to explain to you . . .'

'Right. I can't talk any more,' said Yusef.

Before Blair could say another word, he had hung up the phone.

Blair set the phone down on the coffee table and covered her eyes with her hands. Of course he was angry and disappointed. He had been betrayed by Celeste and now by Rebecca. What else would he be, but angry? She suddenly realized how ill-equipped she was to do anything on his behalf. Rebecca, an experienced reporter, had been the ideal person to consult, but now she was out of the picture. Who else was there?

Blair sat for a while rubbing her temples, as Malcolm's cat jumped up on the arm of her chair and made squawking noises. Blair reached out absently and ran a hand over the cat's furry coat. There had to be someone. Then, she had an idea. She wasn't sure if it was a good idea or not, but she needed to try something. She stood up from the chair. There was no need to put on her scarf and jacket – she had never taken them off. She went to the front door and shuddered, looking out at the cold, windy day. Then she pulled the door open, went down the steps and got back in her car.

'I know I don't have an appointment, but do you think Mr Whitman could see me briefly?' Blair asked.

Stacy de Soto, her eyelashes long, her hair arranged in an elaborate updo, ran a manicured fingernail down the page of the old-fashioned daybook. She pressed a key on the intercom with the eraser on a pencil and waited.

'Mr Whitman? Miss Butler is here. She doesn't have an appointment. But she wants to speak with you.' Stacy listened intently to her Boss's voice and then looked up at Blair. 'Ok. You can go on in,' she said.

'Oh thank you,' said Blair. 'I won't be long.'

Stacy looked up at the clock on the wall. 'He's got an appointment in fifteen minutes,' she reminded Blair.

'I'll be out before then,' said Blair.

She went to the door and tapped on it.

'Come . . .' said a voice from within.

Blair went in and closed the door behind her. 'Mr Whitman?'

'Blair,' the attorney said. 'Good to see you.'

'I'm sorry to barge in without an appointment, but I really need your help.'

'Well, I'll help you if I can,' he said.

Blair took a deep breath. 'Did you happen to see the paper?'

The attorney smiled. 'I did. I saw that you got Muhammed's story onto the front page. You're making some progress.'

'Well, you were right about the police. They have no interest in reopening this case. But I enlisted a reporter to help me. Rebecca Moore. Unfortunately, now she's left town.'

'You got the wheels in motion,' Whitman observed. 'That's the important thing.'

'That's just not good enough,' said Blair. 'I mean, that's not going to get Yusef Muhammed out of jail. I don't know what would. But I can't stay here forever, I have a company to run.'

'Yes, I understand,' said Whitman. 'How can I help you?'

'Well, I wondered if there was some way I could pay you a retainer to start legal proceedings on his behalf.'

'What kind of proceedings?' he asked.

'I don't know. Whatever can be done to help get him out of there. File some motions based on this new information we found.'

Whitman frowned. 'I can't take your money. Right now, with what you've got, there's not much I can do.'

'Doesn't the truth matter at all?' Blair cried.

'You'd be surprised how little weight it holds in legal matters. Look, as I told you, the only thing we have to go on is hearsay. That article made a start, but it was mostly speculation. You need to unearth the facts.'

Blair rubbed her hand over her forehead. 'That's what I hoped to do when I enlisted Rebecca. She had a lot of experience chasing down information. I mean, I'm a pretty logical person and I can think of questions to ask, but I've got no legal background. I really don't know where to begin. And she was able to get the story published on the front page of the paper, where people would read it and start to see things a different way. Now, she's gone and I'm afraid people will lose interest if there's no follow-up. I feel like I'm back where I started from.'

'I understand,' he said.

'So what should I be doing?' Blair asked.

'Well, you need a witness statement. You need someone – besides your late sister who cannot testify – that can establish Muhammed's whereabouts at the time of Molly's death. Or some physical evidence from the crime that will show that Muhammed was not involved in the murder of Molly Sinclair. That's how you get the case reopened.'

'After all these years?' she cried. 'Where am I going to come up with that?'

'It is a tall order,' Whitman agreed. He was quiet for a minute, then he spoke cautiously. 'You were willing to pay me. Are you willing to pay an investigator?'

'Yes,' Blair said cautiously. 'Yes, I would be, if it was someone competent. I think I owe that to Yusef Muhammed. Do you have someone you can recommend? An investigator that you use for your cases?'

Whitman grimaced. 'I do.'

'You're hesitating,' said Blair. 'Is he any good?'

'He is, but can be a bit difficult,' said Whitman apologetically.

'I don't care about his personality,' she said. 'Is he capable?'

'I have found him to be capable. He used to be a cop.'

'Used to be?' Blair asked. 'Is he retired?'

'In a manner of speaking, he was still young when he was forced to retire because of a disability. He developed a tremor in his hands which made it impossible for him to pass the marksmanship test so he had to resign.'

'That is unfortunate.'

'I use him quite a bit. I find him to be reliable. Not personable, as I said. But reliable.'

'I don't need a friend,' she said.

Whitman nodded. 'Do you have a minute?' he asked. 'I can give him a call.'

'Absolutely,' said Blair. 'I'll wait.'

EIGHTEEN

The road up the mountain was winding and the day was growing dark. Blair drove carefully, using her high beams. She had learned from Brooks Whitman that the man she was en route to see was a solitary sort. After his forced retirement, he liked living as far away as possible from his fellow humans. Whitman had called him while Blair was in his office and had explained her situation to him. The investigator was out on a case, but he had agreed to see her later and now, in the waning hours of the day, Blair was seeking his hideaway in the woods.

Blair was not at all sure that a private detective was the way to go, but she was out of options. Whitman assured her that this investigator was thorough and could be trusted.

'Just don't interfere,' Brooks Whitman said. 'Give him the check and get out of his way.'

'Gladly,' said Blair.

She had hesitated when Whitman told her that Tom Olson had been a patrolman at the time of Molly's murder. Blair was apprehensive that he might be prejudiced in favor of the police department, but Brooks Whitman assured her that Tom Olson prided himself on being impartial. Blair found the driveway and pulled in. The small house looked deserted, with no lights on. The only sign that anyone lived there was a single rocking chair on the front porch. Blair pulled up, parked her car and knocked on the door. No one answered. She knocked again. Now that she was on the porch, she could see that the television was on inside, but still, no one came to the door.

'Hello? Mr Olson?' she called out.

'Right here,' said a grumpy voice. 'Behind you.'

Blair jumped and turned around. Tom Olson was walking around the house toward the front porch, hauling a canvas wood carrier, filled with logs cut into woodstove-sized chunks.

'Oh hi,' she said. 'I'm Blair Butler.'

Tom Olson, a man of about forty, had hair that might have been blond or gray. He had a short beard and mustache that framed his pale, lined face. His eyes were light-colored too and he gave the impression of someone who never went out in the sun. He climbed up on the porch and deftly turned the front doorknob with his left hand.

'Come on in,' he said.

Blair followed him into the compact house and stood, waiting, while Tom unloaded the log carrier into the basket beside the woodstove. There was a fire visible behind the glass door of the stove and the temperature in the room was warm as a result. Nothing else about the room seemed warm. The only sources of light, other than the curtainless windows, were from a fluorescent fixture in the kitchen and the television screen, which combined to give the room a cool, gray glow. Tom walked over to the TV and turned it off.

'Have a seat,' he said.

Blair perched on the edge of a wooden chair. She looked around at the house. The furniture was minimal, but the room was tidy. There was nothing decorative in the room. No books. No magazines. No photos. A laptop sat on the dining room table with a coffee mug beside it.

Tom sat down in an easy chair.

'So,' he began, without preamble. 'Brooks said your sister gave Muhammed an alibi on her deathbed.'

'Yes,' said Blair. 'She told me that she was with Muhammed when he picked up Molly and that they dropped her at her house. I feel certain that she was telling the truth, but Mr Whitman said that it won't hold up in court. He said I need to have some facts to back it up or it will never even get to court.'

'What took her so long?' Olson asked.

Blair hesitated. 'Is it important?'

'You might as well tell me or you're wasting my time,' said Olson.

'She was afraid for my uncle to find out about her . . . and her relationship with Muhammed. They were . . . close.'

'Close how? Lovers?'

'I can't say for sure, but . . . probably.'

'So what changed her mind?'

'I guess when she realized that she was dying, she knew that any hope for Muhammed would die with her. And besides, my uncle couldn't do anything to hurt her at that point.'

'Why tell you?' Olson demanded.

Blair shrugged. 'I guess she trusted me.'

Tom Olson nodded and pursed his lips. He peered at Blair.

'You her only family?'

'Yes, well, she has a son, but he's only ten.'

'So she dumped her guilty secret on you.'

Blair grimaced. 'We went through a lot together as children. When we were kids we relied on each other for everything. Not so much in recent years . . . I mean, she and I had very different lives.'

'Nonetheless, she told you.'

'She wanted me to try to clear his name. I guess she thought I could be trusted to do it. I thought it would be a simple matter of telling the police what she told me, but it has turned out to be anything but simple.'

Tom shrugged. 'A lot of man hours went into putting Muhammed away. They're not going to let him go without a fight.'

'Mr Whitman said you were on the police force when it happened. Do you agree with them?' asked Blair. 'Did you think he was the right man?'

'At the time? Sure.'

'And now? Can you see that this might have been a serious miscarriage of justice?'

Tom Olson shrugged. 'I don't know about that. I'll look into it.'

Blair hesitated. 'There are just a couple of things which Rebecca Moore and I discovered that I thought might be relevant . . .' Blair waited for him to encourage her to speak, but Olson said nothing. Blair forged ahead. '. . . We found out that Muhammed dropped Molly at the end of her driveway that day. He was certain about that. We don't know how Molly got to the spot in the woods where her body was found, but a mailman, who was asleep in his truck in the woods, heard something like a big thud, which might have been a body being dumped. Also, a neighbor heard somebody – not Molly – banging on the Sinclair's door that afternoon, and pleading for help.'

Tom Olson nodded in a non-committal way. 'Could be relevant. Might not.' The detective didn't seem to have any more to say.

'I just want to be clear. I'm hiring you to investigate this in order to help Muhammed.'

'If that's how it turns out . . .' he said.

'I promised my sister that I would try to get justice for him,' said Blair.

'Look, all I have is your say-so. No offense, but I need more than that.' Tom pressed down on the arms of his chair and abruptly rose to his feet. 'I'll look into it. That's all I can promise you.'

That's all I'm going to get, Blair thought. It didn't seem like nearly enough.

'You're leaving town?' he asked abruptly.

'Well, I . . . yes, I have go back. I have a company in Philly to run. Why? Is that a problem?'

'Not for me,' said Tom. 'I don't need anybody looking over my shoulder.'

Blair stood up and pulled a check from her pocket. 'Is this enough to get started?' Blair asked, handing it to him.

Olson reached for the check with his left hand, examined the amount and then tossed the check on the old trunk that served as a coffee table.

'Is that a yes?' Blair asked.

'I'll see what I can find out for you,' he said.

'Ok, well . . . thanks,' said Blair. She also handed him her card with her phone numbers and email. 'I want to know, whatever develops.'

'Will do,' said the investigator. 'Can't promise anything.'

'I understand that,' said Blair.

'Don't call me every day. If I have something to say, I'll call you.'

'That's fine,' said Blair. 'I'm pretty busy as a rule.'

The meeting seemed to be at an end. 'All right then. Thank you.'

Tom Olson waved her off as if he were swatting a fly and picked up a poker to prod the fire in the stove.

Blair hesitated, but the investigator seemed to have nothing more to say. Suit yourself, Blair thought. Without a backward glance, she left the little house and got back into her car.

You're doing the right thing, she thought. You've hired someone to look into this. You've fulfilled your promise to Celeste. It's all you can do.

When Blair got home, there was no one in the house and no sign of Malcolm. Immediately she felt a little jolt of panic. Ellis drove in to the driveway a few minutes later and entered the house. Blair met him at the door.

'Where is Malcolm?' she asked.

'Went over to his new family's house,' he said in a mocking tone. 'Sleeping over.'

Blair was relieved and happy to hear it. 'He wanted to go?'

'I guess so. He got off the phone and asked me to drive him there.'

Blair looked at her uncle with a slightly more compassionate eye than before. 'I know you want him to be happy, just like I do,' said Blair.

Ellis snorted. 'I want him out of my hair,' he said.

'You want me to fix you some dinner?' Blair asked, trying to be conciliatory.

'I'm going out myself,' said Ellis. 'Taking Darlene to the VFW buffet.'

Blair did not take offense that she was not invited. The VFW buffet did not interest her in the least. And besides, this sounded like a date. She did not want her bemusement to show.

'That will be nice,' she said. 'Seems like you and Darlene are becoming kind of close.'

Ellis looked at her accusingly. 'Something wrong with that?'

'No. Certainly not,' said Blair.

'You can get your own dinner,' he said. 'There's food.'

'Oh sure. I'll grab something from the fridge. I have to pack.'

'You going somewhere?' asked Ellis.

'Yes, actually,' she said. 'I'm leaving. Going back to Philly.'

'You might as well,' said Ellis.

'That's what I thought,' said Blair. 'I'll probably leave early.'

'Less traffic,' said Ellis, jingling his keys as if impatient to be on his way.

'I'll see you,' she said.

*   *   *

That night, Blair found it hard to sleep. She could not deny that she felt a certain relief at the thought of going home. She had never belonged in this house, in this town, except for a brief moment when she and Molly had been friends. At the thought of Molly, Blair felt the old sadness, but there was no use dwelling on it. She had done all she could to find justice for Molly and for Muhammed. It was time to return to her real life.

The gray light of dawn was coming through the gauzy curtains when Blair finally fell into a deep sleep. She was awakened by the keening of a saxophone. At first she thought it was her alarm, and then, as she swam to consciousness, she realized that it was her ringtone.

'Hello?'

'Blair. It's Janet. Janet Sinclair.'

'Hi Janet,' Blair muttered, confused.

'Listen, Blair. I just got a call from Lucille . . .' When Blair, still groggy, did not respond, Janet continued, '. . . From Yusef Muhammed's mother.'

'Yes, of course,' said Blair, frowning in the darkened room.

'She's at the hospital. Muhammed was rushed there from the prison very early this morning.'

Blair suddenly felt wide awake. 'Why?'

'He tried to kill himself.'

'Oh no,' said Blair.

'I'm afraid so,' said Janet. 'He left a note saying that he had no hope left. Something like that.'

'Oh God,' said Blair.

'I think he took it hard that Rebecca had given up on his story.'

And that I was going away, seemingly given up on him too, Blair thought guiltily.

'Where is he?' she asked.

'At the Yorkville Hospital, Lucille is up there now. I told her you would go up there and see him. I thought that might help.'

'I will. I'm going,' said Blair. 'I'll just get dressed.'

The hospital was quiet when Blair arrived, the early shift just going on duty, replacing those who had seen the ill and broken through the night. Blair bought a cup of coffee from a vending machine and then walked up to the desk. The receptionist was almost unnaturally cheerful for the hour.

'I'm looking for Yusef Muhammed,' said Blair. 'He was brought in here earlier from the prison.'

'Oh yes,' said the receptionist. She hit a few keys and studied her computer screen. 'He's still in the ER. Are you a member of the family?'

Blair remembered her experience at the prison. 'I'm his attorney,' she said.

'Ok,' said the receptionist, and began to give her instructions on where to go.

'I know where it is,' said Blair. She decided she would rather follow the signs herself and curtail this conversation. She could hardly believe how smoothly her ruse had worked, but Blair did not want to press her luck. She immediately started down the hall to the elevators.

She rode downstairs and followed the signs for the ER. Once she arrived, it was easy to locate Muhammed. There were two armed uniformed officers standing outside one of the cubicles that was walled-off with flimsy fabric.

The officer nearest her stopped Blair before she could get to the curtain.

'Hold it there. Who are you?'

'My name is Blair Butler.'

He looked down at the clipboard he was holding. 'I don't have any Blair Butler on my list.'

'I'm his attorney,' Blair protested.

'I.D. please,' he said.

'I'm sorry,' said Blair, trying to sound exasperated. 'I just heard about my client and I came running over. I didn't bring any I.D.'

'Can't let you in then.'

'I have a right to see my client,' Blair insisted, wondering how much trouble she was going to get into for impersonating an officer of the court.

Just then, the fabric curtain was pulled back and Yusef's mother, Lucille Jones, emerged from the cubicle. Blair recognized her from years ago. Lucille looked distressed and exhausted. Blair's eyes widened as the older woman gazed directly at her.

'Thank you for coming, Ms Butler,' said Lucille. 'Do you want to talk to Yusef?'

'I do,' said Blair.

'I'm going to go get me a cup of tea,' said Lucille. 'You go on in.'

The officers seemed helpless to contradict the mother, bowled over by shock and sorrow.

'You know this woman?' asked one of the officers.

'I should do,' said Lucille indignantly. 'This is my son's lawyer.'

'Ok, ok,' said the officer to Blair. 'Go ahead.'

Lucille held back the curtain and Blair slipped past her into the cubicle, whispering her thanks. Lucille nodded, dropped the curtain and went in search of her tea. Blair sat down in the chair beside the hospital bed.

Muhammed lay on the white sheets, his eyes closed and his dark skin color leeched to a blotchy beige. The bed was surrounded by monitors and blinking lights. He was tethered to the machines in half a dozen places by clear tubes. His left wrist was fastened to the bed with a handcuff. Around his neck was a ragged, red and bruised multicolored wound. Hanging, she thought. He tried to hang himself.

Blair sagged and had to will her stomach to calm down at the thought. How desperate could a person be? He was an innocent man who had already served fifteen years for a crime he did not commit. She had dangled hope in front of his eyes, and then, without much thought, had torn it away.

'I'm sorry,' she whispered.

Muhammed's eyelids fluttered and he moved his head slightly. His deadened gaze settled on Blair. He didn't say a word.

Blair took a deep breath. She had planned to go back, to get busy on the lifesaving work of creating human tissue on a computer printer. It was important work. It would offer hope and options to people who had neither down the road. She believed in what she was doing and she enjoyed it. People looked at her with admiration and wanted the knowledge she possessed. But looking at this man here, languishing from his near-successful suicide attempt, she felt ashamed of the choice she had made. Right at this moment, whatever she planned to do back in Philadelphia did not seem as important as this one life. This man was in a hopeless situation. She had promised to help him, and then she had walked away.

'Sorry for what?' he croaked in an almost inaudible, raspy voice.

'Well, for a lot of things,' said Blair. 'For one thing, I'm sorry about Rebecca. It turned out she was only in it for herself. And I'm sorry that I was ready to leave with the job undone. I hired a detective, figuring he could take over and do more than I could do . . .'

'Tom Olson . . .' said Muhammed, disgust audible in his quiet, despairing tone.

'He was a cop on the case!'

'Well, yes, I did know, but he assured me . . .' Blair looked at Muhammed, who had closed his eyes again.

'Fifteen years ago he arrested me,' said Muhammed slowly. 'This is the guy you choose to help.'

'I'm sorry,' said Blair. 'He said that he would be unbiased . . .'

Muhammed let out a harsh cry of disbelief. 'He called me last night. He said there was no hope that I would ever get out of prison.'

'He said that?' Blair asked, confused.

'He wasn't kidding,' he cried, and then he began to cough and gag at once.

'I'm sorry,' Blair said. 'Are you all right?'

Muhammed nodded, although the sickening cough continued.

Lucille suddenly appeared at the break in the curtain. 'Yusef?' she cried. 'Are you ok? Is my son ok?'

'Oh no,' said one of the cops on sentry duty. 'One at a time. Not till the lawyer leaves.'

'Let me in there. My boy is sick in there,' Lucille protested.

Blair stood up and motioned to Lucille. 'I'll be right out.'

Muhammed shook his head slightly on the pillow. A tear leaked out of his left eye and ran down to his ear.

Blair hesitated and then reached out a hand and placed it on his. His fingers were icy cold.

'Listen to me. I know you did not kill Molly,' she said. 'I won't leave until you get justice,' she said.

There was no response from the man cuffed to the gurney.

Even as she said it, Blair did not know how she could live up to that guarantee. Rebecca was gone and Tom Olson had as good as administered threats. There was no one who was going to help her, Blair realized. Her heart sank at the realization that she had almost escaped, but fate had held her back. She would not walk away again, she thought, from this life that was precious beyond measure to no one but God and Lucille Jones. It depended on her determination. There was no wriggling out of her responsibility. It was that simple and that impossible.

'I swear,' she said.

NINETEEN

Blair stood on the porch and banged on the front door. Tom Olson's car was there and she could hear someone moving around in the house. But no one answered.

'You might as well open the door,' she said in a loud voice. 'I'm not leaving.'

Finally, she heard the locks being turned and the door was pulled open. Tom Olson glared out at her. He was barefoot, wearing plaid flannel pajama pants and a frayed T-shirt.

'Do you know what time it is?' he asked.

'Of course,' said Blair. 'May I come in?'

Tom turned his back on her. 'I suppose. It's freezing. I need to get dressed.' He walked toward the back of the house.

Blair came inside. She could smell coffee brewing. There was the beginning of a fire in the woodstove, but the room was still freezing. She glanced at her watch. Seven a.m. She didn't care. It served him right.

She went and sat down on the upright wooden chair where she had sat yesterday. Tom was gone for a few minutes. He emerged in a heavy, chamois shirt, jeans and unlaced work boots. He paid no attention to her presence, but went to the woodstove, opened the door and threw in some more sticks and closed the door again. Then he walked over to the kitchen counter, and poured himself a mug of coffee from the coffeemaker.

'You want one?' he asked.

Blair shook her head.

Tom sat down across from her in his easy chair and stared at her. 'I realize that you hired me when I took your money, but that doesn't mean you can come calling whenever the hell you please,' he grumbled.

'I hope you haven't cashed that check,' said Blair, 'because I want my money back.'

Tom looked at her with narrowed eyes. 'What's the problem?' he asked. 'Results too slow? Did you think I'd have all the answers in twelve hours?'

'I've just come from the hospital,' she said evenly. 'Yusef Muhammed tried to kill himself last night.'

Tom did not flinch or betray any emotion. 'I take it he didn't succeed?'

'No thanks to you,' said Blair.

Tom frowned at her. 'Now just a minute, how do I get blamed for this?'

Blair glared at him. 'You called him yesterday. You reminded him that you had been one of the officers who arrested him and you told him that I had hired you to investigate the case. I believe your exact words were that, "as far as you were concerned, he was never getting out of jail."'

Tom lifted his mug to his lips with a shaking hand. 'That's true. He probably isn't,' he said.

'Bastard,' said Blair, under her breath. 'Just get me my check.'

Tom ignored the insult. 'He hung up before I could explain why I said that. Can I explain it to you? Since you're sitting right here?'

Blair trained a withering gaze on him and did not reply.

'Fine. I'll tell you anyway. Do you know how many prisoners are currently incarcerated in the U.S.?' He did not wait for her to answer. 'About one and half million. Do you know how many were exonerated last year? One hundred and fifty-seven. One-five-seven. And how many of those people currently incarcerated maintain their innocence? I'll tell you. All one and half million. Every goddam one.'

Blair shook her head. 'I'm really not interested in a diatribe about people in prison and bleeding heart liberals. Just give me that check.'

Tom sighed, set his cup down carefully and stood up. He went into the desk in the far corner of the living room, opened the drawer and pulled out a piece of paper. He walked back to where Blair was sitting and handed it to her. Blair glanced at it, folded it and put it in her pocket. Then she stood up.

'This terminates our arrangement,' she said.

'Whether you believe it or not,' Tom said, 'I only said that because I didn't want to give that guy any false hope. Those statistics are reality.'

'Well, you accomplished that,' said Blair sarcastically. 'It should make you feel good to know that he really took your words to heart.'

Tom resumed his seat. When he spoke his tone had a faintly defensive note.

'Just because it seems like mission impossible doesn't mean that I wasn't going to try and do the job,' he said.

'Whatever,' said Blair, heading for the door. 'I'll do it myself. Investigating can't be that difficult, judging from the fact that you make a living at it.'

To her surprise, Tom smiled.

'Touché,' he said.

Blair shook her head and reached for the doorknob.

'Look I made a few notes on the case last night,' he said. 'If you insist on leaving, you might as well take them,' he said.

Blair turned and looked at him. 'Why?' she asked.

'I told you. I was planning on doing the job.'

'Why give them to me?'

Tom shrugged. 'I won't need them. It might help you out.'

Blair stared at him, tempted, but not wanting to admit it.

Tom beckoned to her with one hand.

'Come back. Sit for a minute. They're on the desk.'

Blair wanted to walk out and slam the door, but she couldn't really see the point of a dramatic gesture. She had already taken back her check. Meanwhile, Yusef Muhammed's life was on the line and she didn't really know where to begin. And time was of the essence. If Tom Olson had notes, she could at least take a look at them. She came back to the stiff-backed chair and sat down. Tom went over to the desk and shuffled through some papers there. He assembled a sheaf and brought them to Blair. Blair took them, and looked at him, surprised.

'This is all from last night?'

'I'm a believer in being prepared,' he said.

Blair began to look through the pages. There were lists of questions to be answered and people he planned to interview. There was an entire page of physical evidence which he wanted to review. There were notes about Molly, about Yusef Muhammed, about Celeste. There were several street maps of Molly's neighborhood. Blair glanced up at Tom, who had resumed his seat and was watching her over the rim of his coffee mug.

'You did a lot of work here,' she said begrudgingly.

'Believe it or not, I was looking forward to this investigation. What you said about your sister interested me. I mean, legally, it's not really helpful. People have a much exaggerated idea of the worth of a deathbed confession . . .'

'I found that out,' said Blair ruefully.

'But you seem completely convinced that she was telling the truth as she knew it. And, at that point, why should she bother to lie?' he said.

'That's exactly what I think,' said Blair.

'When I began to go over this stuff, in light of Celeste's admission, I saw a lot of potential holes in the investigation. Those notes will give you a place to start,' he said.

Blair sighed and began to look through the pages again. Then she looked up at Tom Olson.

'It seems like you were actually getting ready to pursue this case.'

'That was my plan.'

'So why did you precipitate Muhammed's suicide attempt with your callousness.'

'I explained that,' he said stubbornly.

'All the same, you needlessly harassed a man, falsely imprisoned, whom you were supposed to be helping.'

Tom did not reply. He gazed at her with a cool, distant expression on his face. Blair understood that he was not going to apologize.

'I do need help with this,' she admitted. 'I have to see it through, but it's a bit overwhelming.'

'Do you want me to take another stab at it?'

Blair sighed and stared at the papers in her hands. 'I suppose I do.'

'In that case, I am willing to give it a try,' Tom said.

Blair didn't know whether to feel relieved or wary. 'Look, I've decided that I can't walk away while this is all up in the air. But I'm not going to sit around this town waiting for you to get results. I want to be involved in every step of this. Either give me jobs to do or let me accompany you.'

Tom shrugged. 'You can tag along, until you get in my way,' he said. 'I won't have that.'

'Understood. And I suppose you'll want this check back,' she said, pulling it from her pocket and holding it between her fingers.

'You're damn right,' he said.

Blair walked over to him and handed him the check. He put it in his shirt pocket and patted it proprietarily.

'When do we start?' she said.

'Let's talk about what we do know,' he said. 'Starting with the crime.'

The sky turned from an early morning bluish gray to a pale gray midday, as they sat in Tom's living room and went over the day of Molly's death in detail. Tom asked Blair to tell him everything she knew about that long ago day. Finally, he sat back in his chair, ruminating.

'What are you thinking?' she said.

'You say that the kid playing hide and seek next door . . .'

'Jenna,' said Blair.

'This Jenna told you that she had heard someone banging on the door of the Sinclair's house, asking for help,' he said, frowning.

'That's right,' said Blair. 'But she didn't hear anyone answer the door.'

'So, that must have occurred before Molly got home. The house was empty. Her parents were away, and, as far as we know, Molly never went into the house.'

'That's right,' said Blair.

Tom pulled out the street maps and studied them, tapping his steepled fingers against his lips. 'This house next door was the Knoedler's.'

'Yes, that's their name,' Blair agreed.

'I know them,' said Tom. 'I answered a couple of calls there when I was a patrolman.'

'Calls about what?'

'Domestic disputes,' he said. 'Randy Knoedler was a mean drunk.'

'Mean, as in violent?' said Blair.

Tom nodded. 'We picked him up for battery a couple of times.'

'You know, come to think of it, I remember that Janet was worried about Molly staying alone in the house, because they had a neighbor with a bad temper.'

'That would be Randy,' said Tom. 'We would arrest him and then the wife would refuse to press charges.'

Blair's heart skipped an anxious beat. 'Are you thinking he was the one who might have come after Molly?'

Tom seemed lost in thought. 'This is what we need to find out. Who was this unidentified visitor? Could it, in fact, have been a neighbor? Someone who ran over there to escape an angry . . . family member? Or did the visitor come in a car?' He looked up at Blair. 'Did the eyewitness, or ear witness in this case, hear a car?'

'She didn't say,' said Blair. 'We could ask her.'

Tom frowned at the map and did not reply. Blair pulled her chair around and looked at what he was studying.

'This is a recent map,' she said. She pointed to the house perched in the midst of a sloping, manicured lawn which she had visited. 'This house wasn't there fifteen years ago.'

Tom looked at her, eyebrows raised. 'No, you're right. It wasn't,' he said. 'We need a map of that street as it was back then.'

'Where do we get that?' Blair asked.

'City Hall,' he said, 'and I think we definitely need to revisit the Knoedlers. This . . . person that the kid heard knocking could be important. Let's take a ride.'

'I'll drive,' said Blair.

He hesitated and she thought he was going to protest, but then he said, 'Sure. Just remember, if you do drive, you may be in for a long day.'

'Not a problem,' said Blair, gazing back at him impassively.

'All right then,' he said. 'Let's go.'

TWENTY

Blair drove, while Tom spoke on his cell phone to someone from the police department. His end of the conversation was monosyllabic, almost as if he did not want Blair to know what he was talking about. He ended the call just as they arrived on Main Street and he started to point out to her where to turn to reach City Hall.

'I know where it is,' said Blair irritably. 'I used to live here.'

'There have been some changes,' he said.

'Not that many,' said Blair. She pulled into a parking spot directly across the street from City Hall and the two of them got out of the car. They crossed the street and mounted the steps. Once inside, Blair's familiarity with the place ended, but Tom seemed to know exactly which office to head to. He went into Zoning and Permits, and Blair followed behind him.

'Hey Tom,' said the woman behind the counter, with a flirtatious smile.

'Melanie, how are you?' he said.

Melanie was a woman in her late thirties, wearing an elaborate updo, lots of eye makeup and a sweater which was too tight and clung to the rolls in her midriff.

'I'm peachy,' Melanie said. 'What brings you here today?'

'Well, my client and I,' Tom said pointedly, indicating Blair, 'need to take a look at one of your topographical maps, from say . . . fifteen years ago.'

'Of what part of town?'

'Fulling Mill Road,' he said.

The woman nodded and went over to a shelf of large books which were arranged side by side in an old bookcase. She struggled to pull one loose and carried it to the counter where Tom and Blair were waiting. Tom thanked her and flopped the old book open on the counter. A musty smell rose from the pages. It seemed as if those pages had rarely been turned.

Blair and Tom leaned, shoulder to shoulder, over the book of maps and drawings of the area. It took Blair only a moment to get the hang of it. Then she was quickly able to turn the topographical drawings and aerial maps into a three-dimensional image of the place in her mind's eye.

'There,' she said, pointing to a pencil-drawn box with footage numbers along the perimeter. 'That's the Sinclair's house.'

Tom nodded and looked.

'This is the Knoedler's,' said Blair, pointing to another box further down the street which had been divided into large lots.

'And on the other side,' said Tom, indicating the page with his open hand. 'Nothing. Woods and trees.'

'Really?' said Blair, frowning at the page.

'I told you there have been changes. A lot of new construction for one thing,' said Tom.

Blair looked at the date on the book's spine. The aerial maps were clearly correct for that year. 'I didn't remember it like that. I mean, I remember there was a lot of woodland, but it looks like those lots were completely undeveloped.'

'Until we get to this spot,' Tom said, pointing to a large parcel of land on the winding road. 'That's the old Warriner place. It's got two buildings on it. Beyond it there's another equally large, isolated parcel where this road winds its way up the mountain.'

'I see that,' said Blair.

'But that would be a treacherous walk to Molly's house from here. That's got to be at least a mile.'

Tom closed the book up and called out to the clerk. 'Thanks, Melanie.'

'Did you find what you were looking for?' Melanie asked pleasantly.

'Maybe,' he said.

Blair shivered as they stepped outside and got back into her Nissan. She looked over at Tom.

'So, where to first?'

'We'll start at the Knoedler house,' he said.

'Ok,' said Blair.

'But first, would you mind stopping at the Wawa up there,' he said, pointing to the gas station and convenience center, which was doing the best business in town, judging from the coming and going in the parking lot.

'No problem,' said Blair. She pulled in and parked.

'I'm going to get myself a sandwich,' he said. 'Can I get you anything?'

Blair shook her head. 'I'm not hungry.'

Tom got out of the passenger side and loped up to the door. He opened it, allowing a young mom and her toddler in a stroller to exit before he disappeared inside.

Alone in the car, Blair felt grateful that the former cop was back on board. If he didn't find this case absorbing, he was doing a good job of feigning interest. Her stomach growled and she wished, suddenly, that she had asked him to buy her a sandwich after all. She knew she could take a minute, go out and get one – after all, they were operating on her dime – but it would slow them down and she found herself not wanting to lose the time.

The door of the convenience store opened. Tom came out carrying a large cup with a straw in one hand and a paper wrapped sandwich in the other.

Blair leaned over and opened the car door. Tom slid inside. He put the drink down in the cup holder between the seats. Blair could see now that there were two straws inserted in the lid. He unwrapped the sandwich, divided it in two and handed a half, complete with paper, over to Blair.

'You looked hungry to me,' he said.

Blair looked at him in surprise.

'It's ham and cheese. You're not a vegan or something, are you?'

Blair smiled and shook her head. 'No.'

'Ham and cheese seemed like the safest bet,' he said.

Blair accepted the sandwich and took a bite. 'I was hungry,' she admitted. 'I've been up since the crack of dawn.'

'I know. You were knocking at my door.' Tom took a sip from the drink and held up a second straw. 'This one's for you if you want it,' he said. 'It's iced tea.'

'Thanks,' she said reaching back behind the seat and lifting up a clear plastic bottle. 'I've got water.'

For a few moments they ate in silence.

'So you grew up around here,' he said.

Blair nodded, keeping her eyes on the windshield. 'After my

mother died, my sister and I moved in with Uncle Ellis. He was my mother's half-brother. Much older than her.'

'Ellis Dietz,' Tom said.

'That's him,' said Blair.

'Does he still have all that Nazi stuff?'

Blair's face reddened. 'You knew about that?'

'Everybody knew about it. When I was a kid, we all wanted to see it. It was like something out of a World War II movie.'

'Yeah, well, living with it was horrible.'

'I'm sure of that,' said Tom. 'Your uncle was considered a local crank.'

Blair sighed. 'He certainly was.'

'Is he still?'

Blair frowned. 'He seems to have a lady friend these days who is having a positive effect on him. A little too late for me and my sister, but it's a good thing overall. Her name is Darlene. She's a hospice worker. She just moved here to live with her brother. Joe Reese? He drives a bus.'

'Oh yeah, I know who he is,' said Tom.

'Do you know everyone?' she asked.

Tom shrugged. 'I know a few people.'

'So you've always lived here?' Blair asked.

'You don't have to say it like that,' he chided her. 'Some people like it here.'

Blair shrugged. 'I guess. For me it will always remind me of my mother's death, living with Uncle Ellis and the shame of having that Confederate flag on the porch. And now I can add the memory of my sister dying here.' Blair shook her head. 'Not a lot of warm, fuzzy memories. It seems like you have fonder feelings for this place than I do.'

Tom shrugged. 'I don't know. My ex-wife and I bought that house I live in together. Back then it was my dream house, now it's just a place that reminds me of what a wreck my marriage was.'

Blair glanced over at him. 'Mr Whitman said you had to leave the police force because of the tremor in your hand.'

Tom nodded.

'But I notice you still carry a gun,' said Blair. 'How come?'

'Well, I couldn't shoot to the degree of accuracy that the job demanded,' Tom said. 'But I can still shoot the damn thing. And I have found that a gun is a useful tool to have on hand in this kind of work. Even if you don't shoot it, it has persuasive powers.'

Blair laughed, disarmed by the frank way he spoke, although she had a feeling that he was normally a bit more taciturn.

'I can imagine,' she said. All of a sudden a sinuous blast of saxophone filled the car. 'Mother, mother . . .' a plaintive voice wailed. Blair rummaged in her pocket for her phone.

'What's goin' on? Is that your ringtone?' Tom asked. 'That song is ancient.'

'I know but I love it. It was my Mom's favorite. Marvin Gaye. I always thought his voice was just . . . haunting.'

'I think he was a tortured soul,' Tom said. 'You know he was killed by his own father.'

'I did know that,' said Blair, as she located the phone and lifted it to her ear. 'Hey Eric. What's going on?' She mouthed the word 'Work' to Tom.

'You done?' Tom said.

Blair nodded and wadded up the remains of her sandwich in the paper wrapper and put it in his outstretched hand.

Tom opened the car door and got out. Blair briefly explained to Eric why she was going to be delayed in returning, while Tom carried the trash to a can near the entrance to the store and then came back to the car. He slid in and buckled his seat belt, as Blair ended the call and stuffed her phone back in her pocket.

'Ready?' Blair asked.

Tom nodded.

Blair began driving through the woods where Molly was found and then rolled up to the intersection with Fulling Mill Road.

'This is the street,' she said.

Blair turned left and almost immediately encountered the Knoedler's driveway. She turned into the drive and slowly approached the house. There was a car and a pickup truck parked in the driveway. Blair pulled up behind them and indicated to Tom that they should get out.

They walked up to the door and knocked. After a few moments they heard shuffling noises and then the door opened. Carol Knoedler blinked at them with a pleasant, puzzled expression on her face.

'Mrs Knoedler,' said Blair. 'I was here the other day. I'm Blair Butler. I was asking you about Molly Sinclair. About her murder?'

'Oh sure,' she said vaguely. She peered at Tom.

'This is Tom Olson. He's a private investigator.'

Carol nodded. 'Are you having any luck?' she asked.

'Nothing concrete yet. Is Jenna here? I was wondering if I could speak to her again too.'

'She's upstairs,' said Carol. 'I'll call her. Come on in.'

Blair climbed up the front steps and followed her into the house. Tom came in behind her and closed the door. Carol went to the bottom of the stairs.

'Jenna,' she called up. 'Someone to see you.'

Blair thanked her and Carol nodded obligingly, although Blair had the feeling that Carol did not clearly remember her visit of the other day.

'Would you like a seat?' Carol asked.

'Oh, no thanks,' said Blair.

Tom looked around him and then spoke up. 'Randy Knoedler? Doesn't he live here?'

'He used to,' she said.

'He doesn't live here anymore?'

'No,' said Carol stiffly. 'We're divorced.'

Jenna was coming down the staircase. 'Who doesn't live here?' she asked.

'Your father,' said Carol.

Jenna's pleasant expression immediately darkened. 'Why are you asking about him?'

Tom was unfazed by the warning in her tone. 'Was your father living here when Molly Sinclair was killed?'

'What difference does that make?' Jenna demanded.

'Well, your father was arrested several times for assault.'

'Oh, that had nothing to do with Molly,' said Carol.

'A series of assaults, as I recall,' said Tom.

'He was just . . . stressed out,' said Carol nervously. 'Sometimes he would . . . lose his temper.'

Jenna turned on her mother. 'I can't believe you're making excuses for him,' she said.

'It was all a long time ago,' said Carol in an anxious, placating tone. 'Water under the bridge. Best to forget about it.'

'She finally divorced him,' said Jenna. 'He made everyone's life miserable.'

'Which was how long ago?' asked Tom.

Jenna shrugged. 'About . . . what?'

'Eight years ago,' Carol said quietly.

'What does my father have to do with this anyway?' Jenna asked.

'I'm just wondering if he was living here at the time of Molly's death,' said Tom. 'He was known to have a violent temper.'

'He didn't kill Molly Sinclair, if that's what you mean,' said Jenna, holding up her hands. 'He wasn't like that.'

'You mean he kept it in the family?' Tom offered helpfully.

Jenna did not reply, but looked at him with a resentful gaze.

'I was just wondering if maybe someone from this house ran next door that day, looking for help . . .' Tom ventured.

'No, that's ridiculous,' said Jenna. 'No one would do that.'

'You're sure,' said Blair.

'Of course she's sure. We wouldn't have,' said Carol.

'Jenna, can you recall—?' asked Blair.

'*No.* I'm sorry. I'd like to help you but . . .'

'I'm sorry,' said Tom, 'but I need to know. What precipitated the divorce?'

'My kids made me do it,' said Carol in a soft voice.

'That's none of your business,' said Jenna tartly. 'You should leave now.'

'Ok, all right. We're leaving,' said Blair.

'Where can I find your Dad?' Tom asked in a firm voice that brooked no excuses.

'He lives in Arborside,' said Jenna.

'Address?' asked Tom.

'Loring Road,' said Jenna. 'It's a tiny town. You'll find him.'

'Would you mind if we looked in that little shed on the way out?' Tom persisted.

'What for?' Jenna demanded.

'Just trying to picture what happened,' said Tom.

'Knock yourself out,' said Jenna coldly, taking her mother by the elbow and starting to lead her away from the door. 'Come on, ma. I'll make you some tea.'

'Thank you, honey,' said Carol.

Jenna closed the door behind them. Blair and Tom hesitated, as if waiting for it to open again and then Tom started back to the car.

'What do you think?' Blair asked.

'Well, Randy Knoedler was a wife beater with a violent temper. It's possible that while the kids were busy with their game, he and Carol got into it. Who knows? I know she denied it, but maybe she ran next door for help.'

'I suppose it's possible,' said Blair. 'But don't you think the kids would have known that?'

'Would they? Kids can have very selective memories. Those kids lived in a dangerous atmosphere. I'll bet they were used to tuning it out.'

Blair had to admit this possibility. 'Maybe.'

'What sort of girl was Molly?' Tom asked. 'Was she timid, or, if she came across them fighting, might she have tried to . . . I don't know . . . intervene?'

'She was not timid,' said Blair slowly. 'She spoke up. I always admired that about her. Is that what you think happened?'

'I started wondering about that when you mentioned the Knoedler's. All the cops knew Randy. He was a nasty piece of work.'

Blair nodded thoughtfully. 'Now what?' she asked.

'Let's take a look in that shed,' Tom said.

Blair nodded and backed the car down the driveway till they got to a wide spot near the shed. She drove into it and turned the car around. Then she turned off the engine. She looked back at the house, but there were no lights on in the front rooms.

They got out and went up to the shed. The door was fastened with a latch that was about to fall off. Everything about the Knoedler's property looked as if it had seen better days. Blair lifted the latch and pulled open the door.

There was a dank odor which seemed to escape in a cloud from the shed.

'Let me go first,' said Tom. He ducked his head to walk inside the shed and then motioned to Blair to follow. She went in behind him. There was a jumble of athletic equipment, garden tools and rusty bicycles in the shed.

'Good hiding place,' Tom observed.

Blair squatted down and looked out the little window cut into the wall. 'Can't see the Sinclair house from here.'

Tom leaned over and looked out the window. 'No, but if you look through those trees, you can just see the driveway. She could easily have heard someone in the driveway, probably clearly enough to recognize their voices.'

Just then, the door to the shed was flung open and a tall young man in sweats with a bony face and clenched fists stood there glowering at them.

'Connor,' Blair explained uneasily.

'What are you doing poking around here?' the young man demanded.

'Your mother said it was all right,' said Blair.

'My mother is in the house all upset, because of you.'

Tom raised his hands in a placating manner. 'Your mother said we could take a look. We're just leaving,' he said.

Connor hesitated and then backed away from the door far enough to let them leave the shed.

Tom waited until Blair was out of the shed and near the car before he addressed the young man.

'Do you ever see your Dad?'

'No. Never,' said the young man, glowering.

'Do you have an address for him?'

'No. He lives in Arborside.'

'That's only about an hour from here,' said Tom.

'Not far enough,' Connor agreed.

'Thanks,' said Tom. 'That's helpful.'

'I'll tell you something. My father was a mean bastard, but he didn't hurt that girl.' Connor insisted.

'How can you be so sure?' Tom asked.

'Why would he? He had us,' said Connor bitterly.

'I'm sorry to be bringing it all back,' said Blair.

'It never left,' said Connor.

'I'm surprised your Mom finally got the nerve to throw him out,' Tom observed. 'Most victims of domestic violence are too intimidated.'

Connor looked off into the distance, a bleak look on his bony face.

'I told her if she didn't, I'd kill him myself. She knew I meant it.'

Tom reached out and patted the young man's wiry arm through his sweatshirt.

'That was brave of you. You did the right thing,' he said.

Blair shuddered as she turned on the engine and revved it, as Tom got back into the car.

'They're lucky to have gotten rid of that bastard,' she murmured.

'Lucky?' said Tom.

'Everything's relative,' said Blair.

Tom frowned. 'They're lucky he didn't kill them.'

TWENTY-ONE

Leaving the Knoedler's drive, they passed the entrance to Molly's house and continued rolling past several large homes built far back from the street, including the one where Blair had spoken to the owner. The road twisted as it wound its way up the mountain and was intersected by several other roads. Blair glimpsed houses set back in the trees.

'I don't really remember any of this,' she said. 'After Molly died I never came over this way.'

'Keep going,' he said.

She continued driving slowly as a few flakes of snow began to swirl around the car.

'Turn in here,' he said.

It was the last property on the street. The road continued on, but the mountain rose up on either side of it and there were only trees visible, as far as Blair could see. She turned into the driveway and then slowed down to a crawl.

'Wait a minute,' she said. 'This is familiar.'

'Over that hill is the reservoir,' said Tom. 'And the power station. I don't think anyone could have come from there. This is the last residence for a while. It was always called the Warriner place.'

'That must have been Eileen Reese's maiden name,' said Blair. 'Warriner. Remember I was telling you about my uncle seeing Joe Reese's sister, Darlene? She lives here. Joe Reese is her twin. He was married to Eileen who grew up on this place. It used to be a farm. I don't think they work it anymore, but it's a sprawling property.'

'You just realized that now?' he asked. 'That you know this place?'

'I've only been here one time,' Blair admitted. 'I followed my uncle's truck. He was driving like a madman. Trying to lose me, I suspect,' said Blair. 'Anyway we came up on it from the other direction. The reservoir side.'

Tom nodded and squinted out at the house as they approached it. 'Looks like no one's at home. No lights on.'

Blair agreed. Darlene's car was not parked anywhere in sight, nor was Joe's.

'Darlene works in hospice care. Joe's a bus driver. They're probably both at work.' She stopped the car and looked around at the farmhouse, which was nearly as run down as Uncle Ellis's house. The barn was in no better condition.

'Want to get out and look around?' Tom asked.

'Look around at what?' Blair asked.

'Well, Joe Reese and his wife were living here when Molly died.'

'I suppose they were,' said Blair. All she could think of was how furious Uncle Ellis would be, if he found out that she and a private detective were snooping around Darlene's house.

'I don't think we should be poking around here. Besides, Joe Reese told me at dinner that he and his wife were away on a church retreat when the murder happened,' Blair insisted.

'Well, even so, practically everyone else on this street is a newcomer. These are the only people who might actually remember something.'

Blair sighed to cover her apprehension. Tom chose to ignore her. He got out of his side and walked up to the house. He peered in the windows. No one was there.

'What are you looking for?' Blair asked irritably.

'I don't know,' he said. 'Just getting a feel for the place. Everything between here and the Sinclair's was woods in those days. So, I guess I'm just curious.'

He came down from the porch and Blair thought he was coming back to the car. But then he veered off toward the barn, he looked into a darkened window. Blair walked behind him in the muddy indentations of the gravel drive. She turned and looked at the house silhouetted against the trees and up at the sky as the gray afternoon light faded.

Blair shuddered. 'I'm going back to the car.'

Tom turned to follow her and then stopped. Blair turned back to look.

Joe Reese, wearing work boots, overalls and a fleece vest, was coming around the side of the barn, holding an overflowing garbage can.

He reached for the door of the barn and then started and cried out, when he saw them standing there. 'What the hell?' he said.

'Mr Reese, I'm sorry to scare you,' said Tom. 'We thought no one was here.'

'Who are you?' Joe Reese demanded.

'I'm Tom Olson. I'm a private detective. I used to be a police officer. We've met before. And this is Blair Butler.'

'I know her,' Joe said.

'Hope we're not disturbing you,' said Tom. 'We called out but no one answered and we didn't see a vehicle.'

'What do you want?' Joe Reese peered at Blair. 'Does your uncle know you're here?'

'I don't think so,' said Blair. 'It's not really his concern.'

'We didn't mean to startle you,' Tom said apologetically.

'You didn't. I was just putting this trash in the barn. I store it out here in the big cans until I have enough to make a dump run. Don't have animals, so the barn's not good for much else these days,' he said.

'No,' said Blair, not certain what to say.

Joe stopped and stared at Tom. 'So, you never said what brings you up here?'

Tom was forthright. 'We are looking into Molly Sinclair's murder. It happened about fifteen years ago. You might remember . . .'

Joe peered at Blair. 'You were talking about that murder when you and your uncle came to dinner.'

'I was,' Blair admitted. 'I'm still trying to get some new information about it. That's why I hired Mr Olson here.'

'Well, I don't know a thing about it. I wasn't even in town when it happened. My wife and I were away on a church retreat,' said Joe.

'I remember you saying that,' said Blair.

Tom frowned. 'When you got back to town, was there any sign that someone might have been making themselves at home on your property, while you were gone? Can you remember?'

'I guess I'd remember that,' said Joe indignantly. 'Why would somebody be here on my land?'

'I don't know. An empty house. The owner away. Look, we know that somebody came to the Sinclair's house on the afternoon that Molly died, banging on their door, pleading for help. We were trying to figure out where they came from. We looked at an aerial map at city hall and there just weren't many places along this road that this visitor could have been coming from. So we drove out to have a look.'

'Well, good luck with that. Trying to figure out what happened fifteen years ago,' said Joe, with a chuckle. 'I can't remember what happened last week.'

'It's not going to be easy,' Tom agreed.

'You sure it wasn't that guy they have in jail?' Joe asked.

'Pretty sure,' said Tom.

'Well, I can't help you,' said Joe.

Tom shrugged. 'Sorry to have bothered you.' He turned and began to walk back to the car, gesturing for Blair to follow him.

'Oh, it's no problem,' said Joe, shaking his head. He picked up the trash can and turned to open the door to the barn.

Blair looked back at Darlene's brother as he went into the barn. He was wearing a fleece vest over a plaid shirt and there was something stuck to the back of the vest. She thought about walking up to him and pulling it off his vest, but she hesitated, wondering if it was a bit too intimate a gesture to make toward this virtual stranger.

'Mr Reese,' she said. 'You've got . . .'

Joe did not seem to hear her, so she took a few steps closer to him.

'Mr Reese,' she said. 'Joe.' She extended her hand to pull the offending object off his vest and then she stopped. At that close distance, she recognized what the object was.

Joe heard her this time and turned around. 'What do you want?' he asked.

Blair shook her head.

'Didn't you just call out to me?' Joe asked.

'No,' said Blair. 'Nothing. It was nothing.'

Tom, already at the car, looked back at her impatiently. 'Blair. Keys?'

Blair began to hurry toward the car. 'Coming,' she said.

'Well, that was a waste of time,' Tom said, as Blair turned on the engine.

Blair did not reply. She made a K-turn and started down toward the road, slowly negotiating the rutted driveway.

Tom glanced at Blair. Then he frowned, and looked at her more closely.

'What's the matter?' he said.

Blair shook her head and waited at the end of the drive, looking in both directions. It was that time of day when some people had their lights on and others didn't. She had a new model car which made the decision for her. But she didn't want to pull out into anyone's path, who might have failed to turn on theirs.

'Something's on your mind,' Tom insisted.

Blair kept her eyes on the street as the daylight faded and the snow blew around them. 'When he was going into the barn, I looked back at him . . .'

'And,' Tom said.

'It's probably nothing,' said Blair.

'What?'

'He had that fleece vest on.'

'Yeah . . .'

'There was something stuck to the back of it.'

'Something like what?' he asked.

Blair hesitated. 'It was a sock.'

'Well, that'll happen when you put things in the dryer together,' said Tom. 'Or don't you do your own laundry?'

'It was a girl's sock. Pink and fuzzy. A child. Or a young girl.'

Tom was quiet for a minute, frowning. 'Could have been the sister's?' he said.

Blair shook her head. 'Darlene would never wear something like that. It was something a child would wear.'

'Maybe . . . it's something she wears to bed, or after a shower.'

His remark reminded her that this man had lived with women and knew what they might wear to be comfortable.

But she shook her head. 'It was too small.'

'He and the wife had no children, right? How about Darlene?'

'No. No children. Darlene has a grown son who lives in Colorado.'

Tom frowned. 'What are you thinking? Did you think it could have been Molly's?'

'After all these years? No,' Blair scoffed. 'I don't know . . . It just . . . gave me a very weird feeling. Here we were, trying to find out about Molly and he has this little girl's sock stuck to his vest.'

Tom stared out the windshield, frowning.

'Why would he have a sock like that at his house . . .?' Blair mused aloud.

'I don't know,' Tom said.

'I just wonder . . .' she said.

Tom frowned at her. 'Wonder what?'

'No. The whole idea is crazy,' Blair cried. 'Besides, Joe and his wife were at a church retreat when Molly was killed.'

'He says,' Tom corrected her.

Blair shivered in spite of herself and put her foot on the gas pedal, turning out onto the highway.

'No. It's not possible. We're getting carried away.' said Blair. 'We're grasping at straws because we don't have anything. It's just so frustrating. I can't stay in this town, but I can't leave til I help Muhammed somehow.'

'You have helped Muhammed,' said Tom. 'You've rehired me.'

'Yeah, well don't tell him that,' she said ruefully.

The two of them rode in silence for a few minutes. There was enough tiredness and discouragement between them to fill the car.

Finally, Tom spoke. 'I think the next order of business is a trip to Arborside to track down Randy Knoedler. A snap out case like Randy . . . I'm not convinced he kept it all in the family.'

Blair nodded absently.

'You look like you've had enough for one day,' he said.

Blair shook her head unconvincingly. 'No, I'm still good.'

'Maybe it's time we went our separate ways for the day,' he suggested.

Blair hesitated. 'Maybe it is,' she agreed.

'Why don't you drive me back to my house,' he said.

Blair did as she was told. She pulled in the driveway and stopped. He got out of the passenger side and looked in on her.

'Don't lose heart,' he said. 'This is a process. It can take time. I'm sure you do the same thing with your computer . . . whatevers . . .'

'Yes, I do,' said Blair. 'But there I know what I'm doing. I miss knowing what I'm doing.'

Tom got out and rapped on the side window of the car. 'I'll be in touch.'

'Ok. Thanks,' said Blair. She watched as he walked, illuminated by the car's headlights, toward the house and up the front steps. He gave her a brief wave and went in. Blair backed out onto the road and headed toward home. Ellis's house, she reminded herself. Not home. Although she wished, more than anything, that she were truly heading home.

TWENTY-TWO

The smell of chicken, dumplings and gravy was coming from the back of the house when Blair opened the front door. She walked back to the kitchen and looked in. Malcolm was seated at the table and Darlene was spooning the steaming chicken stew in his bowl.

'That smells great,' said Blair.

Darlene looked up at her and smiled. 'Sit down. Join us.'

Blair was automatically ready to say no and withdraw, even though she was hungry.

Darlene seemed to recognize that Blair was waffling.

'Your Uncle Ellis had to work late tonight. He asked me to get this boy some supper.' She beamed at Malcolm, who pretended not to notice. 'There's more than enough for all of us, Blair. Have a seat.'

'Ok,' said Blair, pulling out the chair opposite Malcolm. 'I'd like that. If you're sure there's enough.'

Darlene set a plate down in front of Blair and carefully ladled some of the golden chicken dish over it. Then she made one for herself.

Blair looked at Malcolm. 'How are you doing, Malcolm? Did you have a good time over at Amanda's, at the sleepover?'

Malcolm shrugged. 'It's not really a sleepover,' he corrected her. 'That's gonna be my house,' he said.

'That's true,' said Blair. 'Sounds like you're feeling better about that.'

Malcolm shrugged, and took another mouthful of food.

Darlene sat down opposite Blair and Blair glanced up at her. Darlene rolled her eyes, but smiled at the boy. Blair took a bite and savored it.

'Oh Darlene, this is good. Did you just make it?'

'Not today. I had a few containers frozen at the house from the time I did make it. I brought one over and heated it up.'

'That was so nice of you.'

'I'm just as glad to be here with you two. My brother has his men's club dinner at the church tonight. I sometimes feel kind of . . . lonesome out there by myself.'

Blair nodded. 'I was out at your house today. I must have just missed you.'

'Really?' said Darlene. 'What were you doing there?'

'Well, I hired this detective, you know, to look into Molly's death. We were stopping at every house along the road where the Sinclairs lived at the time. Your brother was home so we talked to him for a while. He didn't really remember much about those times. He and his wife were away when the murder happened. Some church retreat they went on.'

'Oh yes,' said Darlene. 'They used to go on a lot of those.'

'Where was that?' Blair asked. 'Somewhere nearby?'

'They used to go to one about three hours from here, out near Gettysburg. My sister-in-law loved those things. I just never could be wholehearted about religion. So many bad things happened to us when we were growing up. It tends to make you a little bit cynical . . .'

'I hear you,' said Blair grimly.

'But my sister-in-law was . . . dedicated. She wouldn't take no for answer.'

'I wonder what they do at those places,' Blair mused.

'Oh, you know. Study scripture,' Darlene said vaguely. 'Counseling. Workshops. Fellowship.'

'Do you remember what it was called?' Blair asked. 'The name of the place they used to go?'

'I don't,' Darlene admitted. 'Although I remember Eileen telling me about it, about how it had a lake and acres of land. You'd think it was a resort the way she described it.'

'Do I have to go to church when I live at the Tucker's?' Malcolm interrupted abruptly.

Blair hesitated. 'What did Amanda say?'

'Nothing,' said Malcolm. 'But I know they go.'

'Well,' said Blair carefully, 'You might want to give it a try with them. But, no one can make you believe anything. That's personal.'

'Well, I'm not going, no matter what they say,' Malcolm insisted, and banged his fist, still holding his fork, down on the table. His plate jumped and then landed in his lap. Malcolm jumped up, squealing.

Darlene tried to dab at the stew on his shirt and hoody, but it was useless. 'You better go upstairs and change,' she said. 'And bring down those messy clothes.'

Chastened, Malcolm did as he was told. Blair mopped up the table and the two women resumed their dinner. After a few minutes, Malcolm came down, dressed in sweatpants and a hoody, obediently hauling his sticky, ruined clothes.

'I better run these through the wash for you,' said Darlene kindly. 'Do you want another plate?'

'Yes, please,' said Malcolm sheepishly.

'That was delicious,' said Blair. 'Thank you.'

'No problem,' said Darlene cheerfully.

Blair got up and scraped her plate. 'Well, I'm gonna leave you two. I've got some work to do.'

Darlene ordered Malcolm to sit. She began to prepare a second plate for him, and then, as he dug into it, carried the clothes out to the washer on the enclosed back porch.

Blair hurried up the stairs to her room. She turned on her iPad and began to search, googling religious retreats in the Gettysburg area. One name appeared repeatedly. Blessed Reunion. Blair tapped on the listing. Immediately, the site came up, complete with prayers printed against a sunset backdrop, photos of smiling people gathered around cafeteria tables and pictures of the retreat's campus in summer. There were lists of the kinds of workshops that were offered. They ran the gamut from youth issues to worship through music. There were all sorts of counseling sessions on everything from substance abuse to gender identity. This church was trying to keep up with the times, Blair mused.

But was this the one, she wondered? There were several men and women listed as group leaders. Blair scrolled through the photos of bespectacled, neatly attired people, looking for the ones who seemed old enough to have been at the Blessed Reunion for a long time. She found one graying gentleman named Adam Sawyer who led marriage counseling workshops. Blair tried to remember. Was that the same workshop which the Reeses had attended that long-ago November? Adam Sawyer's number was listed. Blair hesitated, and then dialed it up.

The phone rang several times and then a deep-voiced man answered.

'Mr Sawyer?' Blair asked.

'That's right,' he said.

'My name is Blair Butler. I found your name on the Blessed Reunion website. I understand that you do marriage workshops. My husband and I are in kind of a difficult place and we were wondering if we might get some guidance by attending one of your workshops.'

'Well, you are welcome, of course.'

'I actually got the idea from a friend of mine, Joe Reese, who told me he and his late wife were helped by your program.'

'Oh, sure. The Reeses. A couple of nice folks.'

Blair felt her heart skip. 'They certainly are,' said Blair. 'Were,' she corrected herself.

'I haven't seen Joe in a couple of years. Not since Eileen died. How's he doing anyway?'

'Well, he's doing as well as can be expected,' said Blair. 'I mean, it's difficult losing your mate that way.'

'So suddenly,' Adam agreed.

Blair wanted to ask more, but she didn't want to betray her lack of knowledge about the Reeses. Besides, she was supposed to be inquiring about workshops for her own marriage.

'I think Joe told me that they first came to Blessed Reunion fifteen years ago,' said Blair. 'Were you running it back then?'

'Guilty as charged,' said Sawyer pleasantly. 'My wife and I have been running these workshops for nearly twenty years.'

'That's wonderful,' said Blair, feeling increasingly ashamed for even pursuing the conversation. What did it prove, after all?

'Well, it seems to work. Our philosophy is that it helps for people to freely share their insights and experiences. My wife handles the women's group and I do the men.'

'They don't meet together?'

'Oh no,' said Adam. 'Didn't Joe tell you? They're separated for the week. That way they can say what they need to say to a sympathetic audience that won't judge them.'

'You mean they're separated for the counseling sessions?' said Blair.

'No, Ma'am,' said Sawyer. 'They're separated for the whole week, except for the occasional meal. They even sleep in separate quarters.'

Blair felt her heart start to race. 'I'm not sure my husband would like that. What if someone decided to . . . I don't know . . . go AWOL for a little while, their partner might not know it.'

'It's been known to happen,' Adam chuckled.

'You don't really keep tabs on them during the workshop?'

'Tabs? No. That's not necessary. These are adults. They're all there for the same reason. Are you concerned about your husband's commitment to the process? Are you thinking he might get here and then want to get away from the retreat perhaps?'

'Well, the whole thing is more my idea than his . . .' said Blair.

'That's normal. One partner is usually more . . . enthused than the other. At least in the beginning.'

'But I'm afraid he might walk out and I wouldn't have a clue.'

'That's possible, of course. But this is a retreat, not a prison camp,' said Sawyer gently. 'If it's any help to you, we do have some wonderful results.'

'I understand,' said Blair.

'Well, you think about it and pray over it. I hope you and your husband will consider coming. I can't promise we can help, but we can try.'

'Thank you,' said Blair.

As she ended the call, she heard the front door slam and Uncle Ellis's heavy tread thudding through the house. She heard him calling Darlene's name, although there was no immediate answer. Then she heard Malcolm hurrying up the stairs and closing the door to his room. For a minute, Blair sat staring out the window of her room at a field of white stars shimmering in the blue-black sky. Then she picked the phone up again and dialed Tom Olson.

'Hey Tom,' she said.

'Hey,' he said.

'Can you talk? Where are you?'

'I'm in the car.'

'Driving?' Blair asked.

'No. I'm parked,' he said.

Suddenly, Blair heard the sound of raised, angry voices from downstairs. She could not hear what they were saying, but it was clearly Ellis and Darlene arguing. She was surprised to hear it. They seemed to get along so well. At least up to this point. Ellis's voice was a thunderous rumble, while Darlene's remained chilly but quiet. The honeymoon's over, Blair thought.

'Blair?' Tom asked.

Blair forced herself to concentrate on the situation at hand.

'Sorry, I was distracted. Look,' said Blair. 'I found that retreat where the Reeses went. I just talked to the guy who runs it.'

'And?' Tom said absently.

'And it turns out that the marriage workshops are segregated by sex. The men and women barely see each other. They arrive together and they can have meals together, but they stay in separate bunkhouses and participate in separate spiritual activities.'

'So?'

'So, Joe Reese could have left there and his wife might never have known.'

'I suppose,' said Tom.

Blair felt disappointed by his reaction. 'You don't sound interested.'

'I am, but right now I'm staking out a bar in Arborside where Randy Knoedler is a regular. I'm waiting for him to show. There was nobody at his house. According to some people I talked to in town, this guy never misses an opportunity to tie one on.'

Blair nodded, but said nothing.

'If this doesn't work,' said Tom, 'I've got the address of the place where he works. I'll go there tomorrow. One way or the other I'll find him before I head back.'

'Maybe you should go in and have a drink,' Blair suggested.

Tom chuckled. 'Maybe I will.'

'Sounds like you're pretty convinced that Randy Knoedler is the key.'

'Not necessarily,' said Tom. 'Just trying to cover all the bases.'

'Well, I won't keep you,' said Blair.

'That was good work you did,' Tom said, hurrying to reassure her. 'I'd tend to rule out Joe Reese but, like you, I find that thing about the sock keeps coming back to me,' said Tom.

Blair did not have to ask what he meant. 'I know,' she said.

From downstairs Blair could hear the sound of the front door slamming, as Ellis shouted. Poor Darlene, she thought. She's getting a glimpse of the real Ellis. The fact is that she is too good for him. She might as well realize it now. Blair reminded herself that she and Tom were busily speculating about Darlene's brother. Her twin. It all suddenly seemed impossibly far-fetched. A bus driver. A Church deacon. A bit dull but a perfectly nice man. Not a man who would bludgeon a twelve year old, and leave her to die in the woods. Blair suddenly felt uneasy. Darlene would be so hurt if she found out about their suspicions. She didn't deserve that.

'It was all so long ago,' Blair sighed doubtfully.

Blair could feel Tom withdraw. 'What are you saying?' he asked.

'It just seems a little . . . hopeless after all this time,' she said.

'Well, it's your money. If you don't feel like paying for it . . .'

'I didn't mean that,' said Blair. 'It's just such a long shot.'

Tom was silent for a moment. 'I do think these are leads worth pursuing. Not that I'm promising anything,' he said.

'I understand,' said Blair. She heard a car start in front of the house. She pulled back the curtain and looked out to see Darlene's little compact car pulling out of the driveway.

'I'll be in touch,' Tom said.

Before Blair could reply, he ended the call. Blair closed her eyes and pressed her lips together. The house was silent again. Too silent.

'Bye,' she said.

TWENTY-THREE

The following morning, Blair knocked on the door of Malcolm's room and looked in.

'I thought I'd make some breakfast,' she said. 'What would you like?'

'Pancakes,' he said instantly. Then he frowned at her. 'Do you know how to make those?'

'Actually, I do,' said Blair. 'It used to be one of my specialties. Give me about fifteen minutes.'

Blair started to pull the door closed when he called after her. 'Do you know if my other hoody's dry? Darlene washed it last night.'

'I'll see if it's in the dryer,' said Blair. She went past Ellis's room, which was dark. She had heard him go out early. She was glad she wouldn't have to see him after the blow-up of last night. He was bound to be in a foul mood. She went downstairs and turned on the lights as she went through the house. It was going to be another gloomy day, she thought.

She was taking the pancake mix out of the kitchen cabinet when she remembered Malcolm's hoody. She went out to the enclosed back porch and opened the door to the dryer. There was nothing inside. She opened the lid of the rusted washer and there were Malcolm's clothes, still wet and flattened against the walls of the washer tub. She pulled them out and put them in the dryer on high. Then she went back into the kitchen and began to read the pancake box. She wasn't fond of pancakes anymore, but she wasn't kidding when she told Malcolm that she had been an expert at making them. Often, pancakes were what she and Celeste ate for dinner during their childhood. Now, on a rare day when she sat down to breakfast, she liked a frittata with vegetables, washed down with a mimosa. But she could still remember how comforting she had found that smell of pancakes when she was a child. It reminded her of Sunday mornings with her mother. Later, after her mother's death, that smell had also signified, to her and to Celeste, that they knew how make a hot meal, which didn't require the begrudging assistance of Uncle Ellis.

Malcolm came into the kitchen.

'Did you find my hoody?' he asked.

'It's in the dryer on high,' said Blair. 'It'll be dry by the time we finish eating.'

Malcolm flopped down at the table and began to study the screen on his phone. Blair went about finishing and plating the pancakes, and set their two plates down on the table. Malcolm immediately picked up his fork and began to shovel them in his mouth.

'These are good,' he said.

'Haven't lost my touch,' said Blair, smiling. As she lifted her own fork, her phone rang and she answered. To her surprise, it was Darlene.

'I'm sorry to bother you,' said Darlene, 'but I think I left my prescription on the kitchen table.'

'I'm sitting right here,' said Blair. 'I'll look.'

There were a couple of transparent, pumpkin-colored plastic bottles with white lids clustered on a tile on the table. Blair began to read the labels. Most of them were for Uncle Ellis. But there was one vial that had Darlene's name printed on it. There was something kind of touching about the way they had consolidated their pill bottles. Love among the old, Blair thought.

'Here we go,' she said. 'These are yours.'

'I thought so,' said Darlene. 'I left in such a hurry.'

'I'll just leave them here,' said Blair. 'You can come get them anytime.'

'That's just it,' Darlene said, and Blair could hear the anguish in her voice. 'I would rather not come over there.'

'Oh,' said Blair, taken aback.

'I don't want to run into . . . your uncle,' Darlene explained. 'I wonder if I could ask you a favor . . . could you possibly bring them to me?'

'Sure, I'll bring them to you,' said Blair. 'Where are you working?'

'Oh, this job is too far. It's about forty minutes away from town.'

'Well, if you need them . . .' said Blair.

'I don't take them till after dinner,' said Darlene. 'Would you mind awfully just bringing them to my house? I'd ask my brother to come get them, but I think he's on a run to New York City today.'

'Not at all,' said Blair. 'I'll be happy to.'

'You're a lifesaver.'

'It's the least I could do,' said Blair. 'But listen. What's this about you and my uncle? I mean you don't have to tell me any details. I just thought things were going well.'

There was silence on Darlene's end, and then she sighed.

'They were,' said Darlene. 'I thought so. But last night . . .'

Blair waited. When Darlene did not continue, Blair said, 'I heard you arguing.'

Darlene hesitated. Then she said, 'You may as well know what happened. I went to use the washing machine. You know, for Malcolm's clothes. Remember he spilled his plate . . .'

'Yeah, sure,' said Blair.

'Well, I was looking for fabric softener in that cupboard above the washer and there . . .'

Blair frowned. 'What?'

'I just couldn't believe my eyes . . . The cupboard was jam-packed with Nazi paraphernalia. A helmet. Pieces of uniforms. Medals with swastikas. SS insignias. Nazi propaganda. It was . . . sickening.'

'Oh, you didn't know that about him,' said Blair.

'Did you?' Darlene asked.

'Oh sure,' said Blair. 'All that shit was on display through my whole childhood. Pardon the expression. But it was horrible. I thought you knew.'

'Good Lord, no,' said Darlene. 'I would never . . . No. My father was a soldier in that war. He was killed by the Nazis before I was even born. When she found out, my mother had a nervous breakdown and had to be hospitalized. That's where my brother and I were born. In a . . . mental hospital. We were sent to different relatives to be raised. It was awful. Don't get me wrong. I'm proud that my father died for his country. But for anyone to idolize the Nazis? When I asked your uncle how he could even think about collecting those things, he said . . . well, never mind. It was just horrible. I couldn't believe my ears.' Her indignation burned through the phone.

'I am so sorry, Darlene.'

'It's not your fault, dear.'

'I still feel ashamed of it,' said Blair.

'Nothing for you to be ashamed of. It's your uncle who should be ashamed.'

'Still, I'm sorry you had to find that stuff.'

'Just as well,' said Darlene tartly. 'Before we got any further along.'

'You make it sound like you don't think you'll get back together.'

'I couldn't,' said Darlene.

Blair heard the finality in her voice. 'Ok. Well, don't worry. I'll bring these pills over to your house.'

'There's a box on the back porch for packages. You can leave them in there.'

'I will,' said Blair. 'I'm so sorry.'

Malcolm was staring at her when Blair ended the call.

'What happened with Darlene?' he asked.

'Oh, she forgot her pills here,' said Blair.

'She's mad at Uncle Ellis,' said Malcolm.

Blair nodded slowly. 'She is.'

'Is she coming back?'

'I don't think so,' said Blair.

'But why?' Malcolm wailed.

She wondered if he knew anything about the Nazis. If he'd even understand. She decided to minimize that part.

'They don't have the same views about things,' said Blair.

'It's cause he likes the Nazis, right?' said Malcolm.

Blair was taken aback. Malcolm was staring steadily at her. Then, she nodded.

'Right.'

Malcolm stabbed his pancakes angrily. 'Why does he do that? Everybody knows they were the worst.'

Blair was relieved to hear him say it. 'That's true. They were evil,' she said. 'I have never understood why Uncle Ellis had this sick fascination for them. Frankly, I'm surprised he hasn't tried to interest you in his horrible collection.'

'He did try,' said Malcolm. 'Mom found out and yelled at him.'

Celeste finally found her courage, Blair thought. 'Your mom and I were always ashamed of having that stuff in our house.'

Malcolm sighed. 'I liked having Darlene around,' he said sorrowfully.

'I know,' Blair said. Thank goodness, she thought, gazing at her nephew, you won't be here much longer. There won't be any fascist memorabilia at Amanda's house. Of course, Ellis would then be free to display every sick item he owned.

As if he had read her mind, Malcolm said, 'I don't get it. Uncle Ellis isn't evil. Why would he like that stuff?'

Blair studied her nephew thoughtfully. Clearly, to Malcolm, Ellis was not a bad man.

'That's a good question,' said Blair, with a sigh.

*   *   *

Malcolm had left for school and Blair was folding the last of the laundry when her phone rang. It was Eric, at the office.

'Blair,' he said, an edge of anxiety in his voice. 'Do you know how much longer it's gonna be till you get back?'

'Not much,' said Blair.

''Cause everyone's trying to cover for you but . . .'

'Eric. If I could be there, I would. I'm hoping to be able to return very soon. I think we're getting closer to some answers here.' She didn't know if that were really true or not, but she said what she had to say to stall him.

'We can't lose this Hahnemann account.'

'We won't,' said Blair with a firmness she did not actually feel, but Eric seemed reassured and asked her to let him know ASAP when her return would be. She said it would be soon, but after she ended the call, she was more conflicted than ever. She wanted to get back to work, but a man's life was at stake. What could be more important? She wondered if Tom had gotten anywhere with Randy Knoedler. She had texted him but there was no reply. She took a quick shower and, as she was getting ready to leave the house, she glanced at her phone again, to see if she might have missed a call while she was in the bathroom. Nothing from Tom. She threw her phone in her bag, along with Darlene's vial of pills and she hurried out the door.

As she approached the Reese place on Fulling Mill Road, she saw that a truck was exiting the driveway, preventing her entry. As she drew closer, she recognized her uncle's pickup. She put on her turn signal and waited. Their eyes met. As Ellis recognized her, his furtive gaze became suddenly angry. She could see him gesturing for her to move on, not to turn into the driveway. Blair watched him as if he were signaling her from the moon. I don't have to listen to you any more, old man. I don't have to do what you say.

Seeing that his angry gesticulations were having no effect, Ellis turned out the driveway and turned in Blair's direction, pulling up beside her in the middle of the road. He rolled down the window of his truck and gestured for her to do the same.

Blair lowered her window and gazed at him impassively.

'What are you doing here?' Ellis demanded.

'I'm doing a favor for Darlene. I might ask you the same question.'

'Just drive on,' he said. 'Stay out of my business.'

For a moment, Blair almost felt sorry for him. Darlene was not his business anymore. 'I heard she didn't appreciate your collection,' said Blair.

'No one wants your opinion,' Ellis said acidly. 'No one is interested.'

A car had pulled up behind Blair and the driver was waiting, without honking the horn. He could see the two drivers talking to one another. Blair glanced in the rearview mirror and then looked back at Ellis.

'Gotta go,' she said.

Ellis started to shout something at her, but Blair pressed the button on the door, and the window slid upwards, drowning him out. She raised a hand in farewell and made the turn into the driveway.

TWENTY-FOUR

Everything looked peaceful at the Reese farm as Blair pulled up beside the dark, quiet house and parked. From the car she could see the wooden box on the side porch, which Darlene had referred to on the phone. Blair slipped the vial of pills into her pocket and got out of the car. She walked across the frozen grass, still crunchy with patches of snow and approached the foot of the steps. She looked up at the back door and that was when she realized that up close, all was not, in fact, perfectly peaceful. The bottom half of the side door to the house was solid, but the top half was mullioned windows. Now that she was close, she could see that the window pane nearest the doorknob was shattered. Hunks and shards of glass were scattered around the bottom of the door. Someone had obviously used force to break the pane.

Blair turned and looked down the empty driveway. What were you thinking, Uncle Ellis, she wondered? It had to have been you.

Everywhere she looked there was glass. Darlene and her brother
had obviously not gone off to work and left it that way. She could
still picture the furtive, guilty look on Ellis's face, as he waited
to turn out of the driveway.

This was actually criminal, Blair thought. She knew that Ellis
was mad at Darlene, but she had never thought he would stoop
so low as to break Darlene's window on purpose. Her first impulse
was to leave the mess just as she found it, put the vial of pills
into the wooden box, and drive away. When Joe and Darlene got
home, it wouldn't take them long to figure out who had done this
and then Ellis would get what was coming to him.

But curiosity overcame her. It looked as if he had broken the
window to get into the house and she shuddered to think what
he might have done inside. What had been his purpose? To wreak
havoc on Darlene's house? How destructive had he been?

Blair picked her way to the door, trying to avoid the shards of
glass on the porch floor. There were still a few ragged triangles
of glass sticking up from the broken pane, and she could see that
there were rivulets of blood running down onto the white painted
frame, where Ellis must have put his hand through the window
to try and reach the lock inside. Blair hesitated. She didn't want to
reach through the treacherous remains of that window pane as
Ellis had. She would probably end up bloody too. Suddenly it
occurred to her to wonder if he had bothered to lock the door
behind him when he left.

She reached down for the doorknob. The doorknob turned and
the door swung open. That was easy, she thought. She stepped
carefully over the lintel and into the dark kitchen. It took her
eyes a few moments to adjust to the darkness and then she looked
around. The room appeared to be completely in order. There was
a little jug of flowers on the kitchen table. A dishtowel was neatly
folded beside the sink and there were several dishes in the drainer.
She flipped the light switch beside the door to get a better look.
Everything was in order except for a line of blood droplets on the
floor which formed a trail through the house.

Being careful not to step in the wet blood, Blair followed the
trail through the rooms. The droplets led through the dining room.
The dining room also seemed undisturbed. Blair continued on. It
was difficult to see the blood spattered on the patterned Oriental

rug in the living room. It was camouflaged by the pattern in the rug. But Blair thought, as she looked around, the living room had also been left alone. Blair passed through it and followed the trail again as it started up the stairs. What a mess, she thought, looking around. What in the world was Ellis thinking? She got to the top of the stairs and saw that the scarlet trail led to a bedroom on the right. The door to the room was closed. Blair felt a sudden anxiety about going in. How violent an act had this been? Could Ellis have found someone at home, unexpectedly, and made them the brunt of his anger? As irritable and bad-natured as he could be, Ellis had never been violent towards Blair or Celeste. Blair wouldn't put it past him, but it wasn't necessarily in his nature, either. Maybe you should just call the police, she thought. She gripped her phone in her hand, wondering. But she decided that she had to know what the police would find when they got there and to see if, perhaps, there was some way she could minimize the damage. She realized, to her own surprise, that she didn't want her uncle to be arrested if there was a way to avoid it.

I'm only thinking of Malcolm, she told herself. That was reason enough.

The boy had been through so much already. He didn't need another upheaval in his life. Uncle Ellis in jail. Not unless Uncle Ellis had done something truly terrible . . . Blair shook her head and made up her mind. She stepped up to the bedroom door and turned the knob. The door slowly swung open and, grimacing in anticipation, she looked inside.

This room, which was obviously Darlene's, was neatly arranged. The brass double bed was made, the bed linens and covers folded in place. The top of the bureau held several framed photos, a comb and a brush. No drawers were opened, nothing pulled apart. But on the bed, laid out as if waiting for the room's owner to return and slip into it, was a knitted cardigan sweater with a sprig of fabric violets pinned near the neckline. A blue and violet wool knit hat and matching gloves were laid out there as well, ready to be donned. There were dark smears on the sleeve of the sweater and a note lying on top of it. Blair walked over to the sweater on the bed and looked down at the note. She could read it without picking it up. She recognized her uncle's handwriting.

'I saw this downtown and I bought it for you. I hoped you would wear it during the holidays. I guess that won't happen now. You may as well have it. I have no use for it. Sincerely, Ellis.'

Tears welled up unexpectedly in Blair's eyes as she read the plaintive note, and looked at the winter ensemble laid out on the bed. Oh Ellis, she thought. What in the world made you decide this would be a good idea? You break into the house and leave this in her room? It's not exactly the way to a woman's heart. It's more like the behavior of a stalker. Still, it was a side of her uncle that she had rarely seen. A side that was hopeful and sentimental, a side that still dreamed of happy holidays with the right person. What happened to you along the way, she wondered? How did a hopeful, romantic heart beat in a Nazi sympathizer? How did those two, polar opposites, co-exist in one person? She looked at the blood on the sleeve of the sweater. That stain would never come out. This sweater would never be worn, she thought.

Blair hesitated, wondering what to do. She finally decided that it was not her business to do anything about this misguided, romantic gesture. It wasn't menacing in any way. Foolish, but not menacing, and certainly not her problem.

She left the door open and stepped carefully to avoid the trail of blood. You should get out of here, she thought. Before anyone comes home and finds you here. She knew that was the smart thing to do. But the thought of Darlene coming home to find this gory trail leading to her room was sickening to Blair. Darlene didn't deserve that. She had been nothing but nice and kind. To Ellis. To Malcolm. Even to Blair.

Blair hesitated and then made up her mind. She went into the bathroom to see if there might be something she could use to clean the mess up. In the bathroom linen closet, a sponge mop with a replaceable top that had clearly seen a lot of use, was leaning against the wall. Blair pulled it out of the closet and looked it over. She couldn't make this sponge top any worse with all the blood. It had already mopped more than its fair share of floors. Blair soaked the sponge under the faucet, and then, squeezing it out lightly, she carried it back to the bedroom and began to mop the trail of blood off the floor. Glancing sadly at the sweater with its bloodstained sleeve, and the hat and gloves on the bed, Blair sighed and then turned away. She would leave that on the bed, along with Ellis's note. It was Darlene's present, whether she wanted it or not.

Blair worked her way out into the hall, then down the stairs and through the house. There was nothing she could do about the blood on the Oriental rug. With any luck, they would never know that it was there. She mopped the dining room, then the kitchen and tried to rinse the sponge out in the kitchen sink. The old sponge head would not come clean. Time for this to be replaced, Blair thought. She looked under the sink, and in the corner cupboard, but did not see any new replacement for the sponge. That was unfortunate, but she wasn't going to worry about it. They could always buy another mop head. At least the whole scene looked a lot less ugly now, she thought. She decided to detach the mop head anyway, toss it out. She would explain it all when she talked to Darlene. Her goal now was just to spare Darlene the sight of the mess.

Blair took the sponge mop head and tossed it into a plastic grocery bag that she found in the cupboard. Now for the glass, she thought. She used the mop handle to knock the rest of the glass out of the broken pane. At least that way no one else would cut themselves on it. Then she got a whisk broom and began to gather up the shards into a dustpan. She managed to clean up the glass pretty well, both inside and out. She emptied the dustpan into the bag on top of the sponge head, and tied the handles in a knot. She looked around, satisfied with what she had done. She thought of putting the bag into the kitchen garbage, but then she remembered the garbage cans in the barn. Take it out there, she thought. Don't leave this mess in the house. The sharp glass might pierce the bag, and someone who picked it up could cut themselves.

She gathered up the bag and closed the door to the kitchen. The empty pane gave the place a forlorn look. She thought about looking for some cardboard to put temporarily in the frame, but then decided she had done enough to clean up after her uncle. She took the bag and, after depositing Darlene's pill bottle in the wooden box, she picked her way down the stairs, across the driveway and down a little slope to the barn.

She walked up to the barn door and pulled on it. The door swung open easily, thanks to the groove it had worn in the dirt from many previous openings. She fumbled against the wall for a light switch and flipped it up. An unshaded bulb hung down on a long cord. The light came on but it was of such a dim wattage that it barely illuminated the space. There was a wall of shadowy, empty stalls across one end of the barn. Two large, black plastic cans were pushed up against the far wall. Blair crossed the barn floor and, as she did so, something shot quickly across the cement floor. She saw it out of the corner of her eye. She turned to look, but whatever it was had disappeared. Blair felt her stomach churn. She had not actually seen it, but she had a good idea of what it was. A rat. What was a barn without a few rats? Barns and rats went together. Although normally, a rat preferred to live in a barn when there were other animals in residence. That way, they had feed bags to raid and grain to burrow in and chew.

He won't come out now, Blair reminded herself. They don't want to encounter people any more than people enjoy encountering them. Still, she hurried across the barn floor to the garbage cans and lifted the first lid.

The can was almost full, the trash thrown in haphazardly, some in plastic bags, some in paper and some loose. The sickening smell of garbage wafted up to her nose. I guess I could use this one, she thought. She decided to look in the other can as well. If they were both in use, she would put her bag in the fuller bin. She replaced the first lid and opened the second. This can was almost entirely empty. All right, consolidate, she told herself. She replaced the second lid, and lifted the first one up again. She took her bag and set it carefully atop the pile of garbage that was in there already. She hesitated for a moment and then replaced the lid. As she crossed the cement floor back to the barn door, something bothered her, though she could not pinpoint what it was. She opened the barn door and stepped out into the fresh air and weak sunlight outside the barn. All right. Enough, she thought. But as she returned to her car and popped the locks with her keys, she was uneasy.

Blair hesitated and turned around, looking back at the barn. For a moment she stood there, undecided.

'None of your business,' she said aloud.

But she could not pretend she hadn't seen it. She walked back to the barn, pushed open the door and flipped the light switch again. She half expected to see the rat, staring defiantly up at her, but the barn was perfectly quiet, as she had left it. She crossed the barn floor to the garbage can and lifted the lid once again. She was glad she had put the glass from the back porch window into a bag and tied it or what she was about to do would have been difficult, if not impossible.

She reached into the garbage can and pulled out, with her fingertips, a small cardboard box, which her gaze had fallen on when she opened that lid the first time. The sight of that box was troubling, but the reason it was troubling had not registered until she was unlocking her car, preparing to leave. Now, she held the box in her hand. The box was not empty. She opened the lid and looked inside, then dropped the box back into the trash, recoiling from what she saw in there. She quickly replaced the lid and then she stared down at it. What is going on here, she thought?

TWENTY-FIVE

Blair's heart began to race. For a moment she thought of picking up that lid again, and reaching back into the can. Pulling out the box and . . . doing what with it, she asked herself? Taking it with her? And for what? It was hardly suspicious, or even surprising that a garbage can would contain an empty box of Tampax, with some of the tampons used and stuffed inside in the wrappers provided. No one would think a thing of it.

But Blair knew that it was wrong. Wrong, as in, out of place. In this house there was no one who would have any need of tampons. They didn't belong to Joe, she thought. They certainly hadn't been used by Darlene. They had no guests. No one who would be young enough to have her period and need tampons. Yet there they were, in the trash. Demanding an explanation.

Get a grip, Blair chided herself. It means nothing. There must be some perfectly logical explanation, and, furthermore, what are you going to do about it? Announce that you were going through their garbage and there's an item you'd like them to explain? It was difficult to imagine a conversation more inappropriate. And why? For what? Since when did people have to account for personal items in their trash? Blair put the Tampax box back into the can and firmly replaced the lid.

Go home, she thought. This is none of your business. You shouldn't even be here. But as she made sure the lid was secure and started to walk across the floor to the barn door, she stopped. There, in the empty barn, a strange scent assailed her. She inhaled deeply and shook her head. She felt as though she was hallucinating. But she was not imagining it.

She smelled something cooking.

Food.

Soup.

There was something so homely, so . . . normal about that smell. It conjured up images of someone putting a pot on the stove, offering a bowl for lunch. It might have been almost comforting.

Except that there was no one here. No one nearby even.

Blair opened the door of the barn and looked out. Everything was exactly as it had been. No car had arrived. No lights were on in the house. I'm losing my mind, she thought. And then, she remembered something. The other day, when she was here with Tom, they thought there was no one at home, but Joe Reese had come walking around the side of the barn. Maybe that was what had happened today. Joe or Darlene had come home and parked around back. Maybe they'd picked up a carton of fresh, hot soup in town and that was what she smelled. Takeout. Obviously there was a car parked somewhere around the other side. There had to be. There was no other explanation.

Blair flipped off the light switch and stepped outside.

'Hello,' she called out. 'Anyone here?'

Her car sat alone in the driveway.

There was no answer.

She walked over to the house and climbed the porch steps. She looked through the window panes in the back door, but there were no lights on inside. She could see the range on the gas stove across the room. None of the burners were lit.

Maybe there was something in the oven, she thought, something that had been scheduled on a timer to begin cooking. She had heard of crockpots, though never actually used one. Suddenly she felt relieved, that she had hit on an explanation that made sense. There was probably a crockpot in the kitchen which was finally beginning to stew its contents, giving off that scent. Blair reached through the empty pane to open the door and walk in again. But even as she went into the house, she was beginning to realize that she was not going to find anything. For the smell had begun to diminish as she left the barn and, by the time she approached the back door, there was virtually no smell at all. She went into the house anyway and looked around thoroughly. Nothing. No one.

Blair did not linger in the house. She had spent too much time there already today and she was beginning to feel distinctly like an intruder. She closed the door behind her and returned to her car. Whatever it is, it has nothing to do with me, she thought. She opened the car door and got in. But even as she slipped her key into the ignition, her mind was racing. Had it been some kind of olfactory illusion that disappeared as quickly as it occurred? For a few moments she sat there, debating with herself. If it had just been some trick of the imagination, the scent would be gone now. What do you care, she asked herself? But she was trained in the sciences. She was used to experiments that she could control. It went against her grain to think that it had just been imaginary, with no explanation.

Once again, Blair got out of the car. She left it running and walked back to the barn. As soon as she opened the barn door, she realized that this was no olfactory illusion. No trick of the imagination. She smelled it again. Food cooking.

'Who's there?' she called out. 'Is someone here?' There was no answer. This time, she left the barn and decided to walk around the perimeter of it, hoping to find the car which had come onto the property and parked there. Or maybe there was someone camping out in the field behind the house. Someone who probably shouldn't be there. She had no interest in startling some squatter. She called out, as she walked along.

'Hello. Anyone back here?'

There was nothing. She stood on the gravelly path behind the high, windowless back wall of the barn and stared across the field beyond it, searching for some sign of a person camped there. But the field, brown and patchy with snow, was motionless except for a rippling breeze that disturbed the dry grasses ever so slightly. As Blair stood there, looking out, the smell of food cooking grew more distinct.

Blair wheeled around and stared at the building behind her. The back wall of the barn was tall and windowless. At ground level there were three matching stall doors that appeared to be tightly shut. They were Dutch doors, divided into top and bottom. The tops of the doors were closed and each door was crisscrossed by boards in the shape of an X. The bottoms were solid. Blair went and tried to open each one, but they were locked, presumably from the inside. Of course they're locked, she thought. There were no animals in the barn. There was no need to keep the stall door open.

Blair stared at them curiously running her hand over the edge of each one. They were perfectly flush with the back wall of the barn. She glanced back out into the field but, apart from some sort of hawk which was circling and making the occasional swoop down, the scene was undisturbed. Blair retraced her steps back around the barn and went inside once more. She crossed the cement floor and walked back to the empty stalls.

There were still some dingy brass and leather pieces of tackle hanging from hooks beside the stalls: a bridle, a girth, a couple of stirrups. Blair opened a stall door and went inside. There was hay scattered on the floors and Blair was sure that a couple of rats made themselves at homes there. The thought of it made her skin crawl, but curiosity outweighed her revulsion. A pitchfork and a shovel, both rusty with disuse, leaned against the back wall of the stall. An Indian blanket, faded and moldy, was tacked up across the side wall of the stall on the end, which gave the place a vaguely Western look.

There was a faint scent of manure reasserting itself in the barn, especially now that the smell of food was fading. For it definitely was fading. Soon it would be gone and she would not be able to say for certain that she smelled anything at all. I will ask Darlene, she thought. Maybe it's something in the air currents around here that carry scents from the nearest neighbor's house. Whatever it is, she thought, it is none of my concern. As she gazed out across the barn floor, she heard scrabbling and saw another furry creature scuttling across the floor.

I've got to get out of here, she thought. She wished she could leave the back way, through the stalls, and not have to cross the barn floor and encounter a rat. But those stall doors looked as if they had not been opened for a long time. She reached out and jiggled the latch on the bottom door of the stall she was in. There was no use jiggling the top lock; the latch was rusted in place. She wasn't going to climb up and hoist herself over the half door, even if it did open. That was a virtual guarantee of painful splinters poking through her jeans. Maybe there was a side door, she thought, over there, beneath the hanging blanket. She went down to the farthest stall, reached for the blanket and pushed it aside. Immediately, she saw that she was right.

There was a door there, although it was locked with a padlock. She reached out and grabbed the padlock, giving it a shake, on the off chance that it might not be fastened. But it was, indeed, soundly locked. She noticed that there was a peephole in the door, as one would normally have on a front door. She leaned in and put her eye to the peephole. At first it seemed as if she were looking at a blank wall. Then, as her eye adjusted, she saw that the door led to an empty room the size of a small foyer. There was a shadowy step up on the far wall, and, almost indiscernibly, another door, again locked with a padlock. What was Joe Reese so busy locking away, Blair wondered? Judging from the look of the house, she doubted he owned anything of much value. She'd seen houses in the priciest neighborhoods of the city with fewer locks than these.

Well, she thought, she would not be getting out through those doors. She gave the padlock another shake, and then let the blanket drop and turned away. She would just have to cross the barn floor again, and hope no rats ran out across the tops of her sneakers.

Blair turned back toward the front of the stall and, as she did so, she suddenly noticed something out of the corner of her eye. It was movement at the foot of the door. Not another rat, she thought. She jumped away, her nerves on edge by now, and glanced down at the cement floor.

She frowned and looked again.

From underneath the door, behind the Indian blanket, three rivulets were trickling out, feebly. Slowly. Blair looked at them in confusion. Calm down. Don't start imagining things, she thought. There's probably some melted snow leaking through the barn walls into that first little room and it found its way out under the closely fitted door. That's all it is.

Nonetheless, Blair lifted the blanket and crouched down beside the padlocked door. She hesitated, then reached out with her fingers and dipped her fingertips into the running liquid. She picked her fingers up and held them to her nose, expecting water, or maybe oil. She inhaled and stared at her fingers in disbelief. She hesitated. She didn't want to do it, but she had to know. She opened her mouth and flicked a drop of the liquid off her finger and onto her tongue. Her eyes widened as the taste registered. She scrambled to her feet, her heart hammering.

Soap, she thought. Soapy water. Somehow, it was trickling out under the door.

In her shock, Blair had to balance herself for a moment against the door. Then she grabbed the padlock and shook it again. It remained firmly locked. She began to pound on the door.

'Hello,' she called out. 'Is someone there? Answer me. Is someone in there?' She looked through the keyhole but there was nothing to see. She placed her ear flat against the door and pounded on it with the palms of her hands. 'Who's there?'

A voice from behind her was steely. 'What do you think you're doing?'

TWENTY-SIX

Blair wheeled around with a startled cry. Joe Reese had quietly entered the barn, crossed over to the stalls and now was standing behind her.

'Oh my God, you scared me,' Blair said accusingly, stepping away from the door and letting the blanket fall back into place. 'I didn't hear you come in.'

'Your car is in my driveway. What are you doing here?' he said.

'Out here in the barn? Or out here at your place?'

'Both.' Joe pursed his lips and waited.

Just be honest, Blair thought. She'd had a reason for coming here, even though her simple errand seemed to have become infinitely more complicated. She launched into her explanation.

'Well, I came out to your place because Darlene left a bottle of pills at our house last night. She called me this morning and asked me to bring them here and leave them in that box on the porch, which I did.'

'Someone broke the windowpane in my door. Was that you? Why were you trying to get into my house?' he demanded.

'No, I didn't break the window,' Blair scoffed, although her denial sounded forced to her own ears. 'It was that way when I got here,' she said.

'That's impossible. There's no glass anywhere.'

'I . . . cleaned it up,' said Blair.

'You cleaned it up,' said Joe skeptically. 'You didn't break it, but you cleaned it up.'

'I know it sounds a little strange, but I didn't want anyone to get cut on it. I cleaned it up and threw it away.'

'So let me get this straight,' Joe said, 'You're claiming you just came here to drop off a pill bottle in the box on my porch. But you found a broken window, so you cleaned it up and then you came out here to poke around in my barn. Excuse me, but that doesn't make much sense.'

Blair couldn't fault him for his skepticism. She knew how unlikely it all sounded.

'One thing led to another,' she said.

'Did you go in the house?' he asked.

Blair thought about lying, but decided against it. 'I had to. I had to get a dustpan and a broom. I put it back after I cleaned up the glass.'

'Why would you do that?' he asked querulously.

Blair sighed. It would not be long before Darlene came home and found the sweater on her bed. She would know that it was Ellis who broke the window and she would tell Joe. What was the point of shielding him from blame?

'All right, look. You might as well know. I was coming here to drop off the pills and I saw my uncle driving away. He had come over here to leave a present for Darlene. He broke the window to get into the house. He put the present in her room.'

Joe stared at her. 'Your uncle broke my window and let himself into my house.'

Blair nodded. 'Yes. I'm not trying to make excuses for him, but he wasn't thinking clearly. He was upset. Darlene was angry at him.'

'To be honest, I hope she is finally done with him.'

'I think she is,' Blair said. 'I'm sorry about your window.'

Joe shook his head. 'Why did she ever get involved with him? Everyone knows he's got a screw loose . . .'

Blair nodded and said nothing.

'Well, this behavior must run in the family,' said Joe. 'I come home and find my window broken and you trying to break into my barn.'

There was a little needling tone in his voice. She had told him the truth, but Joe wasn't about to let this go. She'd ratted out her own uncle and that wasn't enough for Joe.

'Look, I wasn't trying to break in,' Blair corrected him. 'And I had a perfectly good reason for coming out here. The pills. Darlene asked me to.'

'Oh right. The pills . . .' he said humbly.

Blair decided that making excuses would only make her sound more guilty. The fact was that she had a few questions of her own. She pointed to the rug hanging off the wall.

'There's a door behind that rug. Where does it lead to?'

'That's the old tack room. There's no horses so we don't use it anymore.'

'Why is the door locked?' she asked.

Joe shook his head. 'That's really none of your concern.'

'It's a simple question,' she said.

'Well, here's the simple answer. It's locked because I have things in there . . . valuable things. And who gave you permission to come out here and poke around anyway?'

'I thought I smelled something out here,' Blair said stubbornly. 'Food cooking. And then, a trickle of liquid appeared under the door. It was soapy. Like dishwater.'

'How do you know that?' he asked.

'I . . . touched it,' she said. 'I rubbed it on my finger.'

'Off the ground? This is a horse's stall. Why would you do that?' he asked.

Blair felt a sudden surge of anger, whether it was justified or not. His questions made it seem as if she had done something crazy. As if curiosity was somehow . . . akin to madness. She had noticed something odd and she had investigated. Why was he treating her like a criminal?

'I was curious,' she said. 'I was trying to make sense of it . . .'

Joe looked at her with narrowed eyes. 'I told you. There's nothing in there. I use it as a kind of toolshed to hold some lumber and some tools that aren't used anymore.'

'Before you said that you had valuable things in there.' She reminded him.

'This is my house. These are my belongings,' said Joe, in a quiet voice. What business is it of yours what I do in my own barn . . .?'

'I smelled something cooking,' Blair insisted, raising her voice as well.

Joe took a deep breath and composed himself.

'You couldn't have,' he said. 'There's no one else here. Now, get out of my barn and be on your way.'

'You don't even want to know?' Blair asked.

'I already know,' he countered. 'Have you been hit on the head lately? You know, I think I read somewhere that people with brain injuries start smelling things that aren't there. You might want to have yourself checked out.'

'Why were there Tampax in your garbage?' Blair blurted out.

Joe's mouth fell open in disbelief and his eyes glittered behind his glasses. He spoke in a low, menacing tone. 'You went through my garbage?'

'I was throwing away the glass,' she said defensively. Blair realized that she had crossed a line. She was rifling through the trash and claiming to smell someone cooking. She wanted a door unlocked in an empty barn. Anyone would think she was not in her right mind. She could see anger mounting in his face as if she had struck a nerve. And then she remembered the pink sock, stuck to the back of Joe Reese's fleece vest.

What if . . .? she thought.

Everyone had read about such things, seen them on the news. They had been known to happen. What if there were someone being held there, locked in that room? If Joe had nothing to hide, why would he be so reluctant to open the door?

'Could you just indulge me and unlock those doors?' she said. 'This one . . . and the one behind it?'

Anger flared in his cool eyes, and a flush rose in his cheeks.

'You need to get out of here,' he said.

Blair stared back at him. 'It won't take long,' she said. 'Only a minute to unlock each door and then I'll leave you in peace.'

Joe pulled his phone from his pocket.

'That does it. I don't have to bargain with you. You are trespassing on my property. I've been nice about this, but I am going to have to call the police . . .'

Blair knew that what he said was true. She was trespassing. And once the police learned, as they would, that she had also been in the house and cleaned up the trail of blood, she could find herself under arrest. And what was it that she was contending anyway? She suspected that Joe Reese had someone locked behind these doors? Someone who wore pink socks and made soup? The whole idea suddenly seemed preposterous.

She realized how the police would react. Joe was perfectly within his rights to object to her being here, especially with that broken window in the back door of the house. They wouldn't force Joe to open the door. Instead, they'd probably arrest her. She knew how unlikely it all sounded, even though she was nagged by the fact that Joe was indignant, but not curious. Some people were more private than others, she reminded herself. Maybe, for Joe, this invasion of his privacy trumped any curiosity he might have. She needed to think and regroup. Maybe it was time to walk away, at least for now. Apologize, she thought. Apologize and get out of here. Blair raised her hands as if in surrender.

'All right. I'm sorry. I'll go.'

'Too late,' he said, punching numbers into his phone. He held it to his ear. 'Yes,' he said, 'this is Joe Reese on Fulling Mill Road. I'd like to report someone trespassing on my property . . .'

Blair thought about her car, still in the driveway. If she ran out there, jumped in the car and drove away, he would probably drop the whole matter. He just wanted her gone. She could end this right now. That would be the easiest thing. But she wasn't sure that the easiest thing was the right thing in this situation. She glanced at him defiantly and then she reached into her pocket and pulled out her own phone.

'Who are you calling?' Joe demanded in a whisper.

'If you must know, I'm calling the detective I hired to help me investigate Molly Sinclair's death. Tom Olson? If the cops are coming, I'd like him to be here too. He used to be a cop in this town.' She didn't know why she said that, except that she wanted him to know that she had a connection to the police as well. That, and for some reason, she just wanted to let someone know she was here. She bent her head to look at her phone and quickly pulled up Tom's number. Pressed it.

'Yes, I'll wait,' said Joe into his phone in what seemed to be an abnormally loud voice. Almost as if he was pretending to be speaking to someone.

Blair could hear Joe moving around behind her. She put her own phone to her ear and turned to look. He was not talking on the phone. His phone was nowhere to be seen. His jaw was set, his gaze icy and he held an iron shovel, raised above his head. The shovel sliced downward almost as if in slow motion.

'No . . .' Blair cried, raising her arms to try to shield herself. 'Don't!'

She felt the blow and everything went black.

TWENTY-SEVEN

'Hello?' Tom Olson frowned at his phone and then asked again. 'Hello? Blair? Are you there?'

There was no answer. He had only gotten back to town a few minutes ago. His phone started to ring and he saw her name on display. He was glad. He had been planning to call her anyway.

'Blair?' he said again.

Nothing. Tom waited a moment and then ended the call. He put on some water to boil, checked his emails and then went over to his woodstove and threw in a couple of small logs. He sat down and stared into the fire. The trip to Arborside had been tiring and, ultimately, futile. Randy Knoedler didn't want any trouble. He was anxious for Tom to see him as a friend of the police. He claimed not to know anything about the death of Molly Sinclair, and, when all was said and done, Tom was inclined to believe him. He had seen plenty of guys like Randy in the course of his police work, and since. They were more than capable, when they had a load on, of landing a few vicious blows on whichever helpless family member was within reach. It was a combination of malice and sport to them, and certainly, as they saw it, within their rights as the head of the household. To harm a neighbor – that was something else. They could get in trouble for that, Tom thought ruefully. At home, sadly, they were perfectly safe.

Tom picked up his phone and tried Blair's number again. The phone rang and then went to voicemail. Tom knew he should just make himself something to eat or read for a while, but he felt restless. He wanted to talk to Blair. He wanted to compare notes with her.

He was well aware that there was something that attracted him to that girl. All the more reason to stay away, he warned himself. She was going back to Philly and there was no point in trying to start something with someone whose life was so different than his. Besides, he told himself firmly, you're too old for her. She had to be about fifteen years younger than him. He put his head back and closed his eyes. For a few minutes, he tried to rest. But it was no use. He found himself constantly looking at his phone. Blair had not called back.

Let it go, he thought. Don't get fixated on her. The fact was that he was used to the solitary life. Hell, he preferred it. Women were difficult at best. At one time, he was more hopeful. More of a . . . romantic. He thought about his wife, whom he had loved so deliriously when they met. Once they had settled in together, it was as if their relationship buckled under a mountain of petty complaints. They didn't argue about big issues. Children, careers, sex – they never even found time to argue about those things. They were too busy trying to negotiate the minefield of everyday life. His every habit seemed to annoy her: how he dressed, what he ate, where he put things. At first he tried to accommodate her complaints, but gradually he felt as if she begrudged him his very existence. If he tried to point out that she was being petty or a nag, she would dissolve into tears and accusations, which would be followed by the silent treatment. That became the pattern of every day. Tom sighed. The more he tried to please her, the more he seemed to further infuriate her. By the time it was over, he was left with a feeling of failure and relief. Mostly, if he was honest, it was relief. He had grown to dread the sight of her. He did not miss her. He did not miss living with a woman. It wasn't worth the angst.

Tom looked at his watch. It had been an hour since that call came in. He had noticed that Blair didn't play phone games. Or any other kind of game, for that matter. She was blunt. She said what she felt. She called you back. Something had come up, obviously. Still, he had a bad feeling about it. It was always that way when you were around town, asking a lot of questions. People began to resent you.

Tom tried one more time, and got voicemail. The fire needed another log as it was sputtering down. Instead, Tom got up and pulled on his jacket, before he had a chance to talk himself out of it.

A young boy with tired, wary eyes answered the door, a cat rubbing up against the legs of his pants. This had to be Malcolm, Tom thought.

'Yeah?' the boy said.

'I'm looking for Blair,' Tom said.

'Not here,' said the kid.

'Do you know where I can find her?' Tom asked.

The boy turned and bellowed toward the back of the house. 'Uncle Ellis. Where's Blair?'

Tom could hear muttering and the clomping of unlaced boots as Ellis came toward the front door. 'Who wants to know?' he demanded.

'Some guy,' said Malcolm.

Ellis came up to the door, looming over Malcolm and the cat. He peered at Tom.

'Who are you?'

'My name is Tom Olson. Blair hired me to help her with this Yusef Muhammed investigation.'

'Oh. Yeah,' said Ellis. 'Well, she ain't here.'

'Do you know where I can find her?' Tom asked. 'She's not answering her phone.'

Ellis inserted a toothpick between his teeth and began to absently poke it between his teeth. 'Nope. I haven't seen her since . . .'

'Since?'

'Earlier,' said Ellis in a grumpy tone.

'When was that?' Tom asked patiently. He was trying to imagine Blair growing up with this lout as her guardian. How had she turned out so . . . well?

Ellis hesitated, as if he were trying to make up his mind. He pursed his lips, lost in thought and worked absently on his teeth with the wooden pick.

'Mr Dietz?' Tom prodded.

'She went out to Reese's place this morning, on Fulling Mill Road.'

Tom felt his heart miss a beat. He had specifically warned her not to go there alone. 'Did she say why?' he asked.

Ellis hesitated. 'Something she had to return to Darlene. That's Reese's sister.'

'I know,' said Tom. 'But what was so important . . .?'

'I don't know,' said Ellis. 'She's got a knack for going where she's not welcome.'

Like when she came to live here, Tom thought.

'Anyway, I ain't heard from her since then,' said Ellis.

'Did something happen to Blair?' asked Malcolm, who was hovering anxiously behind his great-uncle.

'No, she's fine,' said Ellis.

Malcolm turned to Tom. 'How come you're looking for her?'

Tom avoided the boy's questioning gaze. He wanted to say: *Because she's not answering her phone, and I'm afraid she might have pissed off a dangerous person. So I'm worried about her.* Instead, he shook his head.

'Just want to talk a few things over with her.'

'I told you. She's not here,' Ellis said, in a threatening tone.

Tom grimaced and turned away. He descended the steps and returned to his truck in the driveway.

'What if something happened to her?' Malcolm asked in a panicked tone.

Ellis ran a hand through his greasy hair. 'Your aunt knows how to take care of herself,' he said, closing the door as Tom pulled away. 'Go on, get back inside,' he said to Malcolm.

But Malcolm did not move. He stood watching Tom's truck leave.

'I said *Get*,' Ellis repeated in a loud voice. And then he looked more closely at the boy. There were tears running down Malcolm's face.

'What the hell?' Ellis demanded. 'What are you now? A little girl?'

There were two vehicles in the Reeses' driveway. One was a pickup truck and the other was a compact car with a hospice decal on the bumper. As Tom climbed the steps to the Reeses' back door, he noticed that one pane in the door was missing and covered with a piece of cardboard. He lifted his fist and knocked.

At first there was no response and then someone called out, 'Just a minute.'

Darlene opened the door. Behind her wire-framed glasses, her eyes were red-rimmed as if from weeping, but she gave him an unforced smile.

'Hello there.'

'Ma'am, my name is Tom Olson. I . . . am working with Blair Butler regarding an, um, a cold case?'

'You mean that business with Muhammed and Molly Sinclair.'

'That's right,' said Tom. 'I haven't been able to get in touch with her and her uncle said she may have come out here.'

'Well, she was here at one point. She's not here now,' said Darlene. 'But come in. Come in.'

Reluctantly, Tom followed the older woman to her living room. There a gray-haired guy in a bus-driver's uniform, minus the tie, was sitting, reading the newspaper, while Fox News blared on the television.

'Joe, this is a private detective, Tom Olson . . . This is my brother, Joe Reese.'

'We've met,' said Joe. 'He was here the other day.'

'He was?' Darlene asked. 'How come?'

'Him. And Dietz's niece. Blair.'

'They were?' asked Darlene.

Tom thought of that pink sock, stuck to back of Joe Reese's vest.

'Yes. We had some questions about Molly Sinclair.'

Joe shrugged, as if it were of no importance. 'I forgot to mention it.'

'If you don't mind my asking,' said Tom, 'why did Blair come over here today?'

Darlene sat down in the corner of the sofa.

'Oh, that was for me,' she said. 'I asked her to bring some pills over to me that I left at her uncle's. He and I are no longer . . . on good terms.'

'So you saw her, when she brought the pills?'

'No, I wasn't here. My brother saw her. Didn't you, Joe?'

Joe lowered his paper and looked at Tom with a timid expression. 'I saw her. She was only here for a minute.'

Tom looked thoughtfully at the aging bus driver and wondered if he was telling the truth. It would not have surprised Tom if Blair had used those pills as an opportunity to question Joe Reese.

'I know Blair had a few questions she wanted to ask you. Did she mention Molly Sinclair?'

Joe looked steadily at him. 'No, she didn't.'

'Well, why would she?' Darlene asked, taken aback.

'She dropped off the pills and then she left,' said Joe.

'And did she say where was she going?' Tom asked.

'She didn't say. She seemed like she was in a hurry to be on her way.'

'Maybe she went back to Philly. She's got an important job there,' Darlene confided. 'Her own company. I know she's been anxious to get back to it.'

'She wouldn't leave without telling her uncle, would she?' Tom asked.

'She and her uncle were not on good terms,' said Darlene. 'And now I know why. It turns out that man has a very ugly side which I did not know about. He likes to collect things from the Nazis.'

'Oh yeah,' said Tom.

'You don't seem surprised.'

Tom shrugged. 'He's always been like that. He used to have a big confederate flag on his front porch, got into a lot of arguments with people.'

'Did you know that, Joe?' Darlene demanded.

Joe sighed. 'Well, everyone in town knew he was a nut. I just didn't say anything cause you seemed to like the guy.'

'I wouldn't have liked him if I knew that at the beginning,' Darlene protested. 'Honestly, Joe. You might have warned me.'

'Sorry,' said Joe meekly.

'Well, when I found out,' said Darlene, 'I told him I didn't want anything more to do with him, but he couldn't leave well enough alone. That's how the back window got broken. He decided to let himself in. He thought he would win me back by leaving presents here.'

'He had no right to do that,' said Joe indignantly. 'I'm going to send him a bill for putting in the new window.'

'Anyway, I wouldn't blame Blair for leaving without saying a word,' said Darlene, shaking her head. 'But I'm sure she'll let you know.'

Joe stared into his newspaper, with a faraway expression on his face.

'I hope so,' said Tom.

'If I hear from her, I'll have her call you,' said Darlene.

Tom thanked them. 'I'll let myself out,' he said. As he walked back through the kitchen and out to his car, he kept picturing Blair arriving with the pills. Encountering Joe Reese. Saying . . . nothing? That part of the picture did not fit. He looked out across the driveway at the barn, the dark fields.

Where are you, he thought? What happened to you?

TWENTY-EIGHT

She was freezing cold and the pain in her head thudded so that every inch of her scalp and her face hurt. Even her hair seemed to hurt. Blair tried to open her eyes, but her eyelids felt as if they had been pressed down and sealed together. Her cheek was mashed against the cold cement floor. She wondered if her teeth were still in her head. She ran her dry tongue over them and felt a moment of relief, when she realized that they were still there. And then, as she slowly began to have coherent thoughts, her heart began to hammer. Joe Reese had been wielding an iron shovel and he slammed it into her head. Had he cracked her skull? Was it dangerous for her to even move her head? Was she bleeding? She did not remember anything after the blow.

Where am I, she thought? She wanted to open her eyes, but she was afraid to. What if he were sitting opposite her, waiting for her eyes to open, waiting for her to look up at him? What if he wanted her to regain her wits before he began to hit her again? So he could feel her fear. Enjoy it. She would not put any sadistic impulse past him. Blair started to tremble, partly from the cold, and partly from the sickening anxiety centered in her gut. Her eyes still closed, she mentally took stock of her body. She was wearing her clothes. That was a relief. But her skin felt abraded, as if she had been rubbed, elbows, knees and midriff, by coarse sandpaper. Her right ankle throbbed, as if it had been twisted. Her shoes seemed to be gone.

She felt something flicker over her face, like a butterfly's wing, and then she heard a harsh voice hiss, 'Don't touch.'

The sound of a voice was so unexpected that Blair was suddenly wide awake, completely conscious. She let out a cry and opened her eyes. The room was dark except for a dim light from a hallway.

Blair's eyes adjusted to the gloom and she saw a huddled form, crouched not far from her head. Blair's heart was hammering. At first she thought it might be a dog, seated there on the floor, folded in on itself. Then, she was able to discern that the figure was a small human. She squinted and recognized a child's dirty face. Two eyes, gleaming in the darkness, stared at her from under a tangle of hair.

'Wake up,' the child whispered. Blair could smell decay on the baby's breath.

'Trista, get away,' the harsh voice insisted.

The child started and drew away from Blair.

Blair looked toward the corner of the room from which the voice emanated and saw that there was someone sitting in a molded plastic chair, watching her.

Blair tried to struggle up onto one elbow, but her arms were rubbery and she collapsed back onto the cold, cement floor.

The person in the chair stood up and walked over to where Blair lay. As the figure approached and squatted down beside her, Blair could see that it was a young woman. She was pale as a lunar moth and painfully thin. Her blonde hair hung lank around her face. As she approached, Blair could smell her shabby clothes, which had the odor, both dusty and foul, of unwashed fabric.

She looked Blair over, frowning. 'Your head's bloody. Are you all right?' she asked.

Blair swallowed hard. She did not know how to answer. She opened her mouth to speak, and then closed it again. The thudding in her head was so intense that she could barely keep her eyes open.

'Where am I?' she whispered.

'In the barn,' said the woman. 'The old tack room actually. He beat you up and shoved you in here.'

'He hit me with a shovel,' Blair managed to whisper.

The woman grimaced as she studied the wound on Blair's head for a few moments.

'That looks nasty,' she said. Then, she straightened up and walked over to a shelf on one side of the room. She rummaged around with a basin, then came back to where Blair lay and reached out her hand.

Blair could feel cool drops of water showering over her. She began to shiver. The woman pressed the terrycloth rag she was holding against the wound in Blair's scalp.

'You hold it,' she said. 'Put it where it hurts.'

Blair reached up obediently and accepted the rag from the woman's hand. She pressed it against the wound and immediately she felt an almost magical sense of relief.

'Thank you,' she whispered.

'Don't thank me. Nothing in here is clean. That cut on your head should be cleaned out. At this rate, it'll get infected.'

'Still. It feels better with the wet cloth,' said Blair humbly.

The other woman straightened up and looked down at this stranger, splayed out on the floor.

'Where did he catch you?' said the woman.

'Catch me?' Blair said. As if Joe Reese was a hunter and she was his prey. 'I was here. In the barn, looking around, and he . . . saw me. He told me to leave . . .'

'You should have,' the other woman whispered.

'I guess I should have,' Blair murmured. They were both silent for a few moments, each contemplating her own situation.

'Why were you looking?' the woman asked.

'I was puzzled . . . I began to wonder . . .'

'Wonder what?' said the woman.

'I smelled something cooking. Food cooking.'

'Not cooking. Just heating. In the microwave. It's all we have.'

Blair nodded, her gaze traveling over the sparse amenities. 'And in the trash, I saw Tampax.'

'Mine,' said the woman.

'There was water. Coming from under the door.'

'I did that,' said the woman. 'I heard voices. I wanted to try and attract someone's attention.'

'I noticed it,' Blair assured her.

'There was no use in yelling. I've tried that before a thousand times. I thought maybe if I threw the water against the door it might run down and find its way out. Whoever was out there might see it.'

'It did. It seeped out. I saw it,' said Blair.

The woman nodded, her eyes alight, for a moment, that her idea had worked.

Then the enthusiasm disappeared from the woman's eyes as if someone had blown out a candle behind them.

'I asked him to open the door,' Blair explained. 'First he said he was going to call the police on me. But when I beat him to it, and tried to call a detective that I know . . . that's when he hit me.'

'Did someone come with you?' the woman asked eagerly. 'Does anyone know you're here?'

'No. I'm afraid not. I was alone,' said Blair.

The young woman doubled over as if Blair's words were a blow and let out an anguished groan. She fell to her knees on the cement floor folding her stick-like arms over her stomach. She averted her face.

'Mama,' the little girl pleaded, fear in her voice.

'I'm sorry,' Blair whispered.

'I'm sorry, Mama,' the child echoed, hovering near the kneeling woman.

The woman shook her head and groped for the child's hand. For a few moments they were all silent. Blair felt tears running down her own face. She thought of Tom, warning her not to come here alone. Tom, she thought. Will you look for me? Will you try to find me? Wait, she thought. The phone. Call him. Call someone. For a brief moment her heart lifted. She fumbled in the pocket of her jacket. It only took a moment of groping frantically in all her pockets to arrive at the truth. Joe had taken it from her. It was gone.

Blair closed her eyes and felt the thudding in her head resume, worse than ever. She had been looking for answers about Molly and ended up stumbling into this trap. She thought of Joe Reese, with the pink sock stuck to his vest. This little girl's pink sock. Blair's teeth began to chatter and her stomach churned violently. She retched, but nothing came out of her mouth.

The child started to sniffle and the young woman murmured to her.

'It's ok. It's all right.'

Blair looked at the two of them helplessly. How long had they been waiting for rescue? Praying to be found?

The young woman was struggling to compose herself, to reassure the child. Finally, she turned and gazed at Blair. She put an arm around the child and pulled her close.

'I'm Ariel,' said the woman. 'This is Trista.'

With some difficulty, Blair moved her head so that she could see one and then the other.

'Blair,' she said.

Ariel nodded, and returned to the plastic chair. She sat down again.

'You should get off that cold floor,' she said. 'That won't help any.'

Blair nodded and once again tried to raise herself up on one elbow. She took a deep breath of the damp, fetid air and hauled herself up to a sitting position. The chill of the floor seemed to be seeping up into her bones. Suddenly, the child rushed to her side, patting her on the shoulder and trying to help lift her with her small, grimy hands.

The child's earnest attempt to be helpful was touching.

'Thanks,' Blair whispered.

'Trista. Come here,' the woman commanded.

Immediately, the child let go of Blair and scampered to the woman in the chair. She climbed up into Ariel's lap and Ariel enfolded her against her narrow chest. The chair was so flimsy that it would not have held the weight of two normal people, but Ariel and Trista together appeared to weigh about as much as a starving adolescent. They clung to one another and studied their uninvited guest. Ariel spoke dispassionately to Blair.

'She's never seen any other people but him and me.'

Blair shook her head. 'No one?'

'Nope,' said Ariel. 'She was born in this place.'

Blair's eyes had adjusted to the dimness and she looked around the desolate room. There was almost no furniture and few belongings. There was a bench and a card table. A mattress covered with rumpled sheets was pushed up against the far wall. On the shelves there was a small microwave, a basin, a couple of plates and bowls. A picnic cooler. A stack of magazines. A plastic wastebasket. The paucity of comfort was breathtaking. Blair tried to pretend that she was not sickened.

'How long have you been in here?' Blair asked in a soft voice.

Ariel shook her head. Blair did not know if that meant that she did not want to answer the question, or she simply did not know.

'You mean . . .?'

'I don't know how long it's been,' said Ariel.

Blair closed her eyes and suppressed the urge to weep, but her hands and her lips were trembling with the effort.

'I was fifteen when he caught me,' said Ariel.

There it was again. The image of a creature hunted down, captured. She cleared her throat.

'How old are you now?' Blair asked.

Ariel sighed. 'I don't know.'

Blair stared at her. 'What year were you born?'

'1990,' Ariel said.

'Jesus Christ,' Blair whispered.

TWENTY-NINE

Amanda heard the beep, removed the thermometer from Zach's mouth, and looked at the temperature.

'It's down a little bit,' she said. She looked at her son, whose face was flushed, his hair damp with perspiration. She reached a hand out and placed it on his forehead, as if she was unconvinced by the thermometer and only her own hand could accurately gauge his condition. 'You're feeling a little cooler.'

Zach gazed back at her listlessly. 'Do I have to go to school tomorrow?' he asked.

Amanda shook her head. 'Nope. No school for you, buddy. You can just lie low for a day or two.'

As she shook down the thermometer and replaced it in its plastic case, she heard the doorbell ring. Amanda frowned.

'Someone's here,' said Zach.

'Dad will get it,' she said.

'Can I have another ginger ale?' the child asked.

'I'll get you one. Want some crackers too?'

'Yes, please.'

'Ok. I'll be right back.' She leaned over and kissed him on the forehead. Then she left him fiddling listlessly with his Game Boy and went out into the kitchen. She opened a new package of crackers and pulled out a can of ginger ale out of the refrigerator.

Peter came into the kitchen and looked at her with raised eyebrows. 'We've got company.'

'I heard the doorbell. Who is it?'

'Ellis Dietz. And Malcolm.'

'Ellis? He's here? What does he want? He never comes here.'

'I think he wants to leave Malcolm here. Maybe you better go talk to him.'

'Will you take these into Zach?' she asked, handing him a plastic plate and cup.

'Sure thing,' he said.

Amanda went through the kitchen and into the living room. Ellis was standing on the mat beside the door and Malcolm was standing beside him, yawning.

Amanda put a proprietorial hand on Malcolm's shoulder.

'Hey Malcolm. How you doing, sweetie?'

'Tired,' said the boy.

'I can see that.' She looked up at Ellis. 'What's up? It's kind of late for a visit.'

'Blair didn't come home,' Ellis muttered, 'and, no matter what I tell him, the kid's all worried.'

'A guy came looking for Aunt Blair,' said Malcolm. 'A private eye. He thought something might have happened to her.'

'Probably a false alarm,' said Ellis. 'But he's been bugging me to go look for her.'

'She disappeared,' said Malcolm gravely.

'Oh no!' Amanda cried.

'Oh, she did not disappear. But I had to promise him I'd go look for her just to get him to pipe down. Anyway, I can't be dragging him around,' said Ellis. 'Can he stay with you?'

Amanda frowned. 'The only thing is, Zach is sick. I don't want Malcolm getting sick.'

Ellis peered at her. 'If he's gonna live here, you better get used to that happening.'

Amanda nodded. 'You're right,' she said. She turned to Malcolm. 'Are you hungry? Did you eat?'

'I ate,' he said.

'Well, why don't you go get settled in? Just don't go into Zach's room. I don't want you to catch what he's got.'

'Ok,' said Malcolm. He turned to Ellis and gave his uncle a hug which was briefly, awkwardly returned. 'You find Aunt Blair, ok?' Then he trudged off in the direction of his soon-to-be bedroom, dragging his backpack along the floor.

Peter met him coming through and ruffled Malcolm's hair. 'Hey buddy.'

'Hey,' said Malcolm, trying to stifle a yawn.

'Steer clear of Zach.'

'Manda told me already.'

Ellis opened the front door as if to exit. Amanda grabbed a handful of the sleeve of his coat.

'Wait a minute, Ellis. What made this guy think something might have happened to Blair?'

Peter walked up behind his wife and folded his arms over his chest.

'She ain't answering her phone,' Ellis explained. 'Nobody's seen her.'

'She's used to being on her own,' said Amanda.

'You ain't heard from her, have ya?'

Amanda shook her head. 'No. I haven't.'

'Does she always tell you where she's going?' Peter asked.

'Nah. But that detective who came around had plans to meet her. He got Malcolm all worked up. I don't think there's much to it. But I guess I better go try to find her. She's still my responsibility.'

Amanda and Peter exchanged a glance that was part amusement, part disbelief.

'I'm sure she'd appreciate that,' said Amanda.

'Maybe I could help,' Peter said. 'I could take a ride around town. Ask a few people if they've seen her.'

'You can look for her car,' said Ellis. 'It's a Nissan. A late model gray Nissan.'

'Ok,' said Peter. 'I will. Do you have a photo of her I could show around, to see if anyone remembered seeing her?'

Ellis looked annoyed by the question. 'Just look for the car.'

'Here,' said Amanda, reaching into her pocket. 'I have one on my phone that I took of her with Malcolm,' said Amanda. She showed them the photo she took of Blair in her bathrobe, with Malcolm's arm draped over her shoulders. 'I'll send it to your phone.'

'Good,' said Peter. 'Got it.'

'You try downtown,' said Ellis. 'I'll look in the back roads.'

'Ok. Can I have your cell phone number? In case I find her. You do have a cell phone, right?'

'Of course I've got a cell phone,' said Ellis irritably. He reeled off the number and Peter put it into his phone.

'Do you want my number?' Peter asked.

'I've got your wife's number. That's good enough. Well, come

on if you're coming. I can't stand around here talking all night.'
He glanced at Amanda. 'Thanks for taking the kid.'

'No problem,' said Amanda, as Ellis Dietz walked back out
on the porch and down the steps. Peter went to the coat closet
and got his jacket. Amanda came over to him as he was shrugging
it on.

'You don't think there's anything really wrong, do you?' she
asked. 'I can tell that Malcolm's been crying. His eyes are still red.'

'Well, I hope not. But she has been stirring some things up in
this town,' said Peter. 'If Molly's killer is still living around here,
he might not be happy to have Blair making noise about it.'

'I can't believe anyone would harm her,' said Amanda.

Peter shrugged. 'It doesn't hurt to take a look,' he said.

Eventually, despite the novelty of a stranger appearing in their
space, Trista's eyelids began to droop and she nodded off on the
floor. Ariel came over and looked blankly at her child. Then, she
reached down, scooped her up into her own arms, and staggered
to her feet.

'Come on, baby,' she whispered.

'Where does she sleep?' Blair asked.

Ariel's answer was a whisper. 'There's a closet back here
in the hall. I put our clothes and pillows on the closet floor.
She sleeps on that.'

Blair watched Ariel settle her child onto the closet floor. She
realized that her eyes were getting used to the gloom of the space.
Sweat had broken out on her forehead and pooled under her arms,
adding to the general misery of her conditions. Ariel returned and
tossed a pillow at Blair which she had retrieved from Trista's closet.

'Sit on that,' said Ariel. 'That cold floor will make you sick.'

'Thanks,' said Blair, arranging the pillow beneath her haunches.
'I'm afraid I'm feeling a little bit feverish.'

Ariel gazed at her indifferently.

Blair thought how ridiculous and petty her complaints must
sound to this woman who had been trapped here for years, along
with her child. 'That was clever of you, to make a room for Trista,'
Blair said.

Ariel sat down on her one chair and stared back in the direction
of the closet.

'This way,' said Ariel, 'when he comes in here to rape me, I can put Trista in there and close the door. She still has to hear it, but at least she doesn't have to watch it.' She flashed a pained, chilly smile.

The bluntness of the word and its attendant image, was shocking. Blair winced, as if she had been struck. 'That's . . . horrible,' she said.

'Might as well call it what it is,' said Ariel.

'No, of course. You're right. It's just . . . I'm so sorry.'

Ariel nodded in acknowledgement and they both were silent for a few moments.

Finally Blair said, 'How did he pick you . . . I mean . . . where . . .'

'You mean where did he abduct me?' Ariel asked bluntly.

Blair nodded.

Ariel shrugged. 'At the bus station, I was running away from home. Though I had no idea where I was going to run to. But I had to get out of that house. My mom's new boyfriend had moved in. He was younger than her. She was acting all flirty and pouty around him, always trying to turn him on. Meanwhile, when she was at work, he was sneaking into the bathroom while I was taking a shower and pulling back the shower curtain, or walking into my room without knocking. I finally got the nerve to tell my mom about it and she had a fit. She said it was my fault and that I was a bitch for trying to steal him from her.' Ariel shook her head despondently at the memory. 'She believed him instead of me! I grabbed my backpack and walked out. I didn't know where to go. I just wanted to disappear. So, I went down to the bus station and was hanging around there. This guy who was a bus driver and looked like my gramps offered me a chocolate bar. He started talking to me. Asking me questions. He said he'd let me on the bus and let me ride for free.

'I got on the bus and sat behind him. He talked to me the whole way to New York. Wanted to know all about me. He said New York was too dangerous for a young girl. He said he wanted to help me and I believed him. He reminded me of a little rabbit. He offered me a place to stay with him and his wife, showed me her picture and all. So I stayed on the bus and rode it round trip, right back to Yorkville. I went home with him but there was no wife there. Just me and him. By the time I realized what he was really up to, I was drugged up and locked in here. I was trapped . . .'

Blair thought about Malcolm, running away. Being noticed by Joseph Reese. Rescued by him. Their hero. 'He did have a wife. She was alive back then.'

Ariel sighed. 'Well, she wasn't here when he brought me home. I doubt she ever knew about me. I never saw her. A long time later he did tell me when she died, as if he expected me to feel sorry for him.' Ariel shook her head, still in disbelief.

'His sister lives here now. He has a twin sister.'

'Is she as awful as he is?' Ariel asked.

'She's a nice woman,' Blair said quietly. 'She'd be so shocked if she knew.'

'Maybe,' said Ariel.

They were silent for a moment. Blair thought of Darlene and tried to imagine her countenancing this unspeakable crime. She couldn't.

'I guess now he'll want to have his way with you too,' said Ariel matter-of-factly.

Blair looked up at her in surprise and then realized that Ariel was probably correct.

'I'll kill him,' said Blair through gritted teeth.

Ariel smiled wearily. 'Yeah. You think that . . .' The rest of her observation hung in the air, like a puff of smoke.

Blair looked up at her, sitting in her chair, and wondered how in the world she had survived this ordeal. She shuddered and her teeth began to chatter again.

'What?' Ariel demanded, noticing her expression.

'Nothing. I just . . . it's hard to wrap my mind around all that you've been through. For all this time.'

Ariel nodded and heaved a sigh. 'What were you doing, poking around out here, anyway?' Ariel asked. 'Did someone send you to look for me?'

Blair heard the plaintive note in the question. As if Ariel was clinging to that last little fragment of hope that someone was still looking for her. Still cared what had become of her. She did not know how she could answer without crushing that last flicker of hope. She tried to find some words.

'Not . . . exactly.'

'Never mind,' said Ariel. 'That's stupid. No one even cares that I'm gone.'

'I'm sure that's not true,' said Blair. 'Do you have other family? Or was it just you and your mom?'

'I had an older brother. But he was away, in the army. My grandparents lived in the next town over.' Ariel sat, staring at the floor, her arms hanging limply over the sides of the chair. She lifted one palm up and dropped it again. 'Doesn't matter,' she said dully. 'They wouldn't even know me now.'

Blair nodded sadly. Ariel was probably right. This wasted shell of a woman must bear almost no resemblance to the girl trapped by Joe Reese all those years ago.

'I'm sure they didn't forget you,' Blair insisted. 'They wouldn't.'

'How would you know?' Ariel asked irritably.

'Because,' said Blair, 'you don't forget the people you care about. The people you love.'

'That's what you think,' said Ariel.

Blair noticed that when she spoke, Ariel often sounded like the petulant adolescent she must have been when she was first imprisoned here. As if time had stood still since she became a captive.

'So why were you here?' Ariel asked.

Blair started. 'Oh, I've been looking into the murder of an old friend of mine, actually. It happened a long time ago.'

'What made you look here?' Ariel asked.

Blair tried to think back to how she had ended up here. It seemed like another lifetime.

'My friend lived on this road. They found her body in the woods on the other side. The police arrested a guy and he went to jail for her murder, but I recently learned that it wasn't him who killed her. I have to determine and be able to prove, what really happened or he's not going to get out of jail.'

'The poor bastard,' Ariel said with genuine sympathy.

'So,' said Blair, 'we decided to start again. Start at the beginning. Talk to everyone along this road.'

'Who's we?'

'I hired a detective to help me.'

'Where's the detective now?'

Blair shook her head. 'I wish I knew.'

'Do you think *he* killed her?' Ariel asked matter-of-factly. Blair did not need to ask who she meant.

'I don't know,' said Blair. 'I can't prove it. But how many monsters like him could be living in this town?'

'How many do you need?' Ariel rubbed her eyes with the heels of her hands. 'It only takes one,' she said.

THIRTY

Peter glanced at his watch. He had been out driving around for an hour and had parked several times. He had gone into the local gas station, to ask if anyone had pumped gas into Blair's Nissan. If she was planning on leaving town, he reasoned, the gas station was a logical stop. But it had been a slow night and the lone attendant assured him that he had not filled up a gray Nissan. For the same reason he stopped in the local Wawa and described Blair to the cashier, thinking maybe Blair had bought a bottle of water or a snack for the road. But the cashier was certain she had not seen her.

He stopped into Apres Ski and spoke to Janet and Robbie Sinclair, who were both at the restaurant that evening. Neither one of them had seen Blair.

'Is something wrong?' Janet had asked.

Peter assured her that everything was fine. And, of course, it probably was, he thought, as he got back into his car and pulled out of his parking spot on Main Street. He had traveled only a few blocks when his phone rang. Peter pulled over by the bus station and answered it. Amanda was relaying Ellis's latest message. He had made a circuit of the back roads, so far with no luck. Peter asked about Zach's fever and Amanda said it had come down a little bit.

'I'm gonna head home,' he said. 'I've tried everything I can think of.'

'Where are you now?' Amanda asked.

'Outside the bus station,' he said, glancing over at the stone façade of the old depot, which had buses parked diagonally in the lot. As his gaze passed over the parking lot, he noticed a gray car parked in between two large SUVs.

'Just a minute,' he said. 'I want to look at something.' He ended the call from his wife and got out of his car.

He walked sideways down the embankment to the bus station parking lot, to get a closer look at the gray car. It took him only a moment to register the make and model. He put his face to the window and looked inside.

There was a book entitled 'Robotics' on the back seat, a couple of empty water bottles and a yoga bag with some sort of mandala printed on the front.

'This has to be it,' he said aloud. He straightened up and dialed Amanda's number. Amanda answered instantly.

'Does she do yoga?' he asked.

'I don't know. Wait. I think I remember her mentioning that she does, when we were sitting with Celeste. She was stiff from sitting and said she wished she could go to a yoga class. Why?'

'I think I solved our mystery,' he said. 'It seems that, for some reason, Blair took the bus to Philly this time. Her car is here in the lot at the bus station.'

'Isn't that kind of odd?' asked Amanda.

'Maybe she had some cocktails and didn't feel like it was a good idea to drive,' Peter suggested.

'Yes. Probably something like that.'

'All right. I'm heading home.'

'Thank goodness,' said Amanda. 'I was worried.'

'Everything's ok,' he said. 'Can you call Ellis and tell him? I'll be home in a few.'

Blair tried to make a pallet to sleep on out of the dingy pillow, her coat and a threadbare bath towel that Ariel offered her, from her limited supplies. Earlier, they had shared a can of chili warmed in the microwave. Now the chili sat like a greasy lump in her churning stomach making her want to gag. She hadn't actually thought that she would be able to eat anything, but hunger asserted itself and she forced herself to ingest the dreary meal. Blair hoped she would not have to heave it up into the filthy toilet in the back hall.

Ariel, worn out from making conversation after so many years of silence, lay down first on the narrow bed and pulled up the rank sheets and blankets over her clothes. Blair was far too distraught to be able to rest and she thrashed about in the meager covers until Ariel sat up in the bed.

'You ok?' she asked.

Blair punched the pillow and then punched it again.

'*No, I'm not ok*,' she hissed. 'I feel sick. I'm lying here and I can't believe what has happened to me. I feel like I'm going to crawl out of my skin.'

'You'll get used to it,' said Ariel. 'I used to hope I would die, but I never could bring myself to . . . end it.'

Blair felt tears seeping out from beneath her eyelids. She wiped them away angrily.

'You don't hope that anymore?' she asked in a strangled voice.

Ariel sighed. 'I have Trista now. I have to think of her.'

'I should think she would be a constant reminder . . .' said Blair.

'I don't need any reminder,' said Ariel.

'No,' said Blair glumly. 'I suppose not.' The wound in her head was throbbing, and she recoiled in pain if she so much as grazed it with her finger. She forced herself to concentrate on what Ariel was saying.

'Somehow I have to protect her,' said Ariel.

Blair did not reply. What hope was there of protecting a child from a man who would keep his child and her mother prisoner in this cold, comfortless cell? Blair pictured the pious, aging bus driver and felt such hatred for him that it seemed to scald her from within. She had never been able to imagine killing anyone, but now she really thought that she would be capable of killing him, given the opportunity. She understood why Ariel was skeptical. Surely Ariel had spent hours ruminating about that very thing. But Joe still kept her a prisoner and controlled her life completely. All that ruminating had made no difference.

'Is anyone expecting you?' Ariel asked.

'You mean . . .'

'Tonight. Was there anywhere you were supposed to be?'

Blair realized that this was the second or third time that Ariel had asked some version of the same question. Was anyone going to come looking for Blair? That was the only question that mattered and she did not seem to be able to accept or remember the answer. Or did not want to. She kept asking, as if hoping for a different response. Otherwise, Ariel had shown virtually no interest in Blair since Blair had awakened on the floor. She seemed indifferent to whom Blair might be and how she came to be there.

At first, Blair thought that if their situations were reversed, she would ask a million questions and want to know everything she could learn about the outside world. But the more she thought about it, the more she could understand why Ariel would have no curiosity. After all, curiosity about the world arose from the fact that it was your world. You lived in it. For Ariel, there was no outside world. The world she lived in was this clammy room and hallway. After years in here, she must have felt a profound indifference for what happened in the so-called world. No one from that world had come to her rescue. Who was to say it still existed?

'Is there?' Ariel prodded.

'I'm . . . not really sure,' said Blair.

'Anyone who will miss you when you don't show up?'

Blair thought about it. She had told her colleagues, through Eric, that she would not be returning for a while. Malcolm was just a kid and probably wouldn't even notice she wasn't there. And Uncle Ellis? He would be glad to have her gone. For a moment, she thought hopefully of Tom and then she realized how far-fetched that was. After a rocky start, they got along, but he was an employee. He would only try to find her if he didn't get paid.

Blair's life suddenly seemed unbearably bleak to her. It was as if she was not important in anyone's life. She reminded herself of all the good her work was going to do. People would be able to walk and move again thanks to her and her company. Someday, someone might have her name engraved on a plaque and hang it in the computer lab at Drexel to remind students of all that they could accomplish. But would anyone weep to think that she had not come back?

'No,' Blair whispered. 'No one.'

'That's a big help,' said Ariel.

Blair did not reply.

*　　*　　*

Tom tried to read as the last of the fire in his woodstove turned to embers. He hated the noise of the TV, so reading was his main form of entertainment. He enjoyed settling into his worn leather chair by the woodstove, putting his feet up on the ottoman and losing himself in a book. He favored mysteries and detective novels, although he often found himself impatient with the plots. He thought he could do better, if he would only put his mind to it. One of these days I will write one, he would tell himself. But so far, that day had not arrived. Tonight, he couldn't concentrate on the book he was reading. He had expected Blair to call. He knew he was allowing himself to get too personally involved in this investigation, but he couldn't help it. He wanted to talk to her. Obviously, she had other things to do.

With a sigh he put his book down on the table beside his chair, set his reading glasses on top of it and switched off the standing lamp. He went to the front door and looked out. Everything was quiet, except for the wind, moaning in the branches of the trees. Tom switched off the outside lights, checked to be sure the door was locked and went back to the bathroom to wash up.

He was staring into the bathroom mirror, shaving his neck and the edge of his beard, when he thought he heard a noise from outside. Like the slamming of a car door. He frowned and looked back in the mirror. Probably the wind, he thought. And then, just as he put the razor to his neck, he heard a banging on his front door.

He jumped, nicking the skin, and a line of blood zigzagged down his face and under his shirt. The banging continued.

'All right. Goddamit,' he yelled. 'Just a minute.' He mopped off the pink mixture of shaving cream and blood with a hand towel, and slapped a fragment of Kleenex on the cut. Then he went out into the dark living room. There were no lights on outside, so he could not see who it was banging on his door. He thought about picking up his gun and then decided against it. Intruders didn't knock.

Tom switched on the outside lights and then went to the door and pulled it open. On his porch he recognized the rangy, unkempt figure of Ellis Dietz. Ellis did not smile or apologize for the lateness of the hour.

'I been out looking for Blair,' he said bluntly.

'Come in.' Tom stepped away from the door and Ellis edged past him, trailing the scent of beer. 'Have a seat,' said Tom, turning on the lamp behind his sofa.

'Don't want a seat,' said Ellis. 'Did you hear anything from her?'

A chill ran up Tom's spine. 'No. Why?'

'I been out looking for her,' said Ellis.

'You have? When I came by your house earlier you weren't all that concerned—'

'After you left,' Ellis interrupted him. 'Malcolm got all weepy and bent out of shape. He kept asking me to go find her. Me and another fella have been out looking. We found her car. At the bus stop.'

'Why would her car be there?' Tom asked.

'Exactly! That's what I said. This other fella, Peter what's-his-name . . . Tucker, said he figured she left it there and took the bus to Philly. But she wouldn't do that. No way would she do that. If she was going to Philly, she'd drive.'

Tom frowned. 'She strikes me as doing it that way too. But why else would she leave her car at the bus depot?'

'*She wouldn't!*' Ellis barked. 'That's what I'm saying. She wouldn't.'

'Maybe some kid stole it and took it for a joyride? Drove it there and left it.'

Ellis shook his head. 'The keys ain't in it.'

'You're right. There's something odd. It's definitely . . . unlike her.' Tom peered at Ellis. 'Did you find her phone in the car? I've been trying to call her. I've texted. No answer.'

Ellis sighed. 'No. She must have it with her. I thought she might get in touch with you. You're the only one she knows around here except for Amanda and them. She's paying you to snoop around, ain't she?'

Tom decided not to take issue with this description of his job. He picked up his phone and looked again at his messages. Still nothing from Blair. Tom frowned at the blank display on his phone.

'I think maybe I ought to join this search with you,' he said.

'I don't want company,' Ellis grumbled.

Tom ignored the rude response. 'I went looking for her at the

Reese place earlier. They said they had no idea where she was, but the fact is that they were the last ones to see her.'

'Well, I can't go over there. They'll call the police if they even catch a glimpse of me,' Ellis admitted.

'Joe Reese said you broke the window on their back door?'

'I just wanted to get in the house, to leave something there for Darlene. A peace offering.'

'I don't think it worked,' said Tom. 'Darlene's brother is pissed.'

Ellis waved off Tom's assessment and appeared to be brooding over something.

'What is it?' Tom asked.

'So, if he was so freaking pissed at me, why didn't he call the cops?'

'I don't know,' Tom admitted. 'It seems like he could have.'

'Right. There's his chance to get rid of me for good and all. And he ain't a nice guy, giving me a second chance. But he didn't do nothin'. He looks to me like he knows something and he's not telling.'

'Something about Blair?'

'I dunno,' said Ellis. 'Maybe.'

Tom looked thoughtfully at Ellis Dietz. Ellis was a crank and a bigot and a slob. He seemed to feel nothing but disgust for the job of caretaker to his young relations which had been thrust upon him. And yet, this evening, he was worried. Agitated even. Tom doubted that Ellis Dietz got agitated about his unwanted charges very often. But tonight he was worried about Blair. And that worried Tom.

'Well, I think we've got the perfect excuse for going over there. You just tell Darlene that you need to talk with her, that you want to apologize. They're good Christian folk,' he said sarcastically. 'They'll have to welcome in a penitent man asking forgiveness.'

'They'll slam the door on me.'

Tom shook his head. 'I'll explain how you're so sorry and want to repent.'

'You can't tell him that. He wants me gone.'

Tom shrugged. 'Yeah, but Darlene seems like a reasonable woman. She'll listen to what you have to say.' As he spoke, he pushed Blair's contact number on his phone and held it to his ear. The phone rang, and went directly to voicemail. Again.

'Joe Reese is one of them churchgoing hypocrites,' said Ellis. 'I don't mean to apologize to him. I'll tell you that.'

'It's just a tactic, Ellis. You don't have to mean it.'

Ellis shook his head. 'They're probably asleep now . . .'

Tom pulled his jacket off the hook. 'Let's go wake 'em up.'

THIRTY-ONE

A horrible shriek invaded Blair's dreams and jerked her awake. It took her a moment to remember where she was, and then, as her heart sank with the realization, she wished she hadn't remembered. She heard the shriek again. Ariel rose from the bed across the room and rushed to the closet. Blair could hear the murmur of Ariel's voice, trying to soothe her daughter.

'A monster came in,' the child sobbed. 'A monster.'

Blair's head ached and her limbs shook. She tried to wrap herself in the ragged, makeshift bedclothes. A monster. That would be me, she thought. The sight of a stranger in the space which Trista shared with her mother alone must have been terrifying to the child. The only other person she ever saw was the true monster. Her father. But at least he was familiar.

'It's ok. It's all right,' Ariel murmured.

How did she keep going, Blair wondered? How did Ariel do the things that mothers had to do, when she was faced with an endless imprisonment, an endless series of days in this hellish cave? And then Blair reminded herself that she was in the exact same prison. And now the endless series of days stretched out in front of her as well.

Somehow, Ariel was able to soothe the child and carried her from the closet into her own bed. Trista fell back to sleep in no time, but Blair and Ariel lay awake, in their separate corners of the room, each staring at the ceiling.

'I don't know how you have withstood it,' Blair whispered. 'All this time. Never even stepping outside of this . . . dungeon.'

'I try not to think about it,' Ariel said dully.

'Of course. Sorry,' said Blair.

Ariel was quiet for a moment. Then she said in a voice barely above a whisper, 'I got out once.'

'You did?' said Blair.

'It was a long time ago. Before Trista was born.'

'You broke out of here? You found a way to break out?'

Ariel shook her head. 'He let me out,' she said.

'He *let* you out?'

'Yeah, but I screwed it up. He had this fantasy about me living in the house with him. I guess he'd been thinking about it for a while, because he couldn't wait to tell me about it when his wife left. She went away for the weekend. Some church thing, he told me. That's a laugh, isn't it?'

'Unbelievable,' Blair murmured in agreement.

'Anyway, he told me he would let me out, but that I was still his prisoner and I had to be good and stay only in the house. He made me promise.'

Blair raised herself up on one elbow. Every joint in her body seemed to radiate pain.

'He did? What did you say?'

'What do you think? I promised. I swore on the Bible.'

'What happened?' asked Blair.

Ariel gave a noisy sigh. 'Well, it's not as if he trusted me. He would chain me up anytime he had to leave and he never left for long. But I was good as gold,' she said. 'I did everything he said. After the better part of two days, he decided it was safe to leave me alone in the kitchen, unshackled, just long enough for him to go to the john.'

'What did you do? Did you call for help?'

'Are you kidding? Call and try to explain my situation? To who, the police? In the little time I had? Oh no. I ran. I bolted out the door and ran into the woods.'

Blair felt her heart lift as she imagined Ariel fleeing, finally free.

'Of course he chased me, but I figured he wouldn't be able to see me in the woods and he couldn't run as fast as I could.'

'So . . . how come . . . I mean. Obviously, he chased you down.'

'Not on foot. He got in his truck. Me, I ran through the woods until I reached a clearing, and I saw a house. It was raining, I remember. I ran toward the house. It looked like a log cabin. There was a light on. I ran up to the door and began banging on it, calling out for someone to help me. I could hear a dog barking inside. But no one came to the door. They probably left the light on for the dog.'

There was despair in Ariel's voice, as she relived that long ago day.

'It was no use. I realized I had to keep moving. Run to the next house. I could see it through the trees. But by then he had come after me and found me in his truck. He turned into the driveway and he saw me there, going off the porch. He headed right for me. He almost ran me over. He pinned me between the porch of the house and the truck. I had to run around the truck, but this time he was too quick for me. He grabbed me.'

'You were so close,' said Blair, imagining the misery of it.

'I was,' said Ariel. 'He tied me up, gagged me, put a burlap bag over my head and pushed me into the cab of the truck. He injected me with some drug he used to keep me quiet. I know he always kept that stuff in the truck, but as he was closing the door on me, I heard footsteps on gravel. Someone was approaching the truck, asking what was going on. They must have come walking up the driveway. It turned out that it was the person who lived in the house.'

'How do you know that?'

'Well, I didn't hear another car drive in. Besides, she said so. It was a girl's voice. I heard her confronting him, shouting through the rain, demanding to know what he was doing. For a minute, before I began to pass out, I thought I was saved. I heard him tell her to mind her own business and she said that it was her business, because this was her house. And then, I don't remember anything else. I guess the drug kicked in and I passed out.'

Blair said nothing. She was seeing it all in her mind's eye. Ariel escaping, making her way through the trees and crossing the properties on Fulling Mill Road. Running toward a lighted window and banging on the door. But no one answered. No one had even seen Ariel, running for her life. No one, that is, until the girl came walking up the driveway toward her house.

Suddenly, Blair understood. She understood all that had happened that early evening, long ago. This girl who lived there had just climbed out of a car at the foot of the driveway. She had left a friend's house and accepted a ride from two people she knew, because it was raining. They let her off and the girl began to walk up the driveway and approach her house. Then she saw the unfamiliar truck and a stranger, forcing his prisoner into the cab. And she was outraged. She was not the sort of girl to let such a thing pass without protest.

'I do remember thinking that I was going to be saved,' Ariel continued. 'I don't know what happened. Maybe he talked her into thinking that I was his kid or something. Or that he was playing some kind of game with me or I don't know what.'

Blair felt tears running down her cheeks.

'You know,' Ariel continued, 'I always wondered if that girl, whoever she was, fell for his bullshit or if she ended up reporting it and they just couldn't find me. For a while, after he locked me back up in here, I thought that surely she must have reported it to the police. And that someone would recognize the truck or the license plate from her description and come looking for me. For several days I remember hoping, praying that someone was going to come. After a while though, I gave up on that. I don't know what happened. I guess she didn't tell or, if she did, nobody believed her.'

For a moment, Blair was silent.

'It wasn't either of those things,' said Blair quietly. 'She couldn't tell. He killed her.'

'Killed her?'

It was Ariel's turn to be silent.

'Wait. You weren't there. How do you know that?' she asked.

'Because it was my friend, Molly Sinclair. She had left my house and took a ride with my sister and her friend to get out of the rain. They drove her to her house and let her off at the foot of the driveway that afternoon. The neighbors in the next house overheard you pounding on the door that day, calling for help. Molly must have come upon Reese, just as he was stuffing you into his truck.'

'I still don't get it,' said Ariel. 'How do you know this?'

'Remember I told you that my friend was murdered?'

'Yeah.'

'That girl who confronted him that day – that was my friend, Molly. It had to be. It's all beginning to make sense. She died from a blow to the head. He hit her with something – a baseball bat or a tire iron. Anyway, he hit her hard enough to kill her. I guess he killed her to keep her quiet. Then he took her body and dumped it in the woods across the road.'

'Oh my God,' Ariel breathed.

'That's why she didn't report it,' said Blair.

'I always wondered how anyone could have seen that and not reported it.'

'Oh, she would have, if she could,' Blair insisted, strangely relieved to finally know what happened to her best friend. 'Molly wasn't one to back down, but she couldn't report it. She was murdered, probably so she couldn't tell anyone. The man who drove her to the foot of the driveway that day went to jail for her murder. No one believed him when he said that he dropped her off there. He's been in jail all these years.'

'Jesus. The poor bastard. That was a long time ago,' said Ariel.

'Nearly fifteen years ago. Oh, it makes sense to me now. I could never understand how anyone could hurt Molly. She was never frightened. She always spoke up for the weaker ones. The ones like me.'

'Oh shit,' said Ariel, as she reconfigured the pieces in her mind. 'I misunderstood. When you said you had a friend who was murdered, you didn't mean recently. You were talking about a long time ago.' And then Blair's silence seemed to register with Ariel. 'I'm sorry about your friend,' she muttered. 'Doesn't matter what I thought then. I guess she did try to help me.'

'Yes,' said Blair. 'Of course she did. No matter what, she would have tried to help.'

'How old was she?'

'She was thirteen,' said Blair. 'She was just a girl.'

Joe Reese was still tying the sash on his bathrobe as he reached the back door of his house.

'Hold your horses,' he yelled. 'I'm coming.'

He unlocked the door and opened it. Ellis Dietz and Tom Olson stood on his back porch. Darlene came shuffling into the kitchen, also in her bathrobe, her hair in rollers.

'What is it, Joe?' she asked. 'What's going on?'

'Your boyfriend's here,' he said.

'Oh my word,' said Darlene. She turned away from the door and quickly fumbled to pull the rollers from her hair and stuff them in the pockets of her bathrobe. 'Don't let him in.'

Joe peered out at the two men shivering on the porch. He addressed Tom.

'I'm getting very tired of you people bothering me.'

'Ellis has something he'd like to say,' said Tom. 'Can we come in?'

Joe glared at Ellis, 'I don't want to hear anything he has to say. You have a lot of nerve showing up here, Ellis Dietz. You broke into my house today. I think the cops will want to know about this. Darlene, give the police a call.'

Darlene had run her fingers through her hair and now stood behind her twin.

'Now Joe, let's not have any trouble. Ellis, what are you doing here at this hour?'

'Can we come in, Darlene?' Ellis asked. 'It's freezing out here.'

'Oh, all right,' said Darlene. 'Just for a minute.'

'Now, wait just a minute,' said Joe indignantly. 'This is my house. You don't go telling people whether they can or cannot come in. These two have got no business here at this hour.'

'Oh, I don't?' Darlene said, raising her eyebrows. 'I was under the impression we *both* lived here.'

'I just want to talk to you for a minute,' said Ellis.

'There's nothing to say, Ellis.'

'She doesn't want to talk to you,' said Joe.

'I want to just explain a few things,' said Ellis.

'Come in,' said Darlene, ignoring her brother.

Ellis edged in past Joe. 'Can we talk in private?'

Darlene motioned for him to follow her into the living room.

Joe shook his head. 'So what are you doing here again?' he demanded of Tom. 'I thought we'd seen the last of you.'

'Moral support,' said Tom.

Joe snorted with disdain. 'At this hour?'

'Actually, I decided to drive him over here. He's had a few too many and I didn't want him out on the road.'

'I thought you were here about the girl,' said Joe.

'Oh no. We know all about the girl,' said Tom.

Joe blanched and grabbed onto the back of a chair by the back door. 'You do?'

'Somebody found her car at the bus station,' said Tom. 'So I guess she went back to Philly.'

'Well, that makes sense,' said Joe. 'I guess she took a bus.'

'Although it's odd that she'd leave her car and take a bus,' said Tom.

'I'm sure I don't care what she did,' said Joe impatiently. 'Now, if you'll excuse me, I'm going back to bed.'

'Just one thing. The other day, when Blair and I were here,' said Tom, 'you had a pink sock, like a child's sock, stuck to back of your fleece vest.'

Joe glared at him. 'Well if I did, so what? Is there some law against picking up a stray sock on your clothes?'

'I'm just asking,' said Tom. 'There are no children here, right?'

'No, there are no children here.'

'So how did you get a child's sock on your clothes?'

'I don't know. Maybe Darlene brought it in from one of her hospice jobs.'

'Maybe,' said Tom. 'It just strikes me as odd.'

There was a sudden rumble of raised voices from the living room.

Joe smiled slyly at Tom. 'Well now, why don't you go out in your car and get the motor running. I think your friend, Ellis, is about to get tossed out on his butt.'

Darlene emerged from the living room, shaking her head. 'Ellis, I told you how I feel. There's just no reason why any right-thinking person would collect that stuff. Stop trying to explain it away. I'm sorry, but I am not going to change my mind. Now I want you to leave.'

Ellis stood stubbornly in the living room doorway, trying to somehow justify the unjustifiable. 'I won't keep the stuff,' he pleaded. 'I'll get rid of it.'

Joe went up to him, and poked Ellis in the side. 'Go on now. You heard the lady.'

'Don't put your hands on me,' Ellis warned him.

'All right, don't get excited,' said Joe. 'I just want you to leave.'

For a moment it seemed as if there was going to be a scuffle, but then Ellis dipped his head and conceded.

'All right, I'm going,' said Ellis. He came out into the kitchen. Once Ellis was out of the living room, Joe turned off the lights. Ellis stepped out onto the porch where Tom was waiting.

'We better leave,' Tom said to him.

'Keep your shirt on,' said Ellis in a cranky tone.

Joe began to push the door shut.

Ellis lumbered down the steps as Tom gazed out toward the barn and felt the night wind rise up, chilling him. The door slammed behind them. As he had a few dozen times already that night, Tom glanced at his phone and scrolled to Blair's number. What has become of you, he thought? Automatically, hopelessly, he pressed the number once again.

Suddenly, through the moaning of the wind, from the direction of the dark field in front of them, Tom heard a strange sound. It was the soft, tinny wail of a saxophone wafting sinuously through the night and a high, sorrowful voice pleading 'Mother . . . mother.'

Tom stared at his phone and then quickly ended the call. Marvin Gaye's voice immediately stopped.

Ellis was down the porch steps and halfway to the car. 'Come on,' he growled.

'Wait,' said Tom and then he whispered, 'Listen.' He pressed Blair's number on the phone, and once again, Marvin Gaye began to sing.

'What is that?' Ellis demanded.

Tom looked back at the light in the window of the kitchen door. As if to hasten him on his way, the light was immediately switched off. The house and the driveway were in pitch darkness. Across the field, the barn had a blank, lifeless façade. Tom ended the call and the voice stopped in mid-plea.

'Jesus,' Ellis cursed. 'It's black as a pit out here. What was that noise?'

Tom gazed across the field. 'Blair's phone,' he said.

THIRTY-TWO

Ellis turned and glared at him. 'What are you talking about?' 'Her phone. I just called her number and I heard her ringtone. Her phone is somewhere out there in that dark field.'

'Well, let's go find it,' said Ellis. He trudged across the driveway and began to descend into the field.

Tom glanced back at the house. 'No, we have to leave.'

'Leave?' Ellis yelped.

'Pretend to leave,' said Tom. 'He's expecting us to go.'

'What's her phone doing out in this field? Did she drop it there?'

'She or somebody else.'

'Ring it again. Maybe it will light up.'

'Ellis, not now,' said Tom. 'We don't want to arouse suspicion. Get in the car.'

'The hell I will. If her phone is here . . .' Ellis was making his way slowly into the field in front of the barn.

'Ellis,' Tom barked. 'Do as I say or . . .'

Suddenly the lights came back on in the kitchen and the back door opened. Joe Reese stood there in his bathrobe, peering out at them.

'Why are you still here?' he demanded.

Tom looked up innocently at the man on the porch. He began to pat himself down.

'I can't find my keys.' He turned to Ellis. 'Ellis, they're not over there. I never even set foot in that field. Let me look in the car.'

Without waiting for a reaction, Tom went over to his pickup and opened the driver's side door. He began to rummage around and then straightened up triumphantly, jingling a bunch of keys.

'Here they are. Ellis, come on. I found the keys.'

Ellis frowned and came back to the driveway. He glared up at Joe. 'What are you looking at?'

'I want to see you leave,' Joe said.

'Get in the truck, Ellis,' said Tom.

Grumbling, Ellis did what he was told. Tom put the keys in the ignition and offered Joe a friendly wave as he turned around in the driveway.

'That motherfucker,' said Ellis. 'He knows where she is.'

Tom set his jaw and drove. He took a right out of the driveway and, almost immediately, signaled a turn into an overlook on the other side the road.

Ellis opened his mouth as if to protest and shut it again. Tom pulled into the curved spot along the highway that allowed drivers and passengers to stop and gaze out at the mountains. He put the truck in park and left the engine idling.

Tom was shaking, partly from the cold, and partly from the flood of nervous tension which had swamped him.

'She wouldn't just leave her phone there,' said Ellis.

'No,' said Tom.

'But if she were in the house,' said Ellis, 'Darlene would say so. Even if she's . . . through with me, she wouldn't keep something like that a secret.'

Tom frowned. 'No . . . No, I'm inclined to agree . . .'

'So if she's not in the house . . .' said Ellis, 'where is she?'

Tom shook his head. 'Don't go there.'

The two men sat in silence for a moment.

'Why would he do that? Why would he have her phone?' Ellis demanded. 'Why would he have anything to do with her?'

Tom frowned. 'She may have accused him of something, of a crime.'

'What crime?' Ellis asked.

'What crime is she preoccupied with?'

'I don't know,' Ellis complained.

'The murder of Molly Sinclair.'

'What? That's nuts!' Ellis exclaimed. 'Joe Reese had nothing to do with that. If that's what Blair thought, maybe Joe just took her phone so she wouldn't be able to call around and tell people that.'

'He didn't take her phone,' said Tom in a biting tone. 'He dropped her phone in that field. Or she did. In either case, I think something has happened to her. I don't like to think what.'

'I'll break his neck,' said Ellis.

Tom looked at the other man in surprise.

'What?' said Ellis. 'She's family.'

Tom nodded. 'Right. Maybe we need to enlist the police.'

'They won't be any help!' Ellis protested. 'For one thing, you've got no proof of anything.'

Tom knew that what Ellis said was true. They had nothing but the vaguest suspicions. 'I have friends on the force,' Tom insisted. 'They'll listen to me.'

'They will not. Even if you get 'em to come out here, Reese'll blame everything on me,' Ellis whined. 'He'll tell how I broke in the house.'

Tom looked at him impatiently, knowing that Ellis was right. 'If you've got a better idea, let's hear it.'

Ellis glowered at him. 'I could go in there and choke Joe Reese until he tells me where she is.'

'In other words, you don't.'

'At least it's an idea. While you're pussyfootin' around, Blair's life could be in danger. If she's still alive,' said Ellis.

Tom did not contradict him.

'Quiet,' he said. 'Let me think.'

Blair was burning up. Sweat had broken out all over her body. She thrashed about on her thin pillow and her pile of rags, in a vain effort to get comfortable. The pain in her head was searing and, when she reached up to touch it, something sticky adhered to her fingers. At first she thought it was blood, but then she held her fingers in front of her eyes and saw that the substance on them was not dark or wet, like blood. It was viscous, and foul-smelling. The wound on her head was oozing.

In a way, she was not surprised. He had opened that wound on her head by hitting her with a shovel, which had probably been used over the years to scoop up horse manure and had never even been wiped clean. That gash was like a petri dish full of bacteria. The thought of it made Blair feel sick to her stomach, but when she retched, nothing came out. The little bit of chili, which she had eaten hours earlier, had made its greasy way from her stomach into her bowels, where it now rested uneasily.

Blair groaned and turned over. The hot flushes in her body had suddenly turned to shivers. She began to shake uncontrollably and her teeth chattered from the cold. Help, she thought. But she knew better than to cry it aloud. What help could she possibly expect from Ariel and her toddler? They had been imprisoned for years. What use to ask them for help?

Blair lay on her side, facing the wall, her hands pressed between her knees, trying to warm her icy fingers. Help. Please.

Suddenly, she felt a light touch on her shoulder, which made her jump. She turned her head and looked up into Ariel's frowning eyes.

'What's a matter with you?' Ariel asked.

Blair tried to speak, but her teeth were chattering so that it was difficult. Blair tried to wet her lips and form the words.

'I have a fever,' said Blair. 'I think the place on my head where he bashed me. It's infected.'

Ariel leaned over to look at Blair's wound. Then she grimaced. 'I think you're right,' she said. 'Some kind of crud is coming out of it.'

Blair squeezed her eyes shut. 'Great,' she whispered.

'Look, I think we ought to try to make a plan,' said Ariel.

'A plan for wh . . . what?' Blair asked, her body shaking.

Ariel hesitated, debating with herself, and then took off the sweater she was wearing. She lay it over Blair's back and shoulders. Blair wanted to weep. It seemed like the greatest kindness she had ever known. For a moment, she felt almost warm. And then the chills returned, coursing viciously through her.

'Well,' said Ariel, 'I never know when he's coming here. But we need to be ready. I was thinking maybe . . . with two of us . . . if he came in . . .'

Blair closed her eyes. She knew what Ariel was thinking: maybe they could gang up and overpower him somehow. In theory it seemed a good idea. In fact, it seemed doubtful that Blair could even rise to her feet.

'I can try,' she offered.

Ariel shook her head and sighed. 'You're not going to be any use to me, are you?' she said.

Blair knew that there was truth in what the young woman was saying. Blair was taking up her space and was wrapped in her sweater, and wasn't going to be any help in terms of tackling or attacking her captor. Blair licked her lips and shook her head.

'When that door opens . . .' she said, 'I'll find it in me. I swear . . .'

Ariel looked skeptical. 'I doubt it. You're a mess.'

Blair grabbed at the other woman's forearm. 'Listen. Have you got anything we can use? For a weapon . . .?'

Ariel looked down at Blair's fingers. 'You're burning up,' she said.

Blair felt as if her face was frozen. She struggled to move her lips. 'Think . . .' she said. 'Have you got knives over there with the food?'

Ariel shook her head. 'No knives. I've thought of that. Naturally.'

'Anything heavy . . .? Cans of food? A cast iron pan maybe?'

Ariel sighed. 'No. He's careful. He only brings food in plastic containers. Plastic everything. Plates and utensils.'

'Nothing else?'

'Nothing.' Ariel pulled her own knees close to her chest and rocked back and forth. After a few minutes of silence, she spoke. 'You can hear him, when he's coming in. He unlocks that outer door and then he locks it again, before he unlocks this door. That way you can't rush past him and get out. Believe me, I've tried it. So, after the outer door is locked, he opens that door . . .' Ariel nodded her head, to indicate the door to the old tack room, now her prison.

'Once I tried standing on a chair and hitting him hard as I could when he came in, but I never had anything heavy enough to really hurt him. I grazed him as he came through the door. He made me pay for that . . .'

'How?' Blair whispered.

'He turned off the water in here for days,' Ariel said matter-of-factly. 'The smell from the bathroom was suffocating. And I felt like there were bugs crawling all over me and in my hair. And the thirst . . .'

Blair could more than imagine it. She gagged again, but nothing came out.

'I promised everything to get him to put it back on. He likes to make you beg. At first I wouldn't, but now, since Trista came, I'll start pleading right away.'

'She's his own child. Doesn't that matter to him?' Blair asked.

'He doesn't care,' said Ariel flatly.

Blair squeezed her eyes shut; trying not to imagine what Ariel had endured. If she had even half of her usual strength, she just knew she could make a difference. She could surprise him, overcome him. But all she had right now was a fraction and that fraction was spent trying to control the shaking.

'When he sees the shape you're in, he won't want you,' said Ariel. 'Not till you're better.'

Blair realized that she should be relieved, but all her effort was spent trying to imagine how she would be any better. This fever, this infection, was not going away. Not without antibiotics.

'Does he give you medicine when you need it?' she whispered through parched lips.

Ariel shrugged. 'When he decides you need it. What fun would it be if we died?'

'We have to get out,' Blair whispered.

Ariel's gaze became icy. 'Don't you think I know that?' she yelled. 'Do you think I wanted to stay here?'

Blair shuddered at Ariel's loud yell. But even as she heard it, it started to recede, as if it came from somewhere far away.

Blair shook her head. 'No. Of course not,' she whispered. 'Never.'

'Mommy,' came a plaintive cry from the direction of the closet. 'I'm scared.'

'Look what you've done,' Ariel fumed. 'Coming,' she called out to the child.

'Sorry,' Blair whispered, as Ariel scrambled to her feet and headed toward the closet.

Just then, Blair heard it. It was a thud, like the sound of a door closing and then something nearer rattling.

Blair felt her heart leap to her throat as she realized what was happening. He was outside the door, about to let himself in.

'No,' she whispered. She wanted to call out to Ariel, to warn her. With all her strength she pulled herself up and put her back to the wall, pressing the thin pillow to her chest and holding it there, like flimsy armor. Her head seemed to be spinning.

'No,' she repeated. 'No.'

The door opened.

THIRTY-THREE

He was wearing a pajama top and chinos under a bathrobe and fleece vest. His hair was disheveled, like he had been tossing and turning in bed. A bunch of keys on a chain were attached to a belt loop on his pants and Blair thought, as she watched him carefully re-locking the door, that he resembled a guard in a madhouse. He looked up and his gaze was unreadable behind his silvery glasses.

'Getting acclimated?' he said.

Blair glared at him venomously. 'Never,' she said.

'No need to be unpleasant,' said Joe, and there was a note of warning in his voice. He came closer to Blair and peered at her. 'You don't look well.'

'No sh-shit,' she said, her teeth chattering. 'I have a fever. My head is infected where you hit me with that filthy shovel. I need antibiotics.'

Joe Reese smiled and wagged a finger at Blair. 'Now don't you start barking orders. That doesn't work with me. I don't respond well to commands. Just ask Ariel.'

'Ask me what?' Ariel demanded. She stepped out of the closet, holding Trista, who was still half asleep, in her arms.

'There she is,' Joe exclaimed rapturously. 'My little girl.' He reached out his arms and waggled his hands.

Ariel pivoted away from him and pulled her child close, putting a protective hand around the toddler's head as if to shield her.

'Leave her alone. She's still asleep. What time is it?'

Joe ignored the question. 'Oh, but she'll be glad to see me. Won't you?' he crooned, wresting the baby away from her mother and slipping his pale, beefy hands around the drowsy child.

Trista's head rolled back and then she seemed to awaken. She opened her large, sparkling eyes and looked at the man who was holding her.

'How's Trista? How's my baby girl?' he crooned.

Blair felt her stomach heave at the sound of these words. 'You sick bastard,' she whispered.

Joe either did not hear her or pretended he did not. All his attention was concentrated on the child.

Trista glanced back at her mother and then at the man who was holding her.

'Dada,' she said.

'That's right. I'm your Dada. And you are my little princess.'

At that, the child reached for his glasses and smeared the glass with her sticky fingers trying to remove them from his face.

'Now stop,' he crooned. 'Don't touch Dada's glasses.'

Trista giggled and reached up again for the glinting glasses.

'No, no, don't touch,' said Joe.

Trista giggled at the game and managed to pull one of the earpieces away from his head. His glasses tilted crazily on his nose.

'I said *no,*' Joe shouted, thrusting the child out at arm's length and shaking her.

Trista began to wail miserably, tears filling her eyes.

'Leave her alone,' Ariel pleaded, reaching for her child. 'She's just playing.'

'She needs to learn that *no* means *no.*' He adjusted his glasses on his face.

Ariel turned away, cradling her crying toddler and shaking her head. She muttered something under her breath.

'What was that?' Joe asked.

'Nothing,' Ariel said angrily.

Blair couldn't stand it. 'No means no?' she cried. 'You fucking hypocrite.'

Joe turned on her. 'What did you say?'

'You heard me,' said Blair.

'Don't,' Ariel pleaded.

Blair knew why Ariel was pleading. She didn't want Blair to anger their captor, for fear of his wrath. And Blair knew that she should fear him also. He was a sadist and a killer. Blair thought about what she had learned this evening. Thirteen-year-old Molly had tried to rescue Ariel, and had paid for it with her own life. Blair could not forget that, or pretend it had not happened. She could not ignore it, for the sake of keeping the peace. She felt Molly's spirit entering her somehow, giving her courage.

'You know, I finally understand,' said Blair, 'what happened to my friend, Molly.'

Joe looked at her blankly and then with disdain. 'Oh you do, do you?'

'Yes. Ariel told me about the time she almost escaped from you. How she ran away and you chased her and trapped her.'

'Ariel's daydreaming escapes me!' Joe laughed as if the idea was preposterous. 'She never tried to leave me. She wouldn't. She loves being here with me. She had no one until I found her. She was all alone in the world. You might say we were searching for each other. I had this place ready and waiting for someone. The right someone. But I was very particular about who it was going to be and then I met Ariel. And I knew.' He smiled a sentimental smile at the memory.

'Ariel was in your house. You weakened and allowed her to be in your house. And she ran away,' Blair insisted. 'And you hunted her down like an animal in the forest. Molly tried to intervene . . .'

Joe shook his head as if to say that he felt sorry for Blair. 'You don't know what you're talking about. I rescued Ariel from a miserable life. She's happy here. I don't have to hunt her. Ariel belongs to me. She and Trista.'

'I didn't say anything about any Molly,' Ariel protested pitifully. 'I didn't know any Molly.'

'But it was Molly,' Blair insisted. 'Wasn't it, Joe?' Blair shuddered, and she could not tell if it was the infection or her revulsion at this monstrous man that caused it. 'You know, Molly was only thirteen when you killed her. Thirteen. But she defied you, didn't she? She saw you right away for the coward and bully that you are. That was what she was like. She always stood up for the underdog.'

'Blair, no . . .' Ariel pleaded.

Blair ignored her pleas. She knew that she was betraying Ariel's confidences about Joe Reese and that Ariel was terrified of the repercussions. But Blair could not stop herself. She had to say it out loud to him. Insist on it.

'When I think about it now, Molly was probably lucky that you didn't decide to add her to your little dungeon. What was the matter? Wasn't she your type? Not young enough? Not vulnerable enough?'

Joe came up to Blair and reached for her neck, gripped it and lifted her up off the grimy pallet where she had been resting. She felt herself rise and suddenly her air supply was cut off.

'Molly had a big mouth for such a little girl,' Joe said in a quiet, menacing voice. 'Why would I ever bring that home with me?'

Blair could not answer because she was gagging and gasping for breath, trying in vain to unwrap his fingers from her neck. She could vaguely hear Ariel erupting in feeble protests and Trista had begun to wail.

'Please Joe,' Ariel cried, trying to break his grip on Blair. 'You're scaring the baby.'

Joe stared at the struggling Blair for a minute and then he tossed her back down onto the heap of rags where she had been huddled. Blair collapsed with a hacking cough, then crawled up onto her hands and knees and gasped for air in huge, ragged breaths. Joe lifted his boot and kicked her as hard as he could in the side.

Blair let out an agonized wail and doubled over.

His punishment dispatched, Joe's composure quickly returned. He rummaged in the pockets of his vest and bathrobe, looking for something.

'I brought baby a treat,' he said. From where she lay, clutching her painful side, Blair watched as he lovingly removed a chocolate candy bar and waved it at Ariel, who was still soothing Trista in her arms.

'This is for somebody if she's good,' he said.

Blair watched him in horrified fascination. He seemed to expect cheers and kudos for that measly gift. With a voice weary from years of practice, Ariel made a pro forma exclamation of appreciation.

'I need antibiotics,' Blair demanded, in as loud a voice as she could muster.

Joe's head swiveled toward her as if he had forgotten she was there. 'I'm afraid we don't have any of those,' he said.

'Ask Darlene,' Blair said. 'She has drugs with her for hospice. Maybe she has some antibiotics.'

Joe glowered at her as if offended by her mention of his twin. 'You're going to have to do without them.'

'I can't do without them,' Blair cried. 'I need them. Tell Darlene. Where does she think you are anyway? Where does she think you're going, when you wander out of the house in the middle of the night in that get-up? You look like you escaped from a mental hospital; which is where you should be anyway.'

In a flash, Joe had scuttled over to where she lay and smacked her in the face.

'Don't you dare talk to me like that. My child is over there. I won't allow her to hear that.'

Blair felt a mixture of fear and repugnance to be so close to Joe Reese. What would possess a man to do something so twisted? To keep a woman prisoner for years? To let a child grow up without air, or light, or other human company? To let a woman die from neglect? For clearly, that was his plan for her.

Suddenly, he pushed her back down onto her shredded pallet. He made a moue of distaste.

'You smell terrible,' he said. Then Joe stood up and rubbed his hands together. 'All right,' he said. 'Time for Mommy and me.'

He pulled Blair to her feet, up from her pallet.

'You. Into the closet with my princess.' He gestured for Ariel to give the child to Blair. Ariel bowed her head over the baby's floss-like hair and stifled a groan.

'Go on, now,' he said. 'We haven't got all day.'

Ariel pushed the child in Blair's direction. 'Go in the closet,' she said. 'Don't come out. Just don't.'

Blair and Ariel locked gazes for a moment. Blair tried to let her know how sorry she was, how sick at heart. Ariel gazed back as if from a great distance, as if she was already pulling away from the scene, distancing herself from what was about to happen.

Blair took the protesting little girl toward the closet.

Joe followed behind them almost jovially.

'You two just stay out of the way,' he said. 'Let Mommy and me take our time.' Blair turned to curse him and he kicked her again, this time in the shin. He shoved them both into the closet and locked the door.

It took Blair a moment to catch her breath. Then she managed to get to her feet and fumble around for the light switch. There was none. But a cord was hanging there and Blair pulled on it. The single, low wattage bulb in the closet ceiling lit up. Blair looked around. The floor of the closet was littered with clothes which formed the pallet that was Trista's bed. Trista had clambered to the pillow against the wall and huddled there, holding a dingy stuffed dog.

'Don't stand there,' the child commanded, her lip trembling, and Blair thought that it must somehow alarm her to have Blair looming over her like that.

'I'll sit right down,' Blair whispered. 'Just a minute.'

Blair took another look around. She rattled the clothes bar in the closet, but it was securely fastened to the wall. The clothes were all on the floor because there were no hangers on the bar. No hangers which might be formed into a primitive weapon. He made sure of that. What else, she wondered? She could hear murmuring and grunting from the next room. She tried to drown the noise out with her thoughts.

She moved aside a small jumble of clothing and sat down on the floor. She pushed aside a pink sock and then recognized it. It looked like the mate of the sock which had adhered to Joe Reese's fleece vest. Now, it made sense. The sock was Trista's. It must have come off while she was sitting on her mother's mattress. And one of the many times, when Joe was assaulting Ariel, he had picked up the sock on his clothes.

The idea was repulsive and Blair tried to put it out of her mind. She pushed some other clothes aside. A pair of women's socks were tied together and rested in the heap of clothes on the floor. So Ariel's clothes were in here too, mixed in with her daughter's. There was nothing clean or fresh or new in the pile. It was a sickening jumble of worn, stained, shapeless clothing.

'You're too big for here,' Trista said, and tears stood in her shiny eyes.

'I'm sorry,' said Blair. 'I don't mean to crowd you.'

'When are you going away?' the child demanded.

Blair thought about the question. Would she ever be going away? Would she ever be leaving here alive? She tried to focus on Trista, but her eyes were having trouble focusing and, in addition to the pain where he had kicked her, she felt weak and flushed from her fever.

Stop it, she chided herself. Don't give in. You have to get out of here. There has to be a way. Trista, having lost interest in Blair, rummaged expertly through the mess on the closet floor and pulled out, from among her few toys, a vinyl baby doll which looked like it had been new when Reagan was president. The color was almost worn off its face and eyes, and it was wearing a stained, filthy dress. Joe must have bought it at a rummage sale somewhere. A fine present for his newborn child, Blair thought, someone's old, discarded doll. Trista held the doll close to her and rocked it, cooing.

'What's your baby's name?' Blair asked.

Trista looked at her blankly. 'Baby,' she said.

'I see,' said Blair.

She watched as Trista alternately cradled and then scolded the baby. 'You have dirty diapers,' the child complained. 'I have to change them.'

The groans from the other room were louder now and there was a rhythmic, bumping sound. Rutting pig, Blair thought.

Trista was busily pretending to change the baby's diapers, although, in fact, the doll had no undergarments on. Blair looked at the doll's bare stomach under the pushed up dress. There was a large square cut in the flesh-colored vinyl of the doll's stomach which was closed with a plastic, corrugated latch. A battery compartment. From the size of it, the compartment must hold a pair of D cell batteries. Talk about outdated, she thought. These days, dolls had a tiny microchip in them that made them capable of doing everything from singing harmony with themselves to mapping out directions.

'Does Baby talk?' Blair asked.

Trista shook her head sadly. 'No. Not anymore.'

'She used to talk?' Blair asked.

'She talked before,' Trista said, nodding. 'Dada said so.'

Yeah, years ago, Blair thought, when the doll had batteries in it. And then Blair had a sudden thought which made her break out in a sweat. Easy does it. Steady. Don't scare her, she told herself.

'Baby is so pretty,' Blair said. 'May I hold her?'

Trista clutched the doll to her chest in alarm. 'No,' she insisted.

Blair smiled at her genially. 'Is she your only baby?'

Trista looked at Blair suspiciously for a moment, but then seemed to decide that Blair was safe. 'I have another baby,' she said.

'Can I see?'

Trista hesitated, and then began rummaging through the clothes again. This time she pulled out a black-and-white stuffed kitten. She held it up triumphantly.

'This is my other baby.'

'What's this baby called?' asked Blair.

Blair could tell by the child's frown that she had not given the kitten a name. But she immediately set to work on it.

'This . . . baby . . . is . . . called . . .' The child frowned, thinking. She doesn't know any names, Blair thought. She doesn't know any other people.

'Called . . . Little One!' Trista cried triumphantly.

'Could I hold Little One?' Blair asked, reaching for the kitten and giving it a gentle tug as if to free it from Trista's hands.

Blair's gesture had the desired effect. The child grasped the kitten with both hands, letting the baby doll fall into the pile of clothes.

'No,' she exclaimed. 'Mine.'

She turned away from Blair so that Blair could not reach for the kitten again.

Blair nodded. 'I understand,' she said.

Casually, she reached into the heap of clothes and picked up the discarded baby doll, pretending to gaze at its face. As she did, she reached under the doll's grimy dress and unfastened the battery compartment. She felt a flush of victory when she saw that the dead batteries, two heavy, round D cells, were still inside. Blair immediately slipped them out and stashed them under her leg. Then she snapped the compartment shut again.

'Here,' she said. 'I think Baby is tired. Maybe you should sing her a lullaby so she can go back to sleep.'

The child reached out and gathered the doll up into her arms along with the stuffed kitten.

'They are very tired,' she announced. 'They are going to sleep.'

Blair nodded. Meanwhile, she fished through the pile of clothes until she found that pair of Ariel's socks which she had seen earlier. She untied them and slipped the two batteries inside one of them. Then she tied a knot near where they rested in the toe. Trista, meanwhile, was holding a conversation between the doll and the kitten.

Blair weighed the weapon in her hand. It was heavy, thanks to the batteries. But she knew full well that her window of opportunity was going to be brief.

'What are you doing?' the child asked.

'Nothing,' Blair whispered. 'Getting ready.'

THIRTY-FOUR

Blair wanted to wait, standing up, with her feet planted. But she knew it would upset the child and her anxiety might telegraph a warning. So Blair crouched down on the closet floor. Chills were surging through her, but she could not afford to let them distract her. She was only going to have one chance. One shot. She wished desperately that she was at her best, with all her wits about her. She thought about Ariel saying that she had tried to hit him, to knock him out once, but she wasn't strong enough. At least Blair had something heavy to wield against him. Blair had made herself a jailhouse black-jack with batteries in a sock. It was not a gun or a knife, but it was something. And it was not as if she had a choice. She had to take the opportunity and give it her best. Her best shot. Blair tightened her grip on the knotted sock and waited for the door to open.

It felt as if they had been in the closet for hours by the time she heard him outside the door, fiddling with the lock.

'All right in there,' he chirped. 'Time to come out.'

Blair scrambled to her feet as she heard the click of the padlock and saw the doorknob turn. She was shaking from the effects of the fever, or perhaps from fear, she thought, but she would stand her ground. The window of opportunity was going to be very narrow.

The door began to open and Trista rushed to push herself through the opening calling out, 'Mommy, Mommy.'

'Hey little girl. What's your hurry?' Joe asked genially. He crouched down and reached out, to try and waylay the child as she hurtled through the opening in the door.

His head was bent; a bald spot visible on the crown of his head. Accessible. Now, Blair thought. *Now.*

She lifted up the heavy, knotted sock, lunged forward so that her leg was wedged in the door and brought her makeshift weapon down with all her might on his head. There was a satisfying thwack as the batteries cracked into his skull and he dropped to the floor, with a surprised expression on his face.

For a moment, Blair was paralyzed with disbelief. He lay at her feet. She resisted the urge to kick him. Blair pushed through the door and began to call for Ariel. She rounded the corner into the room and saw that Ariel was still on the bed, half undressed. Her arms were tied to the bedframe above her head and her legs were splayed out, tied to the bedposts. Trista sat on the bed beside her, singing softly to herself, as if having her mother trussed to the bedframe was business as usual.

'Oh my God,' Blair exclaimed. She rushed to the headboard and began to untie Ariel's hands.

'Where is he?' Ariel asked.

'I knocked him out with this,' said Blair, through gritted teeth, setting her makeshift weapon down on the bed. 'But I doubt he'll be out for long.' Her fingers felt clumsy and uncoordinated as she struggled to untie the knots. Losing precious time, she kept thinking. We have to get out. For a moment, she thought perhaps she could leave Ariel there and run. Run for help. But she knew immediately that she could not. The idea of forcing Ariel to watch Blair go through the door, leaving her behind, was crueler than anything Blair could imagine. Not possible. She redoubled her efforts.

One hand was free. Now the next. Blair felt sweat running down the sides of her face, clammy under her clothes. She began to work the other knot free.

Suddenly, there was a groan from the direction of the hallway.

'Jesus, hurry,' Ariel pleaded.

Blair fumbled with the knots and finally one of them came loose. Ariel jerked her own hand free.

'Untie your feet,' Blair commanded. 'I need to get those keys so we can get out of here.'

'Mommy, what is the lady doing?' Trista asked.

'Helping us,' said Ariel as she maneuvered herself around, so that she could reach the restraints on her feet.

Blair went back to where Joe Reese lay on the floor. His head was bleeding and Blair felt a certain satisfaction in that. But his eyes were open and he was starting to stir. Blair went over to him and jerked at the keys on his belt. They were on a metal ring and Blair realized she would have to unbuckle his belt to free them. The thought of it made her light-headed with revulsion. She forced herself to bend down beside him and, with trembling fingers, start to work the belt free of its buckle.

He formed an inchoate sentence and Blair could tell that his gaze had rolled in the direction of her face. She did not look. She freed the tail of the belt and began to pull it from the belt loops, working her way toward the keys.

Suddenly, with the speed of a striking snake, his hand shot toward her and grabbed her wrist. Blair let out a scream. He was holding her more tightly than she thought possible, considering the blow he had suffered.

'Let go,' she screamed.

She tried to scramble away from him, but she only dragged him with her, as he held on tight.

'Let me go, you bastard,' she yelled.

Just as their eyes met, Ariel staggered around the corner. She held the knotted sock in one hand. She stared at them for a moment and then, her face twisted with rage, she raised the weighted sock. With a sharp cry she brought it down on his head. The blow was fierce. The moment it connected, Blair felt his grip on her wrist let go. Ariel struck again. Twice.

'Ariel *stop*,' Blair whispered urgently. 'Don't kill him.'

Ariel stared at the heap on the ground, her jailer for nearly half her life, and raised the sock again. 'Why not?' she asked.

Blair forced her to meet her gaze. 'They could put you in jail for it. That's why. Leave him. We're almost free.'

Just then Trista toddled around the corner and saw Joe, bleeding on the ground.

'Dada!' she cried in dismay.

Blair grabbed the keys from Joe's belt and motioned for Ariel to follow her. Ariel dropped her weapon and reached out to scoop up her child in her arms. 'Don't look,' Ariel said. 'Don't look. We're going.'

It was pitch dark as they stumbled outside. The air was cold and crisp and the sky was full of stars. Blair let Ariel go through the door first, clutching her baby in her arms. She stumbled and nearly fell, but then she regained her balance.

'I freezing,' the child exclaimed.

Ariel pulled her close and stood outside of the barn, staring up at the stars, gulping in the air. 'Look! The sky!' she exclaimed.

Blair hurried out and locked the padlock on the door behind her. Even if he was able to recover enough to stand up, Joe Reese would not get out. She motioned for Ariel to follow her out from behind the barn. They staggered along in the dark. Blair led the way, because she knew the way. Ariel knew nothing of where they were. She probably remembered little of the outside world. Clutching her child, she followed Blair.

They came around the side of the barn and, suddenly, lights went on in the house. Darlene, Blair thought. She will help us. Blair started to walk toward the porch when all of a sudden the back door opened and Darlene walked out. She was in her bathrobe and her hair was in rollers. She was holding a shotgun and she aimed it at the three who were crossing her driveway.

'Who's there?' Darlene cried.

'Darlene, don't. It's me. It's Blair.'

Darlene peered into the darkness. 'Blair? What are you doing here? Who's that with you?'

'Can we come inside? I'll tell you everything.'

Darlene lowered the gun. 'No. You'll wake up Joe. He's sleeping,' said Darlene.

Blair shook her head. 'He's not. He's back there. In the barn.'

'What's he doing in the barn?' Darlene asked.

Blair hesitated. 'It's a long story.'

'Who are those people with you?'

'Look, Darlene. I don't know how to tell you this.'

'Tell me what?' Darlene demanded.

'Your brother . . . Joe has been holding this woman a prisoner out there. And her child. And me.'

Darlene hesitated and then slowly she raised the gun again. 'That's a lie. Don't take another step.'

'Darlene, I promise you,' said Blair. 'He's in the barn. He's hurt. He probably needs an ambulance. You should call for help.'

Darlene aimed the gun directly at Blair. 'Wait a minute,' she said. 'What are you trying to pull?'

'Darlene, I'm not trying to pull anything. I'm telling you the truth. You know me.'

'I don't know you.' Darlene started to descend the steps, the gun trained on Blair.

Ariel watched this unfolding conversation with horror. She saw the woman approaching with the gun and it was too much, too much to be finally free, only to be threatened again. She clutched Trista to her breast and started to run, tripping on the stones in the driveway and falling to her knees.

Darlene swung the shotgun around and pointed it at the mother and baby. 'You stop there. Halt.'

'No, you stop, Darlene,' cried a deep voice in the darkness. 'Stop or I'll shoot.'

Darlene lowered the gun, shocked and puzzled, as Tom emerged into the arc of light from the back porchlight, his hands gripping a revolver.

'Tom!' Blair cried.

'Ellis,' Tom ordered the older man behind him. 'Take that gun away from her before she kills someone.'

Ellis surged up the steps towards the armed woman on the porch. Darlene quickly turned the gun on him, but Ellis just kept coming. 'Darlene, listen. You have to give that to me. Just give it here.'

'You bastard,' Darlene cried and then she burst into tears and lowered the gun. Ellis reached her quickly and pulled the shotgun from her hands as Darlene sagged against him.

'Uncle Ellis?' Blair asked, hardly able to comprehend that her uncle was a part of this rescue effort.

Ellis turned and glowered at her. 'What the hell, Blair?'

Tom rushed over to Blair, Ariel and Trista, huddled on the cold, damp ground. He and Blair exchanged a solemn look.

'This is Ariel,' said Blair. 'And Trista. Ariel, are you all right? Is the baby . . .?'

'We're all right,' said Ariel.

Tom crouched down beside them and picked up his phone, his other hand wrapped protectively around Blair's forearm. He called the police and told them to call for an ambulance. Calmly, he gave them the information they needed.

'How did you know?' Blair whispered.

'We didn't. We just knew that your phone was in this field and that didn't make any sense. We came back here to search for it. Truthfully, we weren't sure what to do next. We were trying to decide, when all hell broke loose.'

Blair shuddered. 'My phone must have fallen from Joe's pocket after he took it from me, after he locked me up in there.'

Tom reached out and squeezed her shoulder. 'It's all right now. You're alive. You're free.'

Ellis and Darlene descended the porch steps. Ellis had set the shotgun down carefully against the porch railing. 'You are done with this gun, woman,' he said.

'Joe,' Darlene cried. 'My Joe.'

'Joe can rot,' Blair said coldly.

'Is he alive?' Tom asked.

'Only because I didn't have a gun,' said Blair. 'He killed Molly. It was him.'

Tom nodded. 'Thank God he didn't kill you.'

Blair gazed at Ariel, dirty, pale and disheveled, rocking her weeping child in her arms. 'Or them,' she said.

And then the flash of lights and the blessed sound of sirens approaching, drowned out all her thoughts and every other sound.

THIRTY-FIVE

'**M**r Muhammed,' said Judge Meredith Shapiro.

Yusef, well groomed, in new glasses and a new – albeit slightly too large – suit stood at stone-faced attention beside his attorney, Brooks Whitman.

'As you know, Mr Joseph Reese has allocuted, as part of a plea deal, that it was he who killed Molly Sinclair. And Ms Ariel

Trautwig, who was Reese's prisoner, has testified that she was present when that murder occurred and that Mr Reese was, indeed, Molly Sinclair's killer.

'But for the fact that your alibi witness lied under oath, Mr Muhammed, you would have never been incarcerated for that crime. In light of the new facts which have come to light in this case, I have granted unusual leeway to your attorney, to allow the testimony of the deceased witness's sister – regarding that witness's deathbed confession – to be on the record.

'The facts in a wrongful conviction are rarely this compelling. I am convinced beyond a doubt that any jury who might hear this case would consider it a grave miscarriage of justice. Therefore, I am vacating your conviction. I hope that – by vacating the conviction – I will speed the process for the inevitable lawsuit which, I am sure, you will be filing against the state. In my opinion, you deserve compensation for your suffering. You are a free man Mr Muhammed and, may I say, I sincerely regret all that you have endured at the hands of the justice system. Godspeed, Mr Muhammed. This court is adjourned.'

Judge Shapiro banged her gavel on the desk.

'All rise,' said the bailiff and everyone in the courtroom was compelled to keep their exuberance restrained, until the judge disappeared through the door.

The first to cry out was Yusef's mother, Lucille Jones, who came around to embrace her son. She clung to him for a long time. Brooks Whitman finally approached them and gently pried them apart. Yusef and Brooks shook hands. Janet and Robbie Sinclair clung to one another and wiped away tears.

Yusef separated himself from friends and family, who had come out to support him, and walked over to the frail, pale-skinned woman who sat silently in front of Blair.

'Ariel,' Yusef said. 'Thank you for testifying. I really appreciate it.'

Ariel held Yusef's gaze and cupped his large brown hand in between her own pale hands. 'I'm glad it turned out this way.'

Blair looked on with a dawning realization. 'You know, I think there's something going on between those two,' she whispered.

Tom Olson nodded. 'It makes perfect sense when you think about it. Who else could understand them? It must be impossible for them to relate to the rest of the world. They were both imprisoned, through no fault of their own, for years. How could they ever explain what they've suffered? But to one another, there's no need to explain.'

Blair glanced at Tom appreciatively. 'You're right. That's really true.'

Tom shrugged. 'I get it right now and then.'

Robbie and Janet got up from their seats and Janet held out her arms to Blair.

They embraced briefly.

'Thank you, Blair,' Janet murmured. 'I'm so relieved that this is over. This would never have happened without you.'

'Maybe, at last, a little bit of justice for Molly.'

'And for us, it's better to know,' said Robbie. 'Somehow, it's easier. Blair, you really were her best friend.'

'I'm glad I could finally help,' said Blair. 'Now, you two need some rest.'

'We do. I'm taking her on a vacation,' said Robbie.

'Good,' said Blair, smiling.

Brooks Whitman came up to them, his face ruddy with excitement. 'We won,' he said. 'Now it's on to the civil suit. That's going to take a while longer. They really need a compensation statute in this state.'

'I agree,' said Blair. 'I mean, why should Yusef have to fight this battle again in court? The state took years of his life, even the judge seemed to agree.'

'Her remarks on the record will certainly be helpful,' said Brooks.

'I can't imagine that this suit will meet much resistance,' said Tom. 'This case has been in the newspapers for months.'

'Neither can I, but I may need you to look into a few things for me.'

'It would be my pleasure to help,' said Tom.

Brooks clapped Tom on the back and kissed Blair on the cheek. 'One for the good guys,' he said, waving as he walked away to join the reporters, who were waiting for comment.

Blair and Tom turned to leave the courtroom when Yusef called Blair by name. She turned and saw him approaching, with Lucille under one arm and Ariel walking steadily by his side. Blair was a little reluctant to meet his gaze.

'I'm very happy for you,' she said. 'This should never have happened to you.'

'No,' he said.

Blair looked into his large, dark eyes behind his glasses. She wasn't sure what she expected to see there. Resentment? Forgiveness? Gratitude? She could not tell by looking at him. He had spent years in jail, keeping his feelings out of sight. Blair was not skilled enough to read them on his face now.

'I'm sorry for all you went through,' she said. 'And for what my sister did to you.'

Yusef was unsmiling, his voice neutral. 'I'm trying to figure out how to forgive her. It's not easy.'

Blair nodded. 'I'm sure not.'

'But,' he continued, 'if not for you, this day would have never come. Thank you for . . . your persistence,' he said.

'You're welcome,' said Blair. 'This outcome is a great relief to me.' She gazed at Ariel, who was standing quietly by. 'How are you doing?'

Ariel shrugged. 'Good days and bad,' she said.

'And Trista?'

'She's with my brother and his wife today,' said Ariel. 'I'm hoping she won't remember much of what happened.'

'That would be a mercy,' said Blair.

Ariel nodded, and leaned in to give Blair a brief hug.

'Are you coming to Lucille's house?' she asked.

Blair sighed. 'I'm not sure. I have to get back to Philly.'

Ariel turned to Tom. 'Make sure she comes. We need to talk.'

'We'll stop by,' said Tom.

Ariel gave them a wan smile, and then followed Yusef out to where the reporters were waiting.

Blair looked at Tom. 'I guess we should,' she said.

Tom nodded. 'It's a big day. Finally, something to celebrate.'

'Ok,' she said. 'I'm still not caught up, but I guess work can wait a little longer.'

'Let's nip out the side door,' he said. 'Avoid the crowd.'

Blair nodded and followed him down a dark corridor to a door with an exit sign.

Tom pushed it open and looked outside, checking in both directions.

'All clear,' he said.

Blair followed him down the steps and out to the street. They walked in the weak winter light out to Tom's truck and got inside.

'I thought Ellis might come today,' said Tom.

'To support Yusef?' Blair asked wryly.

Tom nodded and turned on the engine. 'True. Some things don't change.'

'Still, I'm glad I stayed with him at the house this time,' said Blair. 'Malcolm stayed over too. It was like the bad old days.'

Tom smiled. 'I know you have all the reason in the world to resent him, but I have to say, Ellis was genuinely worried about you when you were . . . in danger.'

'I know it,' said Blair ruminatively. 'I know he was. You know, I can never decide how I feel about him. Part of me never wants to set eyes on him again and then I see how Malcolm still loves him, and I think, that's got to count for something. He's not all bad . . .'

Tom nodded, and they drove in silence for a while. 'How is Malcolm doing at Peter and Amanda's?'

'Fine,' said Blair. 'I guess. He and Zach are into some kind of snowboarding thing.'

'So it's working out for him? Living with the Tuckers?' Tom asked.

'Seems to be,' said Blair. 'He seems happy. Of course, you never know.'

Tom shifted in his seat. He was quiet for a few minutes. Then he said, 'So now that this is over, I guess we won't see much of you anymore.'

'Oh, I'll be back,' said Blair. 'I mean, Malcolm is here. I promised Celeste I would stay in his life and I intend to.'

Tom nodded. 'I think that's a good idea,' he said.

'This morning, Uncle Ellis actually asked me when he was going to see me again.'

Tom smiled. 'Go figure.'

Blair glanced at him. 'And I'd like to see you too. We've made a pretty good team.'

Tom looked at her in surprise. 'You would?'

Blair shrugged. 'Well, sure.'

'Right,' Tom said, and then lapsed into silence.

Blair stared out the truck window at the passing landscape.

From time to time, she thought she detected a spark between them, but she had her doubts if it could ever amount to more than a spark. I don't know why I even mentioned us seeing one another, she thought. Both of us like our lives the way they are. She glanced at her watch. She intended to leave this party as soon as possible. If Tom wanted to stay, she could get somebody else to drive her back to her car.

'I hear music,' he said.

Blair frowned and then nodded. 'Oh yeah.'

'Marvin Gaye,' he said.

Blair smiled, recognizing it. 'Yes, it is.'

'Kind of our song,' he said.

Blair thought there was a suggestion of intimacy in his remark. 'Damn lucky for me that you knew that song,' she said.

Tom pulled up outside of Lucille's house, where Motown was blaring from the windows, and parked. People were coming and going, celebrating the amazing victory.

'You probably won't believe this,' he said, 'but I was once a pretty good dancer.'

'Are you still?' said Blair.

Tom reached out a hand toward her and his hand quivered. 'Want to find out?' he asked.

Blair shook her head. This is hopeless. The world's two wariest people.

'Afraid I'll make you look bad?' he asked wryly.

Blair hesitated. Chicken, she thought. It was just a dance. She took a deep breath and smiled.

'I'm game if you are,' she said.